STILL WATERS RUN DEEP

In 1971 two young expat couples living in Port Moresby struggle with lives that haven't gone according to plan.

Sarah Robinson, an economist, and her husband Andrew, an engineer, long for children, but hide their infertility problems—a subject no-one discusses.

Jack Martin, an agricultural economist, and his wife Jenny, a stay-at-home mum, have two small children—whose arrival forced a marriage before Jack and Jenny were ready for it.

Frustrated by the cards she's been dealt, and plagued by a sense of yearning, Sarah immerses herself in her job, working for Jack in a spectacular country offering the adventure of a lifetime. She gradually blossoms as a woman in the professional workforce but—she falls in love with Jack and reaches a crucial turning point in her life.

Whose happiness will she protect? Will she give up the man she loves?

STILL WATERS

RUN DEEP

LOUISA VALENTINE

Still Waters Run Deep

Copyright © Louisa Valentine 2022

Published by Louise Wilson, South Melbourne, 2022

www.louisewilson.com.au

ISBN 978-0-6450741-5-4 (digital)

ISBN 978-0-6450741-6-1 (print)

Cover design by Annie Seaton, using the image resource 'depositphotos_339776286' and 'Adobe Stock-144111787'

Cataloguing in-publication data is available from the National Library of Australia

CHAPTER ONE

The trade winds which had breezed across Port Moresby since April, through the long dry season, had died away and in November the town sweltered, leaving its residents languid and irritable. Would nothing break this cycle of oppressive heat and motionless air? Black thunderclouds passed mercilessly overhead without dumping their refreshing load on a parched landscape. The six weeks of hell before the wet season arrived bred their own kind of madness. People drank too much, marriages hit the rocks, businesses went broke.

Sarah huffed out her frustration in a loud sigh as the dust-encrusted ceiling fan revolved at a snail's pace, as lethargic as those slumping below it. Even the papers spread out on her battered desk were too tired to flutter in the slight movement of air. Beads of perspiration collected at her elbow and dripped relentlessly onto her papers. She abandoned her attempt at concentrating on her work. 'Will anything *ever* happen around here?' Her voice rang with irritation.

Across the room her colleague grinned at her. 'Be careful what you wish for.'

'Charles Williams!' she retorted, 'this is the last place on earth any sane person would want to be. And you know it.'

He flicked a teasing paper ball her way. 'You were grumpy last November too.'

'So I was. Sorry.' She was about to endure her second period of the doldrums. Action, that's what she craved, action.

Through the grimy louvres, she idly watched a taxi arrive in front of the long, sprawling building. A young man emerged. Not just any young man, even from this distance. His body language as he sprang from the vehicle conveyed a clear signal— dynamism. This man radiated a life force, in contrast to the sluggishness of Sarah's current surroundings.

Anything which exuded energy, or anyone who didn't amble, sparked her interest. She took in the details of his appearance, from his sun-bleached hair cut short to tame its obvious curl, through his height and broad stature, down through his tropic attire of shorts and long socks, permitting a view of skin tanned through exposure to the outdoors, to the tips of his man-sized shoes. His purposeful movements belied the casualness of his dress.

He paid the driver, picked up his briefcase from the kerb and strode towards the main office, disappearing into the verandah's shadow.

A lazy wheel turned a few cogs inside her bored mind. *Could this be our new boss, Jack Martin? He seems far too young for such a position.* As one of Australia's up and coming agricultural economists, he would be the brains behind the Departmental Head, who was a political appointee and figurehead useful for impressing visiting World Bank delegations, but not much else.

She'd been looking forward to his arrival. Like a sponge, she enjoyed soaking up every professional experience she could and a man with his reputation would teach her a lot.

City people were often unaware of the extent to which they relied on the rural sector for their basic existence. Trained in economics, and once a townie herself, she understood that Jack Martin's thesis for his Master's degree, a decision-tree approach for land and water use, held implications for managing the scarce resources of the entire planet.

At a recent briefing session Sarah and her colleagues learned that their new boss would work under a World Bank contract to bring this kind of background training and analytical skill to Papua New Guinea, a.k.a. PNG, a large land mass with major economic resources and massive potential.

The task of creating a modern, viable economy from this tropical backwater was daunting and this country sought help from the new breed of young, university-trained Australians looking for challenge and meaning in their work.

Like the man who had just emerged from the taxi.

Charles had also spotted the new arrival. 'Hey, that's Jack Martin,' he said. 'I knew him at uni and worked with him on another project. Bloody good bloke.'

A buzz of curiosity infected her colleagues, who craned their necks to get their first glimpse of their new boss.

Showing off the inside knowledge gained by his prior friendship, Charles said, 'Thought he was coming from Sydney tomorrow but he must have got a seat on today's plane out of Brisbane, where his folks live. I'll go and say g'day.'

He headed off towards reception and returned half an hour later with the newcomer, and the Departmental Head.

Seeing Jack Martin up close astonished her. Surely this young man, only a couple of years older than herself, couldn't have gained enough experience to win his reputation and this job?

Charles had informed the staff weeks ago that Jack was his legal name, not a nickname for the name John. She liked that name. It suited him. 'Jack' was unpretentious, as he appeared to be, but a strong and manly name, not soft and squishy.

From her position at the back corner of the general office, Sarah observed Jack's broad smile. It disguised his penetrating gaze at each member of staff introduced to him.

She noted his repetition of their name to help commit names and faces to his memory. Yes, his face was alert and arresting, with firm lines and a strong jaw, but his eyes were his dominant feature, hazel-coloured to blend with the rest of his earthy skin and sun-streaked hair tones but well-spaced, keenly observant and somehow reflecting a quality of cleanness, goodness and rightness. His agricultural background implied that Jack was in touch with the basics of life, but Sarah saw no signs of a country bumpkin.

She warmed to Jack's dynamic presence as he made his way through the office, performing the required 'meeting and greeting' routines. He carried the aura of a man who created and expected action.

As the youngest and most junior member of the team of economists, and the only woman in the group, she was the last to be introduced. He walked tall as he approached her, giving his body language even more confidence. His face lit up in greeting and he extended his hand for the obligatory handshake. A little shiver of apprehension rattled her as that dynamic man made brief physical contact with her. It was as if he'd transmitted his energy to her through the two joined hands.

Seemingly oblivious to the confusing sensation he'd provoked, Jack's engaging smile mirrored his friendly approach to the other members of staff. 'Hello, Sarah Robinson. The rose amongst the thorns.' His handshake momentarily increased its pressure before he abruptly released his grip.

She liked his teasing recognition of her being the only female in the office. Appreciating his wry remark, she smiled back.

'I'm told you're the statistical analyst of the group and hold your own with the footy tipping in an office full of footy-mad men.'

She laughed away his small talk. 'That sounds like a Charles comment. But yes, my aptitude for numbers sometimes pays off.' She was determined that he recognise her from the start as a female with a brain in her head.

His eyes locked with hers. 'Then I look forward to working with you.' A burst of mental energy, of engagement, flashed between them.

The moment passed and he disappeared into his assigned office at the end of the corridor, Departmental Head in tow.

His confident greeting style with her had not differed from his style with her other colleagues. She tried to regard the encounter as normally as he evidently did. He left her feeling slightly off-balance, before she wobbled back to equilibrium. Her working world suddenly seemed a lot brighter.

Sarah didn't see Jack again that day, but the hours passed quickly as she tackled her work with renewed enthusiasm. No longer did the tropical oppression seem quite so enervating. Her mood had moved from slightly depressed to mildly exhilarated, and all because one man had shaken her hand that day. How strange.

Lunchtime came. There being nowhere to go at lunchtime in Konedobu, the seat of government administration, it was customary for the men in her group to play a game of darts outside on the verandah during the break. They had a vigorous competition going. Sarah mostly sat on the sidelines, watching the play, eating her sandwich brought from home and drinking her cup of tea. Her love affair with tea was the office joke. She took occasional aim at the dartboard, but she wasn't one of the boys and she let them have their male-bonding fun.

Today the play was rather hit and miss, as the men focused more on exchanging their views about Jack Martin. 'Hey Charles, tell us more about Jack. I've heard he's pretty smart,' said John Bartlett, the young man whose desk was nearest Sarah's. He was a John and not a Jack.

'Yep, that he is,' said Charles. 'One of the best. But he's okay. Got his feet on the ground, he has. But not so flat that you can chew hay seeds around him. Nope, he performs, and he expects others to do the same, mate.'

'Sounds like too much hard yakka to me,' grumbled John. 'I came here to taste adventure, not to kill myself with work.'

'You'll find he's a pretty fair bloke. He doesn't crack a rodeo whip. His modus operandi is amazing.' Charles shrugged. 'Somehow, you just seem to want to improve when he's around. He's a great motivator. It's one key to his success.'

'Good. We need every bit of motivation we can find, before we die of terminal boredom and heat exhaustion.' Sarah's acerbic comment, uncharacteristic for her, proved the impact of the doldrums on her. Or was it the unsettling arrival of her new boss?

'Speak for yourself, Sarah. Some of us are content with our quiet life at work.' John lolled in his corner, his sandalled feet resting comfortably on his desk.

Her lazy colleague often annoyed her. 'Not when it's too quiet.' She'd grown used to working in a man's world, but some men made more congenial professional colleagues than did others. She gave John a curious look. He spent a lot of his time at work yawning. What did he get up to after work?

Sarah couldn't wait for four thirty to roll around, knock-off time. For a change she had plenty to tell Andrew about the events of her day.

CHAPTER TWO

'**M**y new boss turned up today.' She turned down Creedence, belting out her newest favourite album 'Willy and the Poor Boys', so they could talk. 'You'll like him,' she said. 'He's much younger than Pete, and we should have a lot more in common.'

'If you say so,' murmured her husband, always more interested in his cooling ale than her during this cocktail hour before dinner.

'You don't sound too enthusiastic. It'll be easier to get through all the after-hours socialising forced on us in this small community.'

'I find those ag blokes you work with rather boring company. We don't have much in common.'

'True. But I have to get along with your workmates. I'd appreciate the same effort towards mine.' To quell her sudden irritation at him, she took a giant mouthful of her vermouth and ice. 'At least Jack looks like a man of action. Now that he's taken over from Pete, I'm sure he'll generate a lot more activity than poor old Pete ever did.'

Action was why she and Andrew were here. They'd arrived eighteen months ago to join the band of young, adventurous, dedicated Australians helping to develop PNG. She would never have come to the vast island paradise by herself, but Andrew had seized the opportunity to use his skills as a junior engineer.

'That wouldn't be hard,' he mumbled, as he picked up the latest issue of the *Post-Courier* to read the local news.

Sarah flopped back in her chair, disappointed by his usual lack of interest in her work. She grabbed her swizzle stick and attacked the remnants of ice cubes at the bottom of her glass. *This man could drive me to drink.*

But in a moment of brutal honesty, uneasiness crawled from the shadows of her brain into a spotlight highlighting their underlying relationship problems.

She suppressed the niggling thought that had crept unbidden into her mind—not being able to have a baby, but worse, not being able to talk about it, was straining their relationship. Andrew's mind might focus elsewhere, but hers kept focusing on her dreams on her wedding day. She'd pictured children. Close communication. Intimate sharing. None of these key factors featured in their marriage.

Guiltily, she pushed her thoughts away. *Andrew's a good man. It's like he says—everything will be alright if we have a baby. I'm just restless because I don't have a baby. It doesn't feel right. I really must find out what the problem is.*

After four years of marriage they were still childless, unlike their peer group. A population explosion had erupted among the dozens of fertile young couples now surrounding them. Some boasted about their fecundity, others cursed it.

She tried hard to enthuse at the happiness of friends as pregnancies progressed and beautiful babies-in-arms joined their social life. It hurt, but she managed. Babies were delightful adorable creatures to hold, even if they had to be given back.

Sarah watched Andrew swallow the last of his ale. A large, gentle, attractive man, his physical appeal to her had waned in this new place with its new challenges, as their mental wavelengths diverged along different career paths. Their physical bonds were also somewhat strained by tension over her mysterious failure to conceive.

She wondered if other women felt the need to create a family unit as strongly as she did. Unlike those who took their children for granted and followed the parenting model set by their own mothers, she wanted more than that. She craved the chance to create her own family, sure, but different from the one she'd complained about to Andrew during their teenage years.

She studied the lacklustre man sitting opposite

her. Rather guiltily, she compared him with an image which leapt to the forefront of her consciousness. A dynamic man, one hundred percent male, had teased her in the office that day, and his brief but firm handshake and penetrating gaze had sent unnerving signals of electric awareness to her brain.

She shook herself. *That's disloyal, Sarah.* An inner voice rebuked her. *Everyone knows the grass is always greener in someone else's backyard. Just because you're going through a bad patch, don't forget that Andrew is your husband. You love each other. You've been together for years. Get a grip.*

She wondered if Andrew thought about their mutual problem as much as she did. He avoided discussing it and brushed away any small talk about babies, making it hard to suggest investigating what their problem might be. Sometimes she suspected he blamed her for not being like the other wives: the little woman, content to be tied to home duties, cooking and cleaning and pandering to the needs of her man and any children. He seemed uncomfortable that his working wife was becoming too independent.

Tonight wasn't a good time to raise the subject. Once again, he seemed too tired to handle something challenging, and she shook off her uneasy feeling of being an unwelcome trespasser on his comfort zone.

Leave it for now. She sighed to herself. *I'll talk it over with the doctor next time I visit.* It was another

12

compromise in her never-ending internal dialogue. *It's imperative that I do something. Two years off the pill is long enough. It's all very well to say let nature take its course, but nature hasn't. There must be a reason.*

Outsiders believed they had it all. 'You look like the perfect couple,' friends said. Andrew was your typical tall, dark and handsome character, much taller than her own above average height. Despite his conventional good looks and his regular, well-spaced facial features, she could not describe his physical presence as striking.

She'd inherited her Celtic colouring from her father's side of the family—blue eyes, auburn hair and porcelain skin. She could thank both her parents for her thick hair with its natural curl. Like her mother, her build was slim but not skinny. She wasn't athletic like Andrew, who'd been a keen surfer and tennis player in more congenial climates than this, but yes, she supposed they looked like a fine, fit young couple who would expect to breed easily and produce strong, handsome children.

Except they hadn't. It made her sad. And even perfect couples could drift apart. As Sarah contemplated the reticent man she'd chosen as her life partner, it flashed into her mind that they were well downstream in the drifting process.

Their differing careers reflected the temperament preferences which led Andrew to choose practical engineering and Sarah to choose the more conceptual field of economics. The difference had been less obvious when they first joined the workforce, him as a rookie engineer, her as a maths teacher in a country high school, both roles dependent on quantitative skills. In this new environment, she'd begun utilising her formal credentials in economics.

She wished they'd both gained some real-life experience of the world before she became one of the first in her school cohort to marry. 'Well, well, well, who would have guessed?' said one of the catty girls from her school days, met by accident at the beach. She'd ogled Andrew before spotting the ring on Sarah's wedding finger.

She should have kept half an ear on that girl and her mates. They'd been right. Life's not lived out of the textbooks she and Andrew had consumed so voraciously.

As she drifted off to sleep that night, despite her efforts to push it away, a disturbing image of a vital young man with hair on the blonde side, all-seeing hazel eyes, a ready, confident smile and a spring in his step wafted across the recesses of her mind.

CHAPTER THREE

Jack progressively called each of his new staff members into his office to ascertain the status of their current projects and the nature of their skillsets. Sarah's turn came in the late afternoon. He'd been saving the best till last.

Since the day Jenny told him she was pregnant, he'd never looked at another woman. Until yesterday, when he met Sarah. She'd knocked him sideways.

He'd had a sleepless night. That handshake of hers. It crackled with electricity. Those blue eyes of hers. Remarkable. That smile of hers. It lit up her face. If Jenny's romance novels were right, and the possibility of love at first sight was true, then this was it. Zing. The chemistry always missing from his marriage.

On his drive to work this morning he'd sternly rebuked himself. Men were well-practised at damping down their physical responses to women. His brain controlled his emotions, proved by his responsible job at such a young age. He was no longer an experimental teenager. He could treat Sarah entirely professionally.

Before sending for her, he reminded himself of certain promises he'd made, to himself and others, and forced his mind back to the days when he and Jenny were eager young students. The humiliation he suffered among his snooty university friends, busy making fun of his 'shotgun' wedding to Jenny, and the poverty he struggled with as a young married man, had left him determined to make his marriage survive, no matter what. Sarah would be his first real challenge to the course he'd set for himself.

As a young father, Jack could have asked his family for financial help, but he chose not to. He'd told himself he was a man now. He'd stand on his own feet. Baby Tom slept in the opened bottom drawer in their college bedroom. He worked at nights, packing payrolls to earn extra money, and Jenny served shifts in a milk bar on weekends. It was difficult, but they'd both finished their undergraduate courses of study.

When he left uni and went to work in the head office of the Department of Agriculture, his departmental colleagues reminded him of the shining future always expected of him at the time he first entered university. He remembered it too, so he enrolled in his Master's degree as a part-time student, studying in the evenings and on weekends. Both he and Jenny agreed that Tom needed a sibling without a big age gap between the children and Lottie arrived, but his life with Jenny felt flat. He sighed.

Armed with renewed determination, he pressed the button to alert his secretary he was ready for the interview with Sarah. She knocked and entered his office, and his heartrate kicked up. *I can control this*.

'Good afternoon, Sarah. Take a seat.' The rings on her left hand provided even more reason for him to be on guard.

'I've had a quick look at your resume. This field of work is new to you, I see. You were a maths teacher back home.' That field of interest, in itself, marked her out as an unusual woman. 'In a country town.'

'For a couple of years, yes. My husband's job took us there.' She looked him directly in the eye. 'No teaching qualification—but they were very short of teachers in that subject. I did a lot of maths at uni.'

She'd proved his point. A maths brain. He didn't know any other women like this.

'How on earth did you end up in economics?'

'Good question.' She gave a rueful laugh. 'I didn't study it at school. History was my first love there. Economics was a compromise choice.'

'What do you mean?'

'That degree course promised to combine my quantitative skills with theories about how the world allocates its resources. It sounded interesting to me.'

'Me too. It fascinates me, even if many of the concepts are wrong, or only offer partial explanations.'

'I'm beginning to learn that. I've read your thesis. It's good. Interesting. Well argued. Thought provoking. Well written.'

Wow, she has an enquiring mind on top of her looks. No wonder I'm hooked. 'Thanks. Back to you. What did you major in? I'm considering what work might best suit you.'

'Both economics and economic statistics. Strange, for a girl. I know.' She lifted her chin in a gesture of mild defiance, as if proud of herself but at the same time expecting a man to challenge her credibility.

'True. With your particular combination of skills, you'll be the only woman in most offices for a considerable period to come. I'd say we're lucky to have you.' *My lucky charm.*

She gave him a curious look. 'Lucky? Thanks. At first I didn't realise I'd barged into a man's world. Plenty of females in the teaching workforce. Here, I'm getting used to being the odd one out.' She smiled at him, but not submissively. It pleased him she seemed confident in her abilities.

'Being unique can work to your advantage. People notice you.' *Like I did.*

'I appreciate your encouragement. So far things are working out. At uni I had no real idea where my course choices might lead. Spending the past eighteen months in this country, especially in this office, has opened my eyes to the possibilities. On my first day I was hit with linear programming questions, and have since been asked about sampling theory and correcting for large sample errors. It tested me, that's for sure. I didn't remember that from my uni days and had to look it up.'

'Your degree will definitely open many doors for you.'

'Doors? That reminds me. After work today I'm going to a demonstration of a new desk calculator, at a cocktail party at the Papua Hotel. A couple of Ag people were asked to attend, including me, as I've spent hours at the company's office in town, using their current model machine. I suppose they're trying to sell the latest model to us.' She offered him a cheeky grin. 'You're the boss now. Interested? Is there room in the budget?'

He loved that element of *joie de vivre* in her character. 'I see you've been a very useful addition to this department. Just what I need.'

CHAPTER FOUR

Charles Williams bounced into the office.

Sarah looked at her watch. 'What gives with you? Only one minute late today. It's just gone eight o'clock.'

He gave her an 'I've just won the lottery' grin. 'Told you the other day to be careful what you wished for.'

'What's happened?'

'Carolyn's pregnant.' He rushed across and high-fived her.

She was sure her congratulatory smile did not reach her eyes.

Charles, too pumped up to notice, grinned with male pride. 'She's finally agreed we can tell everyone—although she's grumbling that the timing is all wrong.'

'The timing?' In Sarah's world any timing would be a godsend.

'The kid'll be the wrong age for starting school. My wife thinks ahead.'

He laughed along with the other men in the office. Sarah could see it written across their faces—women! The strangest of creatures.

Fresh from his morning meeting with the Departmental Head, Jack came through the doorway. 'Heard that laughter. What's going on?'

Charles told him and earned a hearty, approving slap on the back. 'Make the most of the next few months, mate,' said Jack. 'You'll say goodbye to sleep for a few years once that kid arrives.'

Sarah dabbed at the tears threatening to spill down her face, brushed past Jack and hurried out to the kitchenette to make herself a calming cup of tea. She took the private time she needed, cupping her hands around the hot mug and staring out the window. *What is wrong with me?*

Her mother had easily had children. So had her younger sister. Andrew had brothers.

It was time to stop procrastinating and find out why she was unable to fall pregnant.

Back at her desk, she quietly rang her doctor and asked for his next available lunchtime appointment. He was another import from Australia, as PNG had no local medicos. A young general practitioner, he was developing an interest in obstetrics and gynaecology and Sarah's women friends raved about his care. She would slip across town to his surgery near the hospital. Even if she was late back, none of her colleagues would notice her absence.

Dr Chadwick questioned her about her relevant medical history, then gave her the necessary pelvic examination. She lay on her back with her legs spread wide, tensed her body and stared at the ceiling, trying to pretend this wasn't happening as he inserted the speculum, studied her insides and prodded around with his gloved fingers.

'Sorry,' he said, 'Trying to be gentle. I'm afraid these indignities can't be avoided.'

'I know.' His white coat reassured her that was a professional and knew what he was doing. 'I'll get used to it, eventually. Women do, don't they!' She flinched as he pressed on a tender spot.

'Everything seems to be in the right place,' he declared after a few minutes. 'You can get dressed.' He disposed of his gloves and sat back at his desk to make notes.

Behind the screen she hastily reassembled her clothing and then emerged to face him again.

A sympathetic smile greeted her and in his matter-of-fact voice he said, 'Men are much easier to check for infertility problems. That's the next step.'

She released the nervous breath she'd been holding as she sank into her chair. He'd spoken kindly and was offering her a plan of action.

'I haven't met your husband. Will he agree to

a sperm test?'

'I'm not sure.' This was taking her into unfamiliar territory with Andrew. In his world of calculations and certainty, engineers were invincible. It would require careful handling. Like most men he didn't take kindly to any questioning of his maleness. Engineers, seeing themselves as 'real' men, pooh-poohed visits to a doctor. 'I'll have to wait for the right opportunity to speak to him.'

The doctor nodded, as if he understood the sensitive issues. 'I hope he'll see the logic and come to see me.'

The weeks dragged on into December, the wet season finally arrived, and another menstrual period came and went. Andrew ignored the blood-stained panties rinsed out and hanging on the shower tap to dry and remained oblivious to her dejection over her failed hopes to fall pregnant.

She continued to avoid asking him to make his appointment for a sperm test. Facing their first real challenge as a couple, it struck her that they didn't have a 'discuss anything' type of relationship. Resentment towards him surreptitiously crept in. How had she married someone who didn't notice her moods, only what she did for him as a mate to make his life comfortable?

Anger at herself mounted. *Admit it. Facing the world on your own scared you.* Getting ready for work, she glared at herself in the bathroom mirror. *You're more like your timid mother than you ever wanted to be.*

What was she so scared of? She should bring things to a head, have an argument about it. If only she knew how. As with Andrew, her life experience to date did not equip her for frank discussions.

They'd been inseparable since their high school days. The small world she shared with Andrew, her first and only boyfriend, was cloying, confining, predictable and smothering. But in an almost totally male faculty at uni, the unwanted attentions of admiring fellow students had made her nervous. The effort of warding off their high testosterone overtures had turned her into a scared possum, stranded in the middle lane of the Sydney Harbour Bridge, overwhelmed by the lanes of oncoming traffic.

By her graduation day she suspected that a universe of interesting people lay out there, that life didn't have to be a treadmill of study, duty to one's family and acceptance of responsibilities. But as the eldest of four, she was expected to set a good example, not rock the boat. Trained early in life to get along well both with adults and with peers, she hadn't risked demanding something for herself.

Instead, habits and family expectations had led to her marriage straight out of school and university. The perfect couple. Everyone said so. Looking back,

Sarah saw her and Andrew as virtual babies when they married, childhood sweethearts who looked at life through rose-coloured glasses.

The first significant risk she'd ever taken was moving to Port Moresby, but breaking out of her predictable world wasn't so scary with a trusted companion like Andrew by her side. In this small tropical town, she and Andrew mixed with work colleagues of varying ages and places of origin, discovering a world of friendship they should have explored as teenagers.

Couples took turns at arranging barbecues in their home gardens. Because many expatriate living quarters were located in compounds, it was easy to leave the children safely tucked up in bed, with a network of baby monitors alerting their parents to any cry or emergency. Beer flowed freely until the mosquito candles burned low.

Barbecues comprised much more than Aussie-style burnt steak and sausages. Young wives had fun sharing recipes for meals using local ingredients purchased on Saturday mornings at Koki market, where local growers squatted on their haunches in full sunshine, with their produce spread on mats and plenty of flies buzzing around. It paid to get to the market early.

Sarah and the other wives experimented with barramundi fish grilled on the barbeque and with kaukau, otherwise known as sweet potato, mashed with coconut cream and baked in the oven. Kumu, leaves from a range of bushy perennials similar to basil plants, substituted as greens. Papaya with a squeeze of lime juice tasted wonderful, as did mango mousse. They hadn't eaten this food at home in Australia and loved the new flavours.

After the main bulk of people left these parties, the stayers often played charades, great fun, although some had played it so often that it only took a few seconds to guess what was being acted out.

Andrew's work colleagues occasionally came for dinner on a Saturday night, especially Kevin and Maria Mitchell, who left their children at home asleep in bed, watched over by the resident servant. Sarah could relax in their company, as Maria always delighted in taking a break from her kids. 'Don't even mention them', she'd say, 'they're driving me bonkers.'

After dinner they got out the deck of cards and played rowdy games of canasta or 500, making bets with matches. An oscillating fan going full bore under the table kept everyone cool while not blowing the cards off the table. Sarah enjoyed these games of bluff, pitting her wits against others, but her lack of will to win at all costs tempered her skill with probabilities. She discovered she lacked the killer instinct.

Midweek, she and Andrew sometimes shared a

meal with her own well-liked colleague Charles Williams and his wife Carolyn, the only working wife she knew. They prided themselves on single-handedly solving the world's problems during their fascinating discussions of ideas. It suited Sarah to talk about issues outside herself.

But pregnant Carolyn would soon join the other young wives as a stay-at-home mum. Charles and Carolyn's baby-talk fuelled Sarah's sense of loneliness. She craved her own baby to love.

Outside the inner sanctum of womanhood, she gravitated towards the men. She enjoyed their conversations, engaging with them on an intellectual rather than emotional level and sometimes disclosing her likes, her dislikes, her interests, and her daydreams. But she kept secret from everyone her most important dream, that of motherhood.

CHAPTER FIVE

Sarah's frayed nerves settled when the wet season finally arrived in December. She felt comfortable enough with her new boss to invite him and his wife, Jenny, for dinner. Their two small children too, as the Martins yet had to establish arrangements with trusted babysitters.

In the late afternoon, Sarah heard car tyres scrunching on the gravel driveway and went outside to greet her guests.

'It's this way,' she called. 'You'll never find the front door. We use the back door.'

A little arrow pierced her heart as her visitors came towards her—a young couple with two adorable children. Her brain responded with *Why can't I have a family like this?* Familiar with fending off this troubling idea, she repressed her spurt of envy. Then a new little voice in her head whispered *I want this to be my family.* An icy shiver ran down her spine. Where had the second thought come from?

Jack shepherded his wife and children towards

her. 'Sarah, this is my wife Jenny, and the two little terrors are Tom and Charlotte, known as Lottie.' He introduced his family with considerable warmth and affection in his voice.

'I'm five,' said Tom, jumping up and down with excitement. 'She's only a baby,' he sneered, pointing at his sister.

'Not a baby,' protested Lottie, 'I'm two.'

'Pleased to meet you.' Sarah squatted to shake their hands in a game of formal greeting. They giggled. These angelic-looking children were two delightful bundles of energy.

She stood upright to greet Jenny, seemingly a placid and easy-going woman, standing back with a calm Mona Lisa smile, letting her kids steal the limelight. 'Welcome, Jenny.'

'I've been looking forward to meeting you,' said Jenny. The two women smiled at each other, as if aware of the irony that they somehow shared Jack, one at home and the other at work.

'Likewise. Come, all of you, and meet my husband.'

The man in question ambled down the back stairs to join them in the garden. 'G'day, folks. I'm Andrew.' He shook hands with the adults and gave a nervous smile at Tom and Lottie, who backed off against their mother, as if sensing that this big, tall man might represent stranger-danger.

Sarah felt sudden sympathy for his uneasiness

around these children and dealt with the slightly awkward moment by steering them all towards a drinks table set up in the shade of a large bauhinia tree. She turned to Jenny. 'Will we start with a drink? What would you like?'

'The kids will have orange juice, if you have it, and I wouldn't mind a beer.'

'Okay, coming up.' Sarah didn't drink beer, so she delegated Andrew to organise Jenny's drink while she attended to the children's needs.

'Beer, Jack?' Andrew offered him a can.

'Suits me.'

Perfectly equipped for their male-bonding session, the two men immediately took a few steps towards the bench tucked in a corner of the garden. 'I've heard a lot about you, Jack,' said Andrew. She watched him give Jack a playful jab on the arm. 'I'm wondering how much Sarah exaggerated her stories about you.'

'I hope I pass muster.' Jack turned to look at Sarah, a laughing question mark on his face.

She didn't want the Martins to think she gossiped about them. Andrew had dumped her right in it. Stories? She'd done nothing more than chat to him about her workday events. Of course her new boss would feature, as Andrew had heard everything there was to know about her other colleagues.

She could do with a drink after that. It wasn't often that she needed Dutch courage. Was Andrew going to mess up her career prospects by implying she was like a teenager raving over the latest pop star, just when she'd finally met a boss who took her work seriously?

She'd better keep her wits about her today. No male-female banter. No alcohol. Ignoring the wine bottle in its ice-bucket, she shrugged innocently at the men and poured herself a glass of plain tonic water with a twist of lemon and ice, a refreshing and thirst-quenching drink on a hot day.

She turned towards Jenny with a smile. 'Now that we're all sorted, you and I could walk around the garden with our drinks? Then Tom and Lottie can run about and explore.'

'An excellent idea,' said Jenny. 'They need to use up a bit more energy.' She sighed, as if burdened by the relentlessness of child care. 'The mozzies aren't out yet, so the kids can happily explore away.' She watched them scamper off, then looked around her with interest. 'Your garden is nice and shady for this time of day. Very lush.'

Andrew was not interested in growing things, but Sarah was becoming a passionate gardener and she swelled with pride. 'I belong to the brigade of "mad dogs and Englishmen out in the noonday sun",' she said with a laugh. Chatting with Jenny was proving easier than she'd expected, after her experiences with the wives of Andrew's colleagues, totally obsessed with their kids. Jenny noticed the environment around her. It encouraged Sarah to open up a little about herself. 'I love working on Saturdays with my assistant, Kirua.'

'Your garden boy?'

Sarah nodded. 'His turns of phrase are very entertaining.' The local *lingua franca*, Tok Pisin, was a mixture of many colonial influences, using a much smaller vocabulary than the English language. It required convoluted and long-winded phrasing to convey different meanings. 'Last weekend Kirua slapped himself hard and exclaimed *moskito i-kamap na i-kaikai long mi*. A mosquito came along and ate me.'

Jenny laughed. 'More colourful than saying a mozzie bit me. I've learned the basics of Pidgin English from my house girl.' A veteran of her former posting in a similar tropical climate, she added, 'It's not fair, is it! We're protected from malaria by our chloroquine tablets, our long sleeves, our slacks, our gardening shoes and our gardening gloves, but the locals like Kirua have to endure the risks posed by these deadly mosquitoes.'

'You're so right Jenny, Kirua has so little, but his cheerful attitudes have taught me so much. It's such fun to be with him, listening to his chatter and his giggles as he turns over the heavy black soil and inspects the various worms he disturbs.' She smiled at Jenny. 'I'm doing my best to learn Pidgin, have even enrolled in formal night classes, and he asked me to help him learn English. When I understand what he says, I repeat it back to him in English.'

'Is he a fast learner?'

'Yes, and I love working alongside him. He's so cheerful. So trusting. We've planted up the space with cuttings given by other mad gardeners like me. He scythes the grass and does most of the weeding and watering. We finish around five, when he's tired and often says *Mi bagarap tumas. Mi laik sindaun long as bilong diwai.*' He squats on his haunches under that tree where the men are sitting and I get us both a long, cold, fizzy drink. Lemon sprite, usually. Very refreshing.'

'I bet he loves that. Between you both, your tropical paradise is flourishing.'

'Couldn't agree more,' said Jack as he and Andrew sauntered over, clutching their second beers. 'Apart from the garden,' he said, looking around him with appreciation, 'how are you both finding this place?'

'We've settled in now, but it's just as well you didn't ask us that on the day we arrived.' Sarah laughed at the memory. 'We sat facing each other on the two single beds in our concrete-block, linoleum-floored donga. Gecko lizards ran up and down the walls and clucked alarmingly around us. Remember, Andrew?'

He rolled his eyes heavenward. 'We surveyed the banks of floor-to-ceiling louvre windows, the dust-coated fan rotating slowly overhead, the laminex table between the beds, the two aluminium chairs and the bathroom to be shared with the unknown occupants of the room beside us. Bloody hell. I'll never forget the look on your face.' Andrew looked at his wife and chortled at the memory.

'It sure is a rude shock when you first move to an underdeveloped country.' Jack grinned at them.

'You're not kidding,' Sarah said. 'We wiped the sweat from our brows, and asked ourselves in disbelief, what have we done? Help, let's go home.'

'But soon we escaped that donga and moved into this place.' Andrew waved his arms expansively, master of all he surveyed. 'It's a simple structure, but at least it's a proper free-standing house with three bedrooms and its own kitchen and bathroom, and it's quite adequate for our needs. Cold showers only, of course.'

Three bedrooms! Sarah's smile faded into wistfulness. Did he have to say that? Didn't he notice that she always shut the door into the two spare bedrooms, to save pining over them being empty of occupants. No bassinet, change table, cot or toys. She sighed with relief that neither Jack nor Jenny made a crack about filling up those bedrooms with kids.

Jack glanced at the house. 'On the outside, it looks a lot like ours. All government-provided housing accommodation is pretty stock-standard,' he said.

'Except for ours facing the wrong way on the block. The front door is never used,' Andrew grumbled. He never ceased to be irritated by this break with suburban convention.

Jack laughed. 'We don't stand on ceremony. The back door is fine with us.'

'How did you cope when you hired Kirua?' Jenny asked. 'Hiring household help is normally outside our comfort zone. We have no tradition of this in Australia.'

'True. Another dose of culture-shock. Young first-world city-slickers like us aren't used to third-world conditions. We were told about our obligation to provide employment to others.' Andrew shrugged. 'I left it up to Sarah to deal with it. She was at home for the first month we were here. Sleeping mostly!' His cheeky grin hinted at enthusiastic bedroom action after he arrived home.

Jack and Jenny smirked. They were young, too. Sarah noticed, and blushed slightly. 'The heat and humidity really got to me at first. I was so tired and lethargic. I hadn't started work yet, so I read or slept my way through the afternoons while Andrew was at work.'

A fresh wave of irritation at Andrew washed over her, triggered by his innuendo and his refusal to respect that Jack was her new boss and she was treading carefully. She shook it off and gave him a sugary sweet smile. 'If you recall, you too wanted to sleep off your tiredness when you got home from work.' Tit for tat, she gave her husband a gentle poke on his chest to disguise her exasperation.

'And I didn't sleep all day. In the mornings I shopped and cooked. Cleaned the house. Did the washing.' There, that should set the record straight, that she didn't spend all day waiting for her man to come home and take her to bed. In fact, action in the kissing department of their marriage had noticeably waned.

She turned to her guests. 'That's when I met Kirua. I was pegging on the line when a pair of broad black feet appeared silently below the flapping sheets. Petrified, I hastily pulled a sheet aside, half expecting to find an assailant waving a sharp blade at me, like you hear in the news stories back home. Instead, a jaunty smile greeted me, and he said *Hi Misis, mi laik painim wok.*'

'Luckily phonetics conveys the general gist of Pidgin.' Jenny gave her that fellow-feeling smile exchanged between long-suffering wives left to deal with domestic problems.

'I understood he was saying hello and was looking for work. With just the two of us, out all day, I don't even have enough work to keep myself occupied at home, and accommodation for servants doesn't come with our house. He could see there's nowhere here for him to live. I realised he must already live somewhere close by, to know that we'd moved in here.'

'There's a sizeable encampment of his *wantoks* just down the road from here.' Andrew pointed southwards, in the general direction of the coastline, where a large squatter settlement of incoming Highlanders was expanding.

'We were standing in the garden, so the prospect of outside work came to mind. Testing out my fledgling Tok Pisin, picked up from the lessons on the radio early each morning, I dredged up enough words to say *Yu laik wok long gaden?* Would you like to work in the garden?'

'Good thinking. Any cash work here is good work,' said Jack.

'Of course it upsets me that the cash rate is $1.20 per day, and I earn almost fifteen times that, but then you think of all the economic theory of underdeveloped nations and you realise it has to be that way.'

'We walked around this extensive garden area, with me miming my intentions. I extended my arms to encompass its space and pointed at individual features. Previous residents didn't tend this garden during the long dry season, leaving it parched and barren. He got the message. *Yesa Misis, mi laikim gaden tru. Mi laik tumas wok long dispela gaden.* I can repeat that with confidence now, but at that point I was struggling to understand his words, that he liked the garden and wanted to work here. I just interpreted his body language. You've never seen such a brilliant smile.'

'So how did you figure out his name?'

'By placing my hand on my heart and using his opening line to me. I said "Me, Missus, you?" and he said *Nem bilong mi Kirua.*'

'Okay, Kirua.' We solemnly shook hands. Done deal. I'd hired myself a servant. Before long, I signed up to learn the local language at a free night school. I was pretty proud of myself!' She grinned at her guests.

And so they broke the ice with the Martins. Sarah served the meal early to suit the needs of the youngsters. 'I'm not used to feeding children so I opted for a simple meal. I hope they'll like my version of Shepherd's Pie, with heaps of vegies hidden among the minced meat.'

'Perfect. They'll love it,' said Jenny.

'My suggestion,' said Andrew. 'It's one of my favourites, but Sarah doesn't make it often when it's just the two of us.'

'I don't blame her. It's a lot of work,' Jenny said. 'Plus, it involves lighting the oven.' Jenny made a show of fanning herself, to make her point that the place was hot enough already, without adding a hot kitchen to the mix.

They sat at the table and Sarah carried the ovenproof dish from the kitchen and set down the steaming meal on a thick table mat. She placed a bowl of hot peas on another mat. 'We're not standing on ceremony here. It'll be easier for me to serve the right-sized helpings with you to guide me, Jenny.'

'Of course.' Jenny drew in an appreciative lungful of air. 'That topping of mashed potato and grated cheese, baked to a golden brown, looks and smells melt-in-your-mouth scrumptious.'

'Yum,' said Tom. 'Can I have a big helping?'

'Only if you promise to eat all your peas,' said Jack sternly.

Sarah doled out the food for the children, taking her cues from Jenny. Lottie eyed Tom's plate. 'You've got more than me,' she protested.

'I'm bigger, that's why.'

'Don't forget the tomato sauce.' Andrew distracted them by pointing to a novelty dispenser on the table, shaped like a large red tomato with a green stalk sprouting from its top.

The rounded eyes of her youngest guests warmed Sarah's heart. 'I couldn't resist it,' she explained to their parents. 'Saw it at Steamies in town the other day. Thought it would appeal to the kids.' It had given her incredible pleasure to buy something with children in mind.

'Oops. Damage control.' Jenny grabbed it. 'I'm in charge of this, kids.' She squirted sauce onto their food in the shape of a large red S.

'Superman,' they squealed.

'It's their favourite gimmick at meal times. But

that stalk nozzle sure helps direct the flow more accurately. Great idea,' said Jenny.

'Tuck in,' said Andrew.

Six hungry people obeyed him, saying little until the clatter of cutlery ended. 'Delicious,' said Jack. 'And for once, the kids have cleaned up their plates.'

'But wait, there's more,' laughed Sarah, pleased she'd hit the right spot with her menu choice. 'Predictably, ice cream for Tom and Lottie. Hope it's okay.' She rolled her eyes. Jack and Jenny would understand. You never could tell how many times an item had been half-melted and refrozen when you made a purchase at the town's main trading store. 'My cheese cake concoction for us,' she added.

'You're putting me to shame,' said Jenny. 'I'm not keen on the kitchen. Jack's the main chef in our house.'

'Letting the side down, mate,' said Andrew to Jack. 'I can't boil an egg.'

'Needs must,' laughed Jack. 'But you blokes at Posts and Telegraphs know how those mysterious telecommunications work. Completely out of my comfort zone.'

The banter between the adults and the chatter of the young ones fuelled the longing in Sarah's heart. The life forces in evidence among her guests highlighted the gaping hole in her life. She wished this evening could go on forever, but the tired children were now seeking refuge on their parents' laps, Lottie with thumb in mouth. Nine o'clock saw the Martins loading their two sleepy charges into the car.

'They've been little angels,' said Sarah.

'Luckily. Exhaustion sometimes turns them into prize fighters or clingy, whingeing bundles of misery,' said Jenny with a laugh. 'Tonight they quietly retreated to us, thank heavens.'

'We've had a wonderful time, Sarah and Andrew,' said Jack. 'Thanks so much for the invitation, and for including Tom and Lottie. We'll get you round to our house soon.'

'If ever I get unpacked.' Jenny's gloomy comment reminded Sarah that Jenny wasn't what she'd expected. *Did* she take months to unpack removalist boxes? She moved at a leisurely pace, and spoke slowly, reacting to conversation rather than initiating it, with no sign of the energy, vigour and alertness so obvious in her husband.

As they drove off, Sarah said to Andrew, 'How did you like them?'

'I thought the evening was a great success. Jack's a good bloke alright. His wife seems nice enough.'

'Did you like their kids?'

'Take 'em or leave 'em,' he replied. 'I prefer kids when they're older.'

'I noticed a bit of hesitancy from you when

they arrived. But you've never said that before.'

'You've never asked for my views on the subject.'

'And you've never volunteered them. How old is old enough?'

'Primary age, maybe. Before they reach their teens.'

'What about babies?'

'Women's work.'

She stared at him. This man was turning into a stranger.

CHAPTER SIX

Jack drove carefully. He'd downed a few beers at the Robinson's, but not enough to impair his driving. Touch wood. He glanced in the rear-vision mirror at the two children, fast asleep in their car-seats, their heads lolling. They were his reason for living.

Jenny broke the silence. 'They weren't what I expected.'

'Our hosts, you mean?' He risked a brief glance in her direction, gauging her mood. She stared ahead into the darkness, her shoulders slumped.

'They're a bit like us,' she mused, 'other than the kids, of course.'

'Like us?'

'Yeah, she's on the ball, like you. Deals with stuff. Good organiser. Keeps the conversation going. He's laid back, like me. Moseys along. Enjoys the moment. Rests on his oars. Lacks the force-field of energy needed to make his mark as a personality.'

Jack chuckled. He'd noticed the same thing.

'So you enjoyed sussing them out this evening.'

Jenny bit her lip. 'It worries me, that you work all day with Sarah.'

'Well, it's not quite like that. She's one of my staff, working out in the main office among quite a large group of men.'

'But you've never had a dynamic, attractive young woman working for you before.'

'True, she's the first female I've supervised. Hey, are you jealous of her or something?' He reached sideways and gave her hand a reassuring squeeze.

'Just feeling frumpy. I put on all that weight, having the kids.'

'Most women do, don't they? Except those who live on dry crackers and sparkling mineral water.' She *had* gained some kgs, but how to be tactful yet truthful was currently eluding him.

For once, she saved him the effort of a suitable white lie. 'Thanks, Jack. For putting up with me. I know I'm not what you wanted.'

Her gloomy voice frayed his heart strings because he'd grown to love her—but she'd put into words exactly what he knew to be true.

Especially since Sarah had flashed into his world.

'Hey there, cheer up. Have you ever felt that I don't love you?'

'No, you've been kind and loyal, loving, but

not exactly 'in love' with me.'

'Love grows, you know. And has many shapes and sizes. Passion and drama and purple prose is not compulsory. Have you been reading too many of your Mills and Boon novels?'

She gave him a sheepish grin. 'Maybe. I should give them a rest.'

He took his eye off the road long enough to lean across and plant a quick peck on her cheek. 'I don't regret our uni days, or the decisions we made.' He spoke staunchly, doing his best to console her. 'Would your life mean as much without Tom?'

'Of course not. But you hadn't sown your wild oats. Nor had I, come to think of it, but I never wanted to, after I met you.'

'We've come through. So far, we've survived okay. You may have been my first—and only—proper girlfriend, but I'm not one of those men who feels compelled to play the field.' He had to reassure her—because he was trying to reassure himself.

Sarah had become the first Eve in his life, the first source of biblical temptation he'd had to resist with obstinate willpower.

There was no sign that Sarah felt the same spark. She and Andrew presented to the world as a couple perfectly able to rub along together.

His fascination with Sarah would pass with time.

'You know I'm a man of my word, Jenny. I'll

be keeping my marriage vows. So stop worrying about Sarah.' He looked for a way to change the subject. 'She seems a decent human being and might even become your friend. It's always handy to have women friends in a place like this.'

'Okay, you're right. Definitely scope for a friendship there. I'll gear myself up to return their hospitality.'

He shrugged inwardly. His wife had a frustrating habit of procrastination.

'Soon, Jack, I promise.'

CHAPTER SEVEN

Jack called Sarah into his office on Monday. 'Morning.' He smiled warmly at her. 'Thanks for your hospitality on the weekend. We all enjoyed ourselves.'

'No worries. So did we. It was great to meet Jenny and the kids.' She returned his smile and their eyes locked for a second, sending a shiver of apprehension through her. Or was it anticipation? Of what? How did that saying go—a smile is the shortest distance between two people? His smiles attracted her closer to him than anyone's smiles should. For a moment she gave her intuition full reign and luxuriated in the sense of feeling connected to someone. To him.

'To business. I've been thinking. Unlike my predecessor, I'm keen for every member of my staff to have field trip experience. That includes you.'

Hallelujah! Was he going to overturn the discrimination she'd endured so far, always stuck in the office, writing up the notes of the men's adventures? She sat up straighter in her chair, brushing off her sixth sense, paying more attention to the here and now. 'I've listened jealously to all the men's tales. And Andrew's. I'd love to get out of Moresby and see the country for myself.' There, the Sarah she showed to the outside world was back in control—rational, matter-of-fact.

'It's essential that you do. Goes with the territory. You can't possibly understand our work in the field of development economics if you keep pushing pens here in head office.'

'My sentiments exactly.'

'At your place you impressed me with your tales of working with your garden boy. Your willingness to learn Tok Pisin. Unlike some who come to this country, you have the right attitudes for our work.'

'I admire the locals. They're such a happy lot. Even when they're sitting on the kerb in town, counting out their piles of coins and chattering away. It's like a party.'

He gave a wry grin. 'I wouldn't want to be a bank teller in Moresby. All those customers coming in every few days to withdraw all their money to check the bank hasn't stolen it. Some have amassed quite a nest egg.'

'I think the bank systems are pretty foolproof, as long as they maintain their massive stocks of coins.' She laughed. 'I've watched the tellers sometimes when I go to the bank. They make sure that the coins being returned by one customer aren't seen to be handed over to the next person in the queue.'

'Proves how much work lies ahead to establish a modern economy and build trust in the concept of banking. I'm enjoying the challenge, though,' he said. 'The local people here are fantastic.'

'Yes, it's a wonderful environment, even if it makes me mad to see the local men walking at the front of a family group, under the shade of their umbrella, while the wife tags along behind with the children, in the full sun, with the youngest child carried in a *bilum* bag slung off her head.' She sighed with exasperation.

'We agree one hundred percent. It's too much of a man's world.' He shifted in his seat to line her up in his gaze. 'So here's the thing. Prepare yourself to take an initiation tour. Next week.'

Her face almost cracked open with her grin. She'd jump up and do a happy dance with him but he'd think she was crazy, the exact opposite of what she needed from him. She was desperate for him to treat her as an equal in the workforce.

'My secretary will make appointments for you to meet with various agricultural field officers. You'll be away for the week. In the Highlands. Staying overnight at Goroka, Mount Hagen, Goroka and Kainantu. I hope Andrew will withstand your absence but, since he has to travel for work himself, he should understand.'

She nodded. Too bad if Andrew objected. She couldn't wait. 'I'm thrilled. Thank you, Jack.'

The Highlands straddled the border line between the old German colony of New Guinea in the north and the former British colony of Papua in the south, all administered by Australia since the Great War. Andrew raved about his experiences in the Highlands, but she'd never been outside Moresby. On this trip she wouldn't be tagging along behind him, as she had so far in their married life. She was going alone. Life was happening to her, at last.

She flew on the old, reliable workhorse of PNG, the Fokker Friendship, to the frontier town of Goroka, where the expatriate Arabica coffee plantations were being progressively returned to traditional landowners.

She spent the day sitting in the front passenger seat of a battered old four-wheel-drive truck, while her local driver coached the vehicle along muddy jungle tracks, scattering squealing pigs before them. The smell of the rotting vegetation in a tropical forest did not appeal after the dry bushland she'd been used to in Sydney. That night the temperature dropped to 15 degrees, and next morning she huddled in her cardigan, glad she'd been warned to take some warm clothing with her. She wished she still owned some jeans, but then she'd be too hot when the day warmed up.

The mountains surrounding the town were high and close, forcing planes to keep circling after take-off, gaining enough height to fly over, and not into, the towering peaks. As she flew out of Goroka towards Mount Hagen she peered downwards from the passenger cabin, intrigued, as the little settlement below grew further away with each upward spiral.

From Hagen her journey by jeep took her to remote, densely-populated villages built on steep mountain sides. Here the women grew their kaukau in magnificent terraced gardens, still using their digging sticks and the most primitive of tools. She watched teams of men building access roads with shovels, rocks and their bare hands. Alone with her government-employed drivers, she never had occasion to worry about her personal safety and she soon learned to enjoy their ability to derive fun and enjoyment from the simplest everyday event.

On the way back from Hagen to Goroka, this time in a light plane, a stop-off at Kundiawa was scheduled. Her pilot gave her no warning of what to expect, other than a mischievous grin over his shoulder, his eyes twinkling. He banked steeply, the aircraft wings almost vertical to the ground, and approached an 'aircraft carrier' strip, a grassy stretch cleared from a narrow ridgeline along a spur, with a steep drop falling away on three sides. Her heart stopped pounding when they landed safely. Although it was a weekly event for the local population, the feat also thrilled them, and they spilled out of their huts and swarmed around, chattering and laughing with infectious excitement.

After that cheeky pilot landed her back at Goroka, she took another road trip to Kainantu, a 90-kilometre stretch along the rough and ready 700 kilometres of the Highlands Highway, and home of a large coffee plantation and a sizeable population of expats.

Here her itinerary indicated that a trip in a helicopter would return her to the transport hub at Lae and the Fokker flight back to Moresby. What a thrill to be sitting inside the bubble canopy as the chopper's engines fired up, the rotors vibrated into action and they whirred away from the ground, whop-whopping their way towards the coast.

A photograph taken on her camera by the local ag officer became a favourite souvenir of her trip. It showed her perched on a long plank of timber, supported at intervals by timber posts driven vertically into the ground. Slender upright posts, the front two slightly higher than those at the rear, supported a sagging sheet of corrugated iron above her head, providing shade and shelter from rain. Creating the facia of this primitive structure was a board hand-painted by an expat wag with a sense of humour. It read 'Kainantu International Air Terminal'.

In her heart she thanked Jack for offering her the adventures of a lifetime, and for helping her to build her confidence that she could cope with anything. Her experiences in her five-day initiation tour far exceeded her imagination as a teenaged student in those crowded lecture rooms at Sydney Uni.

In the man's world she inhabited, she was beginning to recognise his willingness to accept her on equal terms as an employee, his treatment of her as 'sexless' on the job, as a remarkable trait. The leaders of the new women's liberation movement in England, America and Australia would rate him as a gold star example of an enlightened man.

CHAPTER EIGHT

Jack and Jenny kept their promise to reciprocate hospitality. In the early part of a tropical Saturday night, Sarah and Andrew arrived at a house aglow with light, fully in use as a family home, lights ablaze in every room. The harmonious voices of the Everly Brothers, pitch-perfect, floated out through the open louvre windows, bemoaning sad tales of young love gone wrong.

Sarah was looking forward to the evening. Because she'd established a respectful working relationship with Jack, any inappropriate remarks from Andrew tonight would not have the impact she'd feared when they'd first met the Martins socially.

'Don't mind Jack and his music,' said Jenny, as she greeted them at the door. 'He doesn't care if it's a golden oldie or the latest and greatest, as long as he can sing along, or dance to it. He's out the back, attending to the barbecue, hence the volume turned up high.'

'The noise won't bother Sarah,' replied Andrew. 'She loves music too.'

Jenny ushered them through the house, where Sarah noted that the layout of Jack's government house at Waigani was a carbon copy of hers. But no-one in the Martin household paid much attention to décor and the arrangement of objects. Nor was Jenny a fussy housekeeper, evidenced by the toys strewn everywhere and a few cardboard removalist cartons stacked in the hallway.

They reached the back door, and the two children rushed over, squealing and jumping up and down with excitement. Sarah picked Lottie up and gave her a big hug. Andrew high-fived Tom, more relaxed with a child of his age than with Lottie.

Jack grinned at his visitors and waved his barbecue tongs in greeting. 'Now that you're here, I'll get started. The kids are hanging out for their sausages. Steak for us. I assume that's in order. Jenny's our bartender.'

An array of drinks and salads beckoned, laid out on the serving table. 'We'll eat out here,' said Jenny. 'Less kiddie mess for me to clean up afterwards.'

After the meal, they moved indoors and Jenny's books, piled on the lounge chairs, had to be pushed aside. As Tom and Lottie scrambled to take possession of the seats, Jack spoke to the excited children. 'Your mother meant what she said.

Bedtime. Off you go.' He held out his arms as they rushed at him, giggling, ready for their goodnight bearhug. Jenny led them away to deal with their toileting and teeth-cleaning rituals.

Sarah offered to read the bedtime story as a way of enticing Tom and his sister into their room, where they would enjoy the novelty of a new entertainer. In their shared bedroom, they snuggled into her, clutching their ragged comforters, and she soaked up the delicious smells of their overheated bodies and their soggy soft toys. Eyes struggling to stay open soon drooped, and she gave each child a kiss goodnight as she tucked them in.

'All's quiet on the western front now,' she said with a laugh as she rejoined the other three. Despite the difference in their household routines, Sarah felt quite at home. It was fun being with the children amidst their chaos.

'You're a natural with kids,' said Jenny. 'I usually have a lot of trouble getting them into bed.'

'If they're asleep, I'm going to put the Everlys back on,' announced Jack, jumping up. 'The kids won't wake again until morning, and I could tell Sarah liked those old-fashioned harmonies. Caught her humming away.' Jack grinned, turned up the music to full volume and joined the recording artists, beefing out 'Cathy's Clown' in perfect harmony with them.

A strange premonition crawled down Sarah's

spine. That song, all about unwanted kisses, struck her as a stark description of her own marriage.

She and Andrew were undeniably struggling as their paths diverged and their interest in each other waned. A wave of lonesomeness washed over her. You can be married, yet still lonely.

She scolded herself. *I'm not lonely tonight. This is fun*. The incongruity of the song's words in her present environment, the miracle of the human voice used as a musical instrument, and the seductive pleasures of harmonising chased away her brief flirtation with the blues.

No matter whether two or more brains worked in synchronisation with each other in an opera or the Everlys, harmonies were central to her enjoyment of music. She'd been like this since early childhood, able to play tunes on the piano by ear. Foolishly, she'd let it go.

What the heck. Life was for living. She chimed in with Jack's warm baritone, bashful at first, quietly humming, then singing the lyrics with gusto, locking laughing eyes with him to keep the tempo.

Jenny and Andrew exchanged amused shrugs, as if tolerant of the strange behaviour of their respective spouses.

Sarah too could not quite believe the unshackling of her repressed self.

What a night. She and Jack took turns at choosing songs by their favourite artists. Jenny and

Andrew occasionally made half-hearted efforts to join in. Clearly not stirred by the power of two minds working closely together, trying to harmonise perfectly, they gave up after mouthing the introductory words of their chosen song, or the chorus line. No foot-tapping, no beating arms in time with the music, no spontaneous singing, like her and Jack.

When time came to leave, Sarah's sparkling face confirmed her feelings as she thanked her hosts. 'I had a marvellous evening. I feel so happy.'

'Yes, thanks very much,' said Andrew. 'Jack, you and Sarah made a talented team with those songs. I've never heard her sing like that. I don't know what prompted her to let down her guard.'

'She should do it more often,' said Jack. 'Look at her.'

Andrew studied his wife's face. 'I haven't seen her eyes shining so brightly since…' He wrinkled his brow as he reached for an example, '… the day we got married.'

Sarah stared at her husband, startled at his unexpected truth. She *was* exhilarated, high on the cuddles with the children, the company of their parents, and the sheer joy of singing in such an unexpected, uninhibited, but co-operative way.

Jenny laughed. 'Thanks for coming. I prefer to read, but Jack loves his music, so it was great for him to find a fellow fan.'

'You'll have to come again,' said Jack. 'We've got all kinds of music here, and it's easier for you to visit us, than for us to lug the kids around in the evenings.'

It was a quiet trip home in the car. Sarah didn't want to break the spell of a perfect evening.

She peered carefully into the darkness ahead. Pedestrians with brown skins and dark clothing were hard to see when street-lighting was so minimal. She was driving because Andrew drank a lot more than she did. He liked his beer, but he was also becoming a committed wine connoisseur, which led to him dozing off at dinner parties. Tonight, she'd been too busy to get past her first drink.

She ignored her glimpses of a growing disharmony between her and Andrew. Especially concerning children. He'd paid no attention to Tom and Lottie tonight, other than high-fiving Tom, which was the least he could do to be polite. It reminded her of his strange *take 'em or leave 'em* comment on the night the Martins came for dinner.

She liked to dance and sing, but his physical outlet was as a tennis player. In the cool of the Moresby evenings she'd learned to play his favourite game, to ensure he had a partner to hit with, but her hand-eye co-ordination for a fast-moving ball left a little to be desired. Other nights he played in a men's squash competition. He never complained that she wasn't sporty. It was as if he didn't care, taking women for granted as one of life's mysteries.

She'd never noticed these differences when they were younger. She wondered which characteristics of hers might bother Andrew. In this country they'd developed a shared love of adventure, but their other interests were gradually diverging.

Pushing her unwelcome, intrusive thoughts aside, she concentrated on her driving, and soon swung the car into their gravel driveway. The refrain of the Everly Brothers' song lulled her into an uneasy sleep.

CHAPTER NINE

On Fridays, Andrew's workmates at the Department of Posts and Telegraphs left their offices in central Moresby and gathered after work at the Yacht Club. It was a relaxing way to end the week.

Articulating her every thought and expressing every emotion about her personal life, like the women in this group, was not her style. As usual she gravitated towards the men discussing current affairs and the latest storm in a political teacup. Unaware the Robinsons couldn't have children, they all took Sarah at face value as a career girl, as a woman not interested in motherhood.

The men also discussed financial strategies for achieving home ownership, the goal they aspired to reach, and they freely offered their opinions to the Robinsons. 'You two are smart, putting off starting a family so you can save up for a house.' Sarah didn't contradict them. This was a private matter between her and Andrew.

Her choice of company avoided the pain of

hearing the women gossiping and comparing the significant life experiences from which she felt so excluded. Hanging around the men did nothing to endear her to the wives, except for Maria Mitchell, wife of Andrew's boss Kevin. Pregnant with her fourth child, she kept everyone entertained with her stories of the various misdeeds of her offspring, making Sarah sometimes grateful to be spared the responsibility of parenthood. The child-free status of the Robinsons was a definite plus for Maria, whose favourite saying to Andrew was, 'Our kids are keeping us in the poor-house.' Her over-the-top personality made Sarah laugh.

This week's gathering held the promise of better times ahead. The Club's balcony overlooked the vast harbour, with dense bushland on the far shore, and a spectacular tropical sunset was proof that the evening downpours of the wet season were waning, exposing them to another long dry period. Breathless, warm, salty air soothed Sarah in its lethargic embrace. Daylight would plunge into darkness as the sun sank over the horizon and the short twilight of the tropics rapidly faded into a velvet blackness, with no city lights to brighten the night sky. Just the stars, faintly reflected in glistening water, and later the moon.

The Yacht Club was at Konedobu, where Sarah worked, but her workmates at the Department of Agriculture, Stock and Fisheries didn't attend the

Friday get-togethers. Staff employed by the various government departments rarely intermingled. Engineers and agriculturalists were especially incompatible as companions, their background training being so different.

Wives kept to the social group surrounding their husband's job, but Sarah straddled both worlds, as a wife in one and as an employee in the other.

Tonight, she wished her own special colleagues were present to share the evening with her. Charles and Carolyn. Jack and Jenny. They would surely appreciate the panoramic scene before them. Especially Jack.

That unbidden thought hit her with a jolt and she flashed back to that singalong night with the Everly Brothers, months ago, and the vibe they'd shared. She knew him better now. He was clearly in tune with his environment and she had a sixth sense that his response to the visual splendours of the landscape before them would be like hers.

She'd zoned out. She refocused on the conversation swirling around her when Maria mentioned a much-advertised program coming up on television concerning male infertility. 'If only,' she said, as she patted her swollen belly and gazed fondly at her existing brood, currently revelling in their game of hide and seek with the other kids.

The men sniggered at the notion that males might be impotent. Prevailing cultural attitudes to that unbelievable idea was the reason for the programme being so widely promoted. Someone in television-land saw the need for necessary community education.

Andrew did not join in the ribald banter. Sarah wondered if niggling doubts existed in his mind about the cause of their failure to conceive. A surge of compassion welled in her. It must be exhausting, having to operate in the 'tough guy' world of men. Maybe he didn't take it for granted that this was women's business and it must be her fault. In his vulnerable moments, perhaps he doubted himself. She herself wished she knew where the problem lay. Doctor Chadwick had said he wouldn't do more tests on her until Andrew had been checked out.

On the way home, Andrew commented to Sarah, as if in passing, 'It's entertaining having all those kids rampaging around. The older ones, I mean. Not the littlies.'

'Yes, I think so too.' She hoped her brief, matter-of-fact response would give him room to expand on his thoughts. Wailing 'poor me, I want a baby' and bursting into tears would shut him down.

'My mates are pretty pleased with themselves for having sons.'

'Pleased about their daughters, too, I hope.'

'S'pose. The point is, they seem to have no trouble having kids.'

This was a breakthrough. Normally this was a

taboo topic, prompting him to change the subject.

'But we do. Have trouble, I mean.' He paused. 'We should watch that program tonight on TV. It sounds like an interesting show.'

This was fantastic. He'd taken a giant mental and emotional step forward. She didn't want her yearning to be too apparent, too threatening to him, so she murmured, 'I agree. We might both learn something, if we can get reception.' Programs from the national broadcaster in Australia were transmitted over unreliable airwaves.

The atmospheric gods co-operated as they turned on the set at eight thirty and sat down to watch. Andrew clutched his inevitable cold beer and Sarah cradled her steaming cup of tea. She found it a strangely refreshing drink in hot climes and a self-calming mechanism in stressful moments.

Afterwards, he was silent for a few moments, but then he said, 'It's made me think. I didn't realise that many men have problems with fertility.'

'Nor did I. But then again, neither of us is a walking encyclopaedia on biology. Other than doing what comes naturally.' She gave him an encouraging smile.

'I thought infertility was basically the woman's problem. I've been wondering why you haven't done something about it.'

Sarah's jaw dropped. Men! She kept her eye on winning the war, not the battle of the sexes, and seized this welcome opportunity to make forward progress with her quest. 'So you agree we could investigate it?'

Andrew looked apprehensive. 'Well,' he began grudgingly, 'as the program outlined, it's easy enough for doctors to check the male.'

'Whereas, for females…' Sarah stopped to let that thought grow wings.

'Bloody hell, what I'd have to do first.' He wrinkled his nose in aversion. 'Producing that specimen. Pretty embarrassing.' Indignation resonated in his voice.

Embarrassing! Did he have any idea of the indignities suffered by women of child-bearing age? Suppressing the urge to laugh out loud, she smiled her encouragement at him. 'But not that hard to do, in the grand scheme of things.' He was an engineer, and she knew an appeal to his logic might work. An emotional 'it's not fair being a girl' outburst would likely fail.

Andrew sat still, silent for a while. 'I keep remembering that story you told me about your dad, when he got drunk at the local pub one Boxing Day and came home and attacked your mum.'

'Good grief! How is that relevant now?' She stared at him, puzzled.

'I think it did you a lot of damage.'

Her mouth rounded into an 'O' as her jaw dropped. What did he mean? Why remind her of the horrible day she'd shepherded her three younger sisters into the back garden to hide them from their father, in case he attacked them next? She'd tried to stop him bashing her mother's head against their bedroom wall, him shouting, her mother screaming.

'It certainly upset me,' she said. 'Our neighbours gathered in the street in front of our house, with their children, my playmates, listening to the commotion, but no-one came to our aid.'

'Leaving you, ten years old, to deal with it.'

She looked at him curiously. Where was this leading? 'Yes, but I had no power as a child against an enraged man. I told you. I ran next door to my neighbour. "Please help me get Daddy away from Mummy," I begged. He returned with me and led Dad out of the house.'

The memories flooded back, of how she'd saved her mother's life but, after her father disappeared from home for a while and then reappeared, everyone pretended it never happened. No-one acknowledged her feelings.

Repressed anger boiled up in her as she said, 'Indelibly imprinted on my brain was the sight of Dad attacking Mum—but Mum not fighting back.'

'By the time I came into your life you'd picked up on her lasting fear of a repeat performance, even though he never attacked her again.'

'Sorry. I shouldn't have inflicted those teenage *I hate my dad* complaints onto you. It's just I never knew why he did it. It was like he'd held back on a lot of stuff until it finally exploded out of him. No-one ever talked about it.'

'He made *you* nervous and stressed, but I always got along okay with your father.'

'I instinctively stood up to him, became the mother of the family, because Mum had been so passive in the face of a threat. It was me who'd acted to fix it.'

'And you've been the responsible eldest child ever since. Looking after people. Your mother. Your younger sisters.'

'Thanks for noticing, after all this time, but why bring this up, especially tonight?'

He gazed at her. 'I think it's why you want a baby so badly now.'

'What do you mean?'

'I've seen how you interact with Tom and Lottie. And the Mitchell kids. I finally connected the dots. You crave having someone to look after and love, to be responsible for, like you've done all your life, especially since you were ten. I'm not enough. You need more.'

Her face crumpled as her tears welled at the realisation that Andrew, of his own accord, had recognised her as a person. 'I really do.' She reached across and squeezed his hand. 'Would you do it? Would you see Dr Chadwick and have a check?'

He remained silent.

'Once you're checked out, we can start on me. That process, for me, will be infinitely more complicated.'

Her pragmatic professional engineer husband finally responded with, 'It's a critical path network problem I never expected.' He stared into space, as if he'd taken his foot off his mental accelerator to coast along while his mind was engaged elsewhere.

She held her breath.

His internal gears visibly shifted and his car sped up again. 'I have to admit, the most appropriate route is for me to be checked first.'

He gave her a rueful grin. 'Give me Dr Chadwick's number.'

CHAPTER TEN

Solemn-faced, Dr Chadwick delivered his shattering news. Andrew had such a low sperm count, with virtually no motility, that a pregnancy stood the same chance as her winning the lottery. Not that he put it quite so bluntly.

'Andrew, we don't fully understand the causes of this condition, but the problem likely relates to having mumps at the wrong time in your childhood.' The doctor's voice trailed away as his concerned gaze switched from Andrew to Sarah and back.

'As a doctor, I can't help you any further. There's a new vaccine for the mumps but, sadly, that's come too late for you.'

His explanation provided no consolation. Andrew slumped in his seat, shoulders sagging, staring at his feet.

Sarah's first instinct was a rush of concern for her husband. Watching his self-image crumble before this blow to his perception of manhood, she reached across and took his hand to comfort him. He did not respond but she tightened her grip as the implications for her hit home. Calm on the outside for his sake, but panicking on the inside, her dreams for her future shattered into a million shards of disappointment, cutting into her breaths and weighing down her heart.

He ignored the implications for Sarah as his confidence in himself plummeted. He didn't look at her and mutter 'I'm sorry.' She didn't cry with disappointment. White-faced and silent, they left the surgery.

Although distraught at this single fatal blow to her dreams of motherhood, Sarah was full of sorrow for Andrew's pain. In the weeks that followed, she wished she knew how to help him. Her childhood lessons from Sunday School played in her mind: never do anything that's not kind. Out shopping together at the market, she held his hand like a young couple in love. In bed at night, she snuggled against him as a comforter.

Each, in their own way, digested the implications of the news as they suffered in silence.

Sarah's maternal instincts, heightened and made more poignant by being part of a community of young families, all breeding like rabbits, grew stronger and more painful. She would never care for, nurture, manage and entertain her own babies. In the moments when that thought took hold she wanted to burst into tears, sob and scream at him 'You snatched my dream away.' She resisted the urge. It wasn't his fault. With the effort of suppressing her disappointment, she lost interest in food and began to lose weight.

Discussing a problem of this nature with anyone was out of the question. No-one opened up about their marriages. Recalling the sniggering that night at the Yacht Club, she knew their highly fertile friends wouldn't understand. Intimate issues had never been broached with their family members, thousands of kilometres away. She'd never witnessed her parents discussing anything together, ever. Counselling services didn't exist anywhere in this underdeveloped country.

His medical diagnosis, which shamed him, she could tell, would have to stay as her secret, a sorrow she bore alone.

Sexual interest in each other died away. It aroused too many painful emotions swirling in the psyche of a man who knew he was 'firing blanks', and a woman who knew she'd never have a baby.

On Wednesday nights she focused with renewed energy on her voluntary role as a maths teacher at night school. In this overwhelmingly patriarchal society, only the men came to lessons. Her class of supposedly sixth grade standard students might consist of five who could add, subtract and multiply but not divide, six who could add and subtract with about a 50% success rate, and eight who couldn't do anything. The organisers tried to juggle the classes to get the most advanced students into her class and redistribute the others, but psychological attachment to their various teachers meant they wouldn't be moved.

It was all a hopeless muddle but they were very keen to learn, so it was quite satisfying to be helping these men enter the modern world. The contrast between her world and theirs was aptly captured in the title of the recent autobiography by a leading local politician, Albert Maori Kiki: 'Ten Thousand Years in a Lifetime.'

Andrew retreated further into his world of work, where a promotion made him responsible for inspecting new projects in several far-flung centres.

That same afternoon he came home and said, 'My forthcoming trip schedule has focused my attention on the need for better home security.'

'Don't worry. I'll be fine.'

'I disagree. Remember that night when we looked up from our books to see a pair of dark brown eyes peering in through the louvres at us?'

'Vividly.' Sarah shivered, wishing he hadn't reminded her. They lived in Korobosea, close to Port Moresby General Hospital, which attracted much foot traffic as well as the passengers pouring off the PMVs serving as public transport. She'd been sure at the time that those dark brown eyes belonged to a harmless stranger, curious about how the other half lived. She and Andrew led a simple life by Australian standards, but still lived in the lap of luxury compared with living conditions for most of the locals.

Her complacency faded. How would she feel if a similar incident happened again, while she was home alone, without Andrew's comforting presence? 'Okay then, you're right. There is a lot of unemployment and ever-increasing levels of petty crime. Our security needs a boost, I agree.'

He nodded. 'We can't build a security fence, this is government property, but I've arranged for gravel paths to be installed right around the perimeter of the house, making it easier to hear the approach of any intruders.'

'Good idea. Thanks. You asked Kirua to do this?'

'Nope. A team of labourers will be here next week, cutting out the paths and spreading the gravel. I'll be here to supervise. You're the master planner of the garden. Come outside and show me where you'd like the paths to go.'

'To be effective they'll need to be hard up against the house, won't they? To deter an intruder from creeping around on my soft garden beds.'

He huffed with impatience. 'Yes, but how wide do you want them? Straight or curved at the corners?

Which plants will have to be moved?'

She recognised this as serious men's business and paid attention. 'Relatively few, luckily.' She smiled her encouragement at him.

They walked down the back stairs into the garden, brushing past the papaya tree outside the kitchen window. She pointed at it. 'I don't want that moved. It's perfect in that spot.'

'Righto. This garden bed is small and tucked in between the stairs and the corner of the house. The pathway will easily skirt this bit.' He made a few notes on the clipboard he'd grabbed as they left the house.

They walked round the corner of the building and along the front of the house, past the few steps leading up to their front door, which was never used. Andrew narrowed his eyes. 'It's obvious why this point of access tempted that curious intruder. Nice soft soil here.'

'Yes, this spot definitely needs better protection. All the plantings near these steps are small foliage plants, struck from cuttings. If they're kept damp, Kirua and I will replant them next time he comes, squeezed in along the front boundary line. We might do something creative to hide the piers supporting the house. Trellis work, perhaps.'

She enjoyed working with Andrew on a joint project. It happened rarely these days, but a minor construction project like this gave him a sense of being in control and compensated slightly for their lack of 'togetherness' in the bedroom.

They reached the side of the house facing the driveway and the street. Andrew looked at the blank wall which had greeted them on their arrival two years ago, now covered with a beautiful magenta-flowering creeper, flourishing on its sturdy stems. 'Even I know this plant. A bougainvillea. It's prickly. There are no windows on this wall. It can stay. This section of the path can safely be a few feet out from the house.'

Rounding the last corner, they reached the car parking area. 'I'll widen the gravelled area here, to eliminate that strip of garden beside the house,' he said.

'I agree. No need to keep the straggle of plants in this spot.'

'Okay. Job done.' He tucked his clipboard under his arm. 'We'll both rest easier by next weekend,' he said. A satisfied smile creased his face.

She'd need to. She'd be spending a lot of time at home alone over the next few months.

Kevin was on the line. 'Got news for you. As Andrew's away, I thought I'd ring you myself. Maria's had the baby.'

'Great. When?' Sarah repressed her brief stab of jealousy.

'Overnight. A girl. Both doing well.'

Sarah forced enthusiasm into her voice. 'Wonderful news. Does she have a name?'

'Isabella.'

'Lovely. Isabella Mitchell. It has a nice ring to it.' She strove for the next polite response. 'Will Maria be in hospital for a few days? Can I visit her?' She had no excuse. Moresby's hospital was just along the road from their house.

It'd be hell holding this new baby but, somehow, she'd screw on a smile for Maria, her friend.

'Dunno. They kick 'em out quick here. Came home to check on the other kids. I'll find out when I get back to Maria. It's fortunate this wasn't her first child.'

'Why, what happened?'

'The hospital was bursting at the seams when we arrived. The only available bed was in a main corridor. That's where Maria gave birth.'

'In the corridor? With people walking past her? No privacy?'

'Nope. Luckily, not a lot of foot traffic at that hour—but some. Then, after they'd checked the baby and Maria had delivered the afterbirth, they handed her a towel and told her to go take a shower while they found her a bed in a ward. Isabella needed a bit more monitoring.'

'I don't believe it.'

'True story. Wait, there's more. Her bed in the

ward lay alongside a panel of louvred windows with a public footpath outside. An hour later she found herself in a tug-of-war with a local who was trying to snaffle her bedsheet and drag it through the window.'

Sarah burst out laughing. 'I guess it makes a change from the usual bag-grabbing efforts of *raskols*. It's hilarious. Were you there when this happened?'

'I missed that part of the fun and games. They'd packed me off to the waiting room after Isabella arrived. They came and got me only after they'd moved Maria's bed further from the windows.' He laughed too. 'Maria took a while to appreciate the funny side. She was pretty exhausted after having the baby. Unexpected feats of muscle power weren't part of her plan.'

'It's impressive the way she copes with everything here.'

'She's a trooper alright. Living here has trained her to be tough.' He laughed again. 'A few years ago I took her with me on one of my trips away, so she could see the country, better understand my job. Sophia was our baby then, and she came with us. On our way from Lae up the Highlands Highway towards Goroka, a gang of *raskols* stood blocking the road ahead, hoping to stop our vehicle and distract us, while a few nicked around behind us looking for stuff to pinch off the back. We had to get out of the truck to deal with them.'

'Scary.'

'Well…kind of. Everyone crowded around, entranced by a white baby. They seemed friendly enough. Then one of the women, bare-breasted of course, grabbed Sophia from Maria's arms and suckled her. Don't know if she did this out of natural instinct, or out of curiosity about the different ways of white babies. I've never heard Maria scream so loud.'

Sarah gulped. 'Was Sophia okay?'

'Mother's milk's pretty safe, I guess. It was the pig fat surrounding the nipple and general standard of hygiene that horrified Maria.'

She laughed. 'Life back in Sydney will seem so tame once you get home. Sophia's friends will never believe that story at her twenty-first.'

Carolyn had her baby a few weeks later. A boy. Richard. Ricky. Charles beamed with pride.

Sarah selected flowers and a cute toy to welcome both new babies into the world. She kept her visits short and sweet to minimise the painful tugs on her heartstrings.

At home alone in the evenings, she came to lonely terms with the notion that the one thing she craved in life was permanently out of her reach, and there was nothing she could do about it. With the heart-wrenching discovery that life is unfair and you can't always get what you strive for, she confronted reality for the first time. Would she and Andrew survive this crisis?

CHAPTER ELEVEN

Jack noticed the sudden change in Sarah. She'd always shown a bright face to the world, but lately, if she let down her guard, a dispirited expression greeted him.

It puzzled him. She'd been the first to extend hospitality to him and his family. Kind and welcoming to them, joining in with the fun of life. Professional in her dealings with the men at the office. Although she held back in front of her male colleagues, she had so much potential in every way. Privately, he regarded her as the most capable member of his staff.

He wanted to cheer her up. She needed a challenge, something new to engage her attention.

The wet season had been and gone, and it was the end of May already. He walked down the corridor to her desk, smiled at her and said, 'I've got a special assignment for you. Come into my office so we can discuss it.'

Her face agog with curiosity, she followed him

and plonked herself into his visitor's chair.

He wasted no time. 'I'd like you to conduct the annual cost of copra production survey.' Her eyes widened in astonishment.

'All the information about previous surveys is in this file.' He pushed it across his desk towards her. 'Take it away and read it. The standard questionnaire is there too.'

She picked it up, flicked through the pages, and gazed back at him.

'My secretary has booked you on a flight next Monday morning and has arranged all the accommodation.'

'Who's coming with me?'

'No-one.'

She gasped. 'On my own, you mean?'

'Yes. You can handle it. You'll be away for several weeks, as per the schedule of plantation visits, but you'll come home on Friday afternoon. I don't expect you to be stranded in some frontier town by yourself on a weekend.'

'Thanks for that. I wouldn't like that either.'

'I want you to perform the survey this year, as it calls for a fresh pair of eyes on the job.'

'I gather the copra industry's in decline, with the competition from oil palms.'

'So you've been keeping your eyes and ears open? It proves why I selected you.'

Sarah nibbled her lip, showing her concern.

'What do you expect me to do, then? I'm a statistician, not an agricultural officer.'

'Then the standard questions on acreage, yields and numbers of employees won't bother you. In addition, I want you to ask about the age of the coconut palm trees. Their health status. Replanting statistics. Look around you. Does pasture grass or broadleaf weeds flourish at ground level? Is the owner operating his plantation as a monoculture? Or has he under planted his palms with cocoa, herb and spice crops? Is he grazing animals?'

'And you think I'm up to this?'

'Of course. A driver and someone from each local office will accompany you so you'll be perfectly safe.'

'I wasn't worrying so much about my safety as my level of knowledge.'

'You're very capable. You'll have a checklist. I need an interviewer who'll carefully consider what they are seeing, what they are being told, and then take accurate notes. Kind of like being a reporter. Scrappy reports from previous years show that some of our blokes got on the booze with the owners instead of attending to their duties.'

'What can I say but thank you? For your vote of confidence in me. For offering me the experience of a lifetime.'

'Just make sure you do a good job.' He dredged up his 'strict teacher' manner from somewhere in his past. From in his present came a faint but insistent little voice, 'I could so easily fall in love with you.' He gave himself a mental slap on the wrists. *Danger. Don't go there.*

'Wow, this will be an adventure.' The stern tone of his spoken words hadn't generated the reaction he expected. In her irrepressible grin he glimpsed the old Sarah.

———

Armed with her questionnaire, and with her support staff, over the next two weeks she did the rounds of the copra plantations. Although she travelled with the men staffing agricultural outstations, she knew Andrew wouldn't act jealous. She didn't 'play around'.

But her imagination tempted her and betrayed her on several of her lonely nights away. What might it feel like to have Jack's arms enveloping her, his kisses arousing her? She berated herself. 'I'm falling into the grass-is-greener trap, just because I'm unhappy. I'm not interested in any of my colleagues—including Jack.'

Most of the plantation homesteads were sprawling structures raised a few feet from the ground, with an iron roof and wide wooden verandahs. Partial screening with mosquito mesh made it possible to sit outside with a drink at dusk. House and garden magazine editors based in Sydney might romanticise these settings, but she discovered a reality of battered buildings and shabby furnishings.

It was years since most places had seen a paintbrush. Ancient rattan sofas and well-worn chairs, scattered along the verandahs rather than grouped for ease of conversation, were lumpy and uncomfortable, far from 'easy'. French doors opened onto the well-trodden timber decks and through them she glimpsed beds offering no promise of a good night's rest. Thanks to the prior arrangements made for her accommodation, she was glad she didn't have to sample any of them.

Sarah saw the indolent lifestyle of plantation owners as an inevitable consequence of spending years in the enervating heat and humidity of the tropics. Her colleagues in Moresby jokingly referred to the owners as the B4s, referring to previous generations of expatriates. In the lazy days before the Second World War, the life of these men had revolved around a few beers at lunchtime, a few gin and tonics at four thirty, and a few whiskies in the evening. Some long-term expats she interviewed maintained these habits. Their hands shook by midday with the symptoms of alcohol withdrawal.

It amazed these relics of a bygone era that an attractive young woman would turn up to conduct official government business. As their house boys plied her with cups of tea, they'd ask, 'Why did that Moresby bloke send a slip of a thing like you this time?' They bent over backward to guide Sarah proudly around their domains, demonstrating the husking and cutting of coconuts, explaining their diseases and the different types of dryers, and showing her an opened cocoa pod with all its innards. The plantation owners and managers told her a great deal more about their operations than was prudent, since a steel-trap mind lurked behind the 'girlie' whose pretty face they rushed to compliment. Jack's reason for sending her as his data collector became apparent.

She returned to the office with dozens of pages of her commentary notes, written on the back of the questionnaires, impatient to share her discoveries with Jack. Her mood was happier too, as the assignment had removed her from after-hours socialising with mothers and babies and had taken her mind off her troubles with Andrew.

Jack made no comment about the obvious diminution in the strain lines around her eyes. He flipped through the pages of responses. 'Bob's your uncle! Well done.' He glanced at her commentaries. 'These additional notes distinguish an adequate job from a superb effort. Here you've noted something important.' He read it aloud: 'Agricultural crops can go in and out of fashion. Coconut oil might make a comeback.'

'Full confession. That wasn't my knowledge

on display. You know that. I simply recorded what one of those old-timers said to me.'

'I knew you'd be a great interviewer.'

Her face lit up as she absorbed his words of approval. He wanted more of this. Sarah was an intriguing enigma, so downcast when she believed no-one was looking and so radiant when she thought life was beautiful. Every day he had to douse the spark she'd fired in him.

He continued. 'Replicating the format of earlier reports is an option but, after seeing your notes, I reckon you'll set a new benchmark for conducting these surveys in the future.'

'Being very familiar with those documents now, I agree they provide inadequate management information.'

'Would you like my ideas on using your field work to best advantage in satisfying the official requirements of the survey?'

'Of course I would.'

Sarah sat still while Jack perused her notes in more detail, and she jotted down his occasional suggestions on the notepad balanced on her knee. It wasn't long before he looked up, smiled across the table at her and said, 'If you base your report on the points I've mentioned, it will come together nicely.'

The expression on her gorgeous face lit with enthusiasm and his pulse quickened in response. Then he reprimanded himself. The challenge of her work excited her, not him. How he wished it otherwise.

He forced his mind back to business mode. 'I'll leave it to you to undertake the detailed analysis, as that's your specialty after all. Can you have your draft on my desk by Friday lunchtime?'

CHAPTER TWELVE

Whenever she compared her working environment with Andrew's, Sarah smiled wryly. On coastal lowlands she tramped around Papuan copra plantations, hot and sweaty, clasping her clipboard and her camera, dodging the occasional fall of a coconut aiming for a target on her head.

In his high-tech world he landed by helicopter on cold, cloud-swathed New Guinea mountain tops. Pretty bloody hairy, he said. On the highest peaks the chopper pilot kept the engine idling while the men performed their duties, in case the motor wouldn't re-start at that altitude. No-one wanted to be stranded up there. But the risk was worth it—this was the country's future.

Andrew's regular absences became a feature of their life and she began taking her personal security precautions much more seriously. In the living area she closed the lower level of metal louvres at night, drew the curtains across the glass ones and ran the ceiling fan on high to counter the stifling air in an unventilated room. Government housing did not provide air conditioning.

On many of her 'alone' nights, if a strong breeze was blowing and rustling all the leaves outside the house, and blowing doors open and shut inside the house, she jumped every time and came over all jittery. On those nights she retired to bed early with a book, trying to forget imaginary prowlers.

She keyed all the connecting doors in the house at bedtime, aware that she could always remove the louvres and use the bedroom window as a fire escape, and she plugged the telephone handset into the socket by her bed in case she needed to call the police.

So far, so good, she'd escaped the notice of anyone trying to rob the place or take advantage of a young white woman living on her own. But one night, after midnight, as she tossed and turned, she heard the faint crunch of footsteps on the loose gravel in the car parking spot near her bedroom.

She lay there, rigid with apprehension, her heart pounding so hard it could set the beat in a symphony orchestra.

Had she heard right? The sound came again. A quiet shuffle, not a scurry of several culprits. Just one person? Was he after her car—or her? He didn't sound drunk, as he was moving stealthily, not stumbling around. She slid out of bed and switched on the light to warn the intruder that someone inside the household was awake.

Grabbing the phone she dialled the emergency number, hoping that whoever skulked outside would hear the rotary dial clicking round and realise she was calling for help. As extra insurance, she yelled into the darkness *Wusat? Kolim nem bilong yu.* Getting no answer, she yelled again, *Lukim yu, polis i kam kwik.*

She hoped that her shouted warning would make the prowler run away. She knew full well that the police were a laid-back lot, unlikely to turn up on her doorstep until the morning. Gun violence had not yet crept into this culture, but rape was increasing with the influx of men pouring in from outlying villages, their women folk left behind. If the intruder was a newcomer from the Highlands, unaware of police habits and still fearing the word 'police', he might abandon his intentions.

She pressed her back against the wall, legs trembling, wishing she had a heavy frying pan or a hockey stick to use as a weapon, if needed.

Running footsteps eased her panic. He'd gone.

Her stomach churned and her bladder urgently needed emptying, but it took half an hour of quietness before she was game enough to unlock her bedroom door and tiptoe down the hall to the bathroom. She congratulated herself for overcoming her fears of this type of aloneness. Her sense of personal power was increasing.

Afterwards, Andrew called her by telephone most evenings to check on her welfare.

On the nights she didn't get much sleep, thinking prowlers were trying to get in, she never feared sleeping in and being late for work. Every morning she was wakened as the PMVs drove past her house, trucks packed with men sitting on the flat tray behind the driver's cabin, those in the middle squatting on their haunches, the rest swinging their legs over the sides, all singing loudly together as a male chorus. She and Andrew both loved their novel alarm clock.

But apart from his obvious concern for her physical safety, they were becoming like ships in the night. Slipping alongside each other on parallel courses, almost invisible to each other. Despite her attempts to show solidarity, to snuggle up to him in the night, he never opened up about his feelings. Body language wasn't enough and she didn't have the words, or the skills to help him.

A king-sized panic at work offered a welcome diversion. The Assistant Administrator had decreed that her section must prepare a case against the Rural Minimum Wages recommendations put forward by a formal Committee of Enquiry. The Committee, comprising visiting university professors and their PhD students, had sat for the past six months, but her section only had five weeks to get all the necessary field data, analyse it, write it up and have it typed.

Jack allocated teams of two to each of the cocoa/coconuts, rubber, coffee and tea industries. Given her experience with the copra cost of production survey, he sent her and Charles to Rabaul for five days to assess the current profitability of that industry and the likely impact of higher rural wages. Rabaul was built within the caldera of an active volcano, but she was too busy collecting data to worry about its dangerous location. It was comforting to have the uncomplicated company of her friend Charles as her travelling companion and the perfume of the frangipani dominating the streets of Rabaul soothed her senses.

'To stay, or to go, that's been my dilemma,' Andrew announced on a Friday evening after his latest trip.

'What are you talking about? Go where?'

'Home. My contract of employment has come up for renewal.'

She inhaled with shock and almost choked on her mouthful of kedgeree. 'Why didn't you tell me?'

'I've been giving it some quiet thought, that's why.'

'It affects me too.'

'It's *my* career we're discussing. That's what counts. My work challenges me and it's worthwhile, doing the country some good. I've renewed my contract. Signed the papers a few hours ago.'

'Just like that. You've made that decision without consulting me.'

'Why not? You've got a job you seem to like. We might as well be here as anywhere else.'

Sarah stared at him, dumbfounded, lost for words. No wonder she felt adrift in this marriage. Nothing was working out. No proper communication—apart from that moment months ago when he'd displayed insight into why she so badly craved motherhood. A stab of loneliness knifed through her.

Gloomily, she reviewed the choices she'd made in her private life.

By marrying Andrew, she'd settled for her comfort zone and safety—for habit and security over discomfort and challenge. From the age of ten she'd assumed the responsibility of keeping her family safe and happy, in a world where disaster might happen but the people closest to her pretended all was well. Nothing to see here—they turned the spotlight on other people's affairs. Too often, she'd ignored her own desires.

She'd attached herself to Andrew, a boy with whom she'd always felt safe. He'd helped her through her teens, been a good listener to her. She'd helped him with his career moves, encouraging him, leaving her home for an intra-state and now an international relocation.

Her internal moral code frowned at all aspects

of selfishness. She'd never previously contemplated the concept that it was impossible to please everyone but her outlook was slowly changing. *I should have listened to my inner voice when I finished uni. I knew another world beckoned. I should have been braver. I should have pleased myself.*

On Monday at work, Sarah mentioned Andrew's plans to Jack. He'd been her boss for more than six months now and she admired and respected his positivity, his constructive approach, his ability to grasp new ideas so quickly and his own hard-working attitude. It was a wonderful confidence boost to work for someone like this. She was glad to have the opportunity for this arrangement to continue.

'That's good news. It means you can stay here too, with us.'

The broad smile on his face triggered another unnerving response and her heart kicked over. This man could smile like no other person she knew. And he smiled with his eyes, not just his mouth, and those eyes looking at her gave her a sudden lift, to think that she pleased him. For too long she'd been living with a sense of failure, but with Jack she could feel like a real winner.

'Stay here too, with us' carried a meaning, for her, that Jack surely didn't intend.

He meant 'with us in the department'. But she

walked on cloud nine in Jack's presence, and his words instantly made her uncomfortably aware that she wanted to 'stay here with him'.

Work was so much more challenging, and rewarding, these days. His supervisory and delegatory skills made all the difference to her enjoyment of her work.

He replicated these skills guiding the other staff. The economists within the group were currently focusing all their efforts on the impending arrival of the World Bank's annual delegation. Sarah helped her colleagues by preparing the management information reports for the Bank's inspection team, tasked with assessing the use of its project funding. The visitors expected to see progress being made towards building the country's eventual economic viability.

Away from the office, she found it harder and harder to contemplate another endless year stretching out ahead of her, encompassing more of Andrew's emotional withdrawal, more lonely evenings caused by his frequent absences, and the strain of tactless friends joshing her about being a career woman. She struggled to maintain her mental equilibrium.

She did little better with her external signs of wellbeing. The heat left everyone sluggish but lately, nearly every day, she dozed off at work if just reading something. She blamed the antibiotics she'd been taking for a sinus infection. Today she was making her third trip to see Dr Chadwick in a month.

As she approached his rooms she knew that he, at least, would surely understand the reasons for her recent weight loss. He kept tabs on her only ongoing complaint as a resident of Moresby, her occasional vascular headaches, a milder form of migraine, brought on by the dilation of blood vessels when her head grew too hot. To her relief she'd been free of actual headaches lately, but the sinus pain around her cheekbones and the thick green discharge of mucous from her nose was almost as debilitating.

She unexpectedly shared the waiting room with Maria Mitchell, still carrying the remnants of her tummy bulge. In her arms she held its cause—her four-month-old infant Isabella, inexplicably screaming.

The doctor called Maria into his surgery and Sarah said, 'Give Isabella to me. I'll look after her for you. You and Dr Chadwick won't be able to hear yourselves think with all that squalling.'

'Bless you. Thanks.' Maria thrust the distressed baby at Sarah and rushed away.

Sarah stood and paced up and down the room, cradling the infant in loving arms as she tried to shush her. The bawling child needed something additional to distract her, so she gently exhaled warm air from her own mouth into Isabella's ear. It seemed to both surprise and soothe Isabella, and the loud protests died away.

Still pacing, Sarah talked to the baby as if she was a person, rocking her, telling her why her mummy disappeared behind the door and when she was coming back, lulling her with a soft voice, bonding with this baby. When Maria returned, Isabella was quite content again.

Maria beamed at her daughter, gooing and gaaing to make her smile, ever the proud and doting parent, at the same time saying, 'Thanks Sarah, you're a marvel. A baby-whisperer. You should have children of your own. You'd make a marvellous mother.' Maria reached out to reclaim her child.

Sarah nearly dropped the baby at that throwaway line. She craved what Maria had. It hurt worse than her childhood memories of having a forbidden sweet taken away as she handed back the precious bundle in her aching arms.

CHAPTER THIRTEEN

Sarah's enthusiasm guiding her work on the copra plantation survey had faded, as if she had nothing to look forward to. Jack was not entirely sure of its cause, but he'd noticed her quietness whenever the men's office banter turned to bragging about the development milestones reached by their babies, or war stories about the devilish behaviour of older kids.

He had a pretty fair idea that *his* Sarah, as he was coming to think of her, was pining for the presence of children in her household. It might explain her increasing air of depression.

Was it even remotely possible that she and Andrew were unable to have kids? She had plenty of brains, more than most but, at her house and at his, she'd shown a maternal streak, a rare and tantalising combination of attributes in any woman. She'd surely be a mother by now if nature had taken its normal course. Was she the problem? Or Andrew?

He'd jump at the chance to try some baby-making with her himself. He chased that intrusive, traitorous thought away and cursed her unexpected effect on him. A jolt of powerful chemistry had zapped him the moment he met her, although she seemed oblivious to its thrall.

Sarah had a husband to whom she was apparently loyal and he had no reason to suspect otherwise. Every week in the office he reminded himself, and his traitorous body, of his commitment to his wife and children. He had no intention of breaking the vows he'd made to himself. He had matured into a dedicated family man, able to control his wayward feelings.

In command of the situation, he'd be a good friend to this couple, letting no-one see just how alluring he found this fascinating creature named Sarah.

Yes, that's what he'd do. He'd hold out the hand of friendship.

He asked the Robinsons to join him, Jenny, Tom and Lottie on a family picnic. Being with the kids might restore the glint of fun to her eyes and the bounce back into her step.

Going on a picnic was special in this amazing country. The local environment, too primitive to attract pampered and well-heeled international tourists, offered its adventurous permanent residents the choice of a variety of interesting and different picnic sites. All of them uncrowded, indeed virtually uninhabited.

The following Sunday, they took both cars and headed into the hills outside Moresby. A dusty and ill-formed road wound its way to Crystal Rapids, a remarkably cool haven on the hottest of days. Mini waterfalls poured off rocky ledges as the cascades of sparkling water rushed past, tumbling downwards in search of the sea. In the quieter sections of this busy torrent, they submerged themselves in shallow pools and washed clean their grimy faces and sweaty bodies.

———

These outings became a regular event.

For Andrew and Sarah, their picnics with the Martins offered the perfect escape from too much time spent alone together. The prospect of years of aloneness stretching out into the future was so depressing. Middle-aged couples whose children had left home found the concept difficult to accept. For a young married couple, the concept was alien.

For Sarah the weekend excursions were a great blessing. Her social skills were perfectly adequate, but by nature she was a true introvert with a rich inner life. Regular contact with congenial company like Jack's and Jenny's freed her inhibitions.

Jack, although technically her boss, had been simpatico from the start, proved by the sing-along at his house. Jenny was never one to fuss over her offspring. Their outings were very relaxed affairs, focusing on simple pleasures. A picnic basket. An Esky for the cold food and drinks. A rug to sit on. A towel, a hat, bathers under outer clothes, insect repellent. An agreed rendezvous point.

Jenny always brought two extra items to a picnic site. A director's chair and a book. Pleasant and friendly to begin, she invariably unfolded the chair, retrieved her latest romance novel from her bag, gave them an apologetic smile, tossed an 'I'm off duty' remark at everyone and slipped into her dream world. It eclipsed the realities of her daily existence and she let her capable husband deal with Tom and Lottie, organise the lunch and chat with Sarah and Andrew. This was her day off from childcare. Her charges clearly accepted this as the norm and doted on their father's attention.

This pleased Sarah. Mutual parenting had been her father's style too, when his daughters were young and he was not at work.

She recalled with pleasure the adventurous weekend family picnics of her primary school years. Her dad had been a capable man of action too and her mother had relished it, been part of his team. He'd stirred his female household into action, transported them to the beach or a bushland site, cooked sausages over a fire and swung the billy to make tea afterwards. Before that Boxing Day episode spoiled everything for her.

Eager as a puppy, Sarah looked forward to her

weekend outings with the Martins. With their mutual interest in things agricultural, she and Jack found enjoyment in pointing out various vegetative forms to Tom and Lottie, whose round eyes sparkled with joy at discovering the world in all its glories of nature. Life was full of such joyous pleasures around childish laughter, she told herself. It had nothing to do with spending more time with Jack.

Over the course of their picnicking sessions, Sarah gradually realised that while Jack's relationship with his laid-back, absent-minded wife did not entirely suit him, he tolerated her ways and obviously adored his two delightfully boisterous youngsters.

When the wet season finished, and flood levels eased, they swam in the warm, muddy Brown River as it snaked lazily to the coast. The women splashed around on the riverbank, paddling with the children. Sarah loved nothing better than picking up Lottie's slippery little body to bring her to safety when she strayed too far from the shore.

The men took greater chances. They swam out into the river and drifted along for a short distance, each with a child riding on their backs, emulating the customs of the local populace. Tom and Lottie held on tightly, their fingers firmly gripping Jack and Andrew's hair, their feet jammed against the men's ribcages, squealing with joy at the fun. This was a job for male muscle power, as the men had to stay vigilant to catch a child who might slip, and they had to breaststroke back against the current to the picnic spot. Basic precautions ticked various risk management boxes: the downstream flow was sluggish; both children could dog paddle enough to keep their heads above water if necessary; and they didn't go far out into the stream.

The famous Kokoda Track further up into the hills beckoned today. Beyond Nine Mile they passed the turnoff to the Bomana War Cemetery, beautifully maintained by the Commonwealth War Graves Commission. 'Andrew, we should stop here,' commanded Sarah urgently. 'I bet Jack and Jenny haven't seen this place.' He turned hard left, towards the parking area, and the Martins obeyed their car's yellow flashing blinker and followed suit.

Inside the entrance gate the Martins' faces paled in shock. Serried ranks of formal white headstones stretched as far as the eye could see, honouring nearly 4,000 people who lost their lives fighting in Papua and Bougainville during the Second World War.

Tom and Lottie ran up and down the rows playing hide and seek while their parents squatted to read details on the headstones. 'Look at this Jack, how sad, most victims were younger than us,' said Jenny.

'Many graves are unidentified. This place makes me cry every time I visit,' sniffed Sarah, 'especially when I remember the numbers lying in those other two PNG war cemeteries, at Lae and Rabaul.'

'It's a sobering place. What a bloody waste.' Jack stared around him, transfixed, as if he couldn't quite believe the magnitude of the events of twenty-five years ago.

Subdued, they left quietly and continued their journey. Thirty-plus kilometres further east they bumped along the dirt road winding through the rubber plantation at Sogeri and parked at Owers' Corner. Sarah and Jenny stuffed towels, drinks, snacks and mosquito repellent into hiking packs which the men hoisted on their backs and they set off down the Track.

At the bottom of the first precipitous incline came their reward, a raging torrent feeding a refreshing swimming hole, so cold it set them shivering. Sarah's hair flattened and water dripped off her nose but she wasn't out to impress Jack in the least, was she? No, absolutely not.

This trip was a taster, not a trek, and after an hour they turned back. The steep walk uphill through dense jungle was slippery with mud and required every ounce of fitness they possessed. Breathless from the exertion, their hearts pounding, they frequently stopped for rests and grateful sips of the drinks lugged in the backpacks. Sarah pitied those poor malaria-ridden, wounded soldiers retreating along this track in the war, helped by locals affectionately called the fuzzy-wuzzy angels. Even her tennis-match-fit husband marvelled at their historic achievement. 'How the hell did they do it?' he puffed.

'Buggered if I know,' panted Jack, lugging Lottie and dragging Tom by one hand up the steepest of the slopes, their short legs unable to deal with the terrain. But Jack typically made them scramble as best they could, the adults keeping slow pace with them. He was teaching them to be independent and self-reliant, not spoilt little brats.

On other days they picnicked in the shade of coconut palms, relaxing beside the blue expanse of a tropical ocean, calm behind its protective reef. Sarah had never been a suntanned bikini-clad bathing belle, as her childhood trips to the beaches in Sydney had too often caused painful sunburn and she'd soon learned to cover up.

On their carefree beach picnics in these latitudes, her sweat-sheened skin did not burn so fast but still needed extra protection, as radiation reflected off the sea and the sand as well as directly beaming from above. If she removed her beach wrap to go for a swim, Andrew helped her apply Coppertone lotion, advertised to contain a sunscreen, to her exposed shoulders and back. A big improvement on the limitations of zinc cream on her nose. She writhed in pleasure at the lotion's slippery feel on her skin and imprinted its distinctive fragrance on her brain with a few deep breaths.

Once she noticed Jack watching this procedure with a strange expression on his face. Not the leer of an ogler. More like the stare of someone silently processing some uncomfortable thoughts. He looked away quickly when she caught his eye but, somehow, he didn't trigger a self-conscious reaction in her, just an unexpected flutter of physical connection to him. The moment evaporated with the heat rising off the sand as she headed down the beach for her swim.

Sarah cherished the days she spent with Jack and his children. Playing with Tom and Lottie came naturally to her. Their piping voices brought joy to her heart. Jack inadvertently taught her extra little tricks for handling them and firmly and consistently disciplined any of their inappropriate behaviour. She learned that lots of cuddles, stimulating activities, sensible food and plenty of rest made small fry like Tom and Lottie delightful company—most of the time.

Charles Williams owned a power boat. One Sunday he invited his work colleagues with their families to a big day out, meeting down at the harbour to go out to Local Island for a barbecue breakfast and then water skiing.

He'd told them that he planned for everyone to

take turns at water skiing inside the reef, where the waves were calm enough to introduce amateurs to the sport.

For once, John Bartlett wanted to be part of the action and he came along with his wife Annie, who Sarah had never met. The Bartletts moved in different circles to the rest of the office crowd. Annie sashayed along the sand, flaunting her buxom breasts and her firm, rounded buttocks in a just-there shoe-string bikini. Such a public display of sexuality took Sarah straight back to her uncomfortable, self-conscious teenage years on Sydney's beaches and reminded her all over again that she was too strait-laced and had never been one of the girls.

John too made her nervous, the way he ogled the women and inserted sexual innuendo into his every remark.

'Surprise, surprise,' he drawled when he spotted her on her knees on the sand, leaning over to help Tom and Lottie build a castle, her breasts at just the right angle for a good view. 'Peachy.'

She straightened up, wishing she'd worn a demure one-piece swimsuit instead of the respectable but definitely two-piece costume she'd chosen for the outing. John was proving to be the childish type who might behave badly and unhook a costume top, playfully, to expose an eyeful of bare breast.

John was quick to demand his turn on the skis,

but despite his swagger and bravado, within minutes he came a cropper. Andrew caught her eye and whispered, 'So much for that try-hard bloke. All gear, no idea.'

She grinned at him, enjoying their private joke, happy to see the smile on his face today. Andrew shone at sport and was relishing the fun and novelty of this new sporting experience. She watched him zooming across the surface, proud of his prowess at mastering the skills of water skiing.

Most of the wives present, other than Annie Bartlett, were busy with parental duties. Sarah had long felt cut off from their company. Their two separate worlds did not overlap much common ground. While she was at work they were at home, surrounded by babies, nappies and toys. They socialised together during the day and built up a memory bank of shared experiences which excluded her. They had no interest in, or understanding of, her professional life in the office.

So full of their own lives, so engaged in their endless conversations about the feeding, sleeping and teething problems of their babies, and so insensitive to the problems of childlessness, the womenfolk did not inspire Sarah with the confidence to confess her troubles. They might say 'Oh, that's too bad, I'm sorry,' as if she'd complained of a headache, then launch into their next anecdote describing little Johnny's latest escapades.

It was a relief when her turn to ski gave her an excuse to leave the cosy mothers' club on the beach. Launching from the shallows on the shoreline, she kept her balance long enough to surge forward on her skis as the speedboat roared into life and accelerated. She thrilled to the pull on her arms, the strain on her thigh muscles, the whoosh of water rushing past her skis, the salt water splashing in her face.

Her sensory feast ended ignominiously when she bounced over a small but treacherous wash from a passing cruiser and made a spectacular dive headfirst into the balmy water.

The tow rope dragged her under before she remembered to let go of it. Her costume began to 'go with the flow' and she worried she and her bottom covering would part company. *I should have worn that one-piece swimsuit.*

Jack was the spotter, facing backwards on lookout duty. As she resurfaced, coughing and spitting from swallowing too much water, he yelled, 'Don't panic. We're coming back to get you.'

Easier said than done. The boat had stalled. Charles crouched at the stern, fiddling with the motor and bellowing instructions to Jack, now seated at the steering wheel, keeping the craft headed safely into the breeze.

Sarah floated awkwardly on her back, her life jacket doing its job, her ski tips out of the water, her feet pedalling under the surface. She struggled to keep the skis as parallel as possible to maintain her body alignment, fighting the pull of the current, which continually dragged one ski apart from the other, as if she was doing sideways splits.

Simultaneously her chest tightened in pain as she battled her fears. This bay was full of tropical reef sharks. Her imagination launched into overdrive as she pictured an inquisitive creature cruising by and spotting her legs, white and tempting targets. At the thought of strong sharp teeth snapping at her thighs, she clenched her jaw so tight her teeth hurt. How would she fight off a shark?

She kept her eyes peeled for dorsal fins and tried to ward off panic by opening her mouth to relax her jaw and taking deep, slow breaths as the minutes ticked by. The waves obliged by rippling gently and she managed to avoid swallowing more salt water. At last, she heard the welcome sound of the motor sputtering to life and burbling steadily.

The boat circled her and Jack called, 'We'll come past again and float the tow rope towards you. You'll have to grab the handle.'

She nodded as she anxiously checked the straps of her costume before her hands would have to reach out for the tow rope.

He watched her actions with a grin on his face. 'Your costume came adrift with that spill?'

She continued squirming and tugged the lower half firmly into position over her buttocks.

'Don't worry, I'm not like Bartlett. I won't look.' His cheeky laugh echoed across the water as the boat began to circle back.

She pretended to glare at him.

As the boat cautiously approached, he tossed the tow rope as close to her as he could and it drifted to within her reach. She grabbed the handle and he gave her the thumbs-up. 'Think you can manage a deep-water start?' His voice carried the note of confidence that of course she could manage.

'I'll try,' she spluttered, heartened by the nervous energy flooding her body.

As the boat idled its way clear of her, he yelled his quick instructions for positioning the tow rope, her skis and her body. The boat revved up and powered away. She concentrated hard, heaved herself upright on the skis again and successfully retained her balance as she was towed in a sweeping circle towards the shore.

'Let go. Now,' shouted Jack, and she glided in to shallow water, slipped her feet out of the skis and waded in.

Smiling with the joy of an unexpected achievement and the sudden release from anxiety, she handed over the skis to the next beginner. Andrew tossed her a towel and grinned. 'You showed Bartlett up, well and truly.'

When Charles and Jack eventually re-joined them on the beach, Charles said, 'You did well out there.' Jack high-fived her.

'Beginner's luck. Tomorrow my sore arms will berate me for dragging them out of their sockets. But what fun I've had today.'

CHAPTER FOURTEEN

Jenny and Sarah were alone at their regular Brown River picnic site while the men entertained the children down by the water. Sarah pottered around, packing up stray items, while Jenny picked up her latest Mills & Boon novel, read a few pages, then tossed it aside impatiently.

'I'm not in the mood for that book today,' she said. 'You can tire of reading about romance. Always a happy-ever-after ending. Let's talk about the real-life version instead. How did you two get together?'

Sarah blinked in surprise. This was new. Jenny seemed to be extending the hand of her casual, sometimes wary friendship towards a more personal relationship.

'At the school dance. My girls' school partnered with his boys' school.' She rolled her eyes. *How corny is that!*

'High school! Precocious!' Jenny grinned at her.

'Not funny. Unadventurous, more like. Risk averse.'

'How old were you?'

'I was fifteen. Andrew was seventeen.'

'Babies.' Jenny made herself more comfortable on the rug. 'I'm settling in for a gossip session. Keep going.'

Sarah raised her eyebrows. 'This isn't like you.'

'It is today!' Jenny grinned again. 'So…?'

'Alright then, if you really want to know. He nervously asked for my phone number on the night.' She recalled the moment with a pang of nostalgia for the time when her world began to open up. 'I felt so grownup!'

'Did he summon the courage to ask you on a date?'

'It took him a week!' She smiled at the memory. 'Of course the whole family heard the call. Our phone was in the living room.'

'So lots of big ears were flapping at this turn of events.'

'My sisters' eyes were like saucers. A boy! On the phone! Mum lurked in the background.'

'I'm loving this 'young love' story. It makes a change from the scheming *femme fatale* ladies in my novels. Go on.'

'He invited me to see a film but, being a swot, I was studying for a dreaded chemistry exam. Besides, Dad wouldn't have let me go to the pictures. He was very strict when I was a teenager.'

'Tough. My dad was the opposite, too lenient.'

'Lucky you. But teenage boys find a way, don't they! Chemistry was my worst subject. When Andrew rang a few weeks later and heard the bad news about my mediocre exam result, he offered to become my tutor.'

'And the rest is history?' Jenny gave a deep sigh of satisfaction.

'Yep. Ten years now. He finished high school the year before me and got into Sydney Uni. Engineering. Then came my turn. Economics.'

'That was a feather in your caps. Your parents must have been proud of you.'

'They were. We were the first members of our respective families to attend university, so we both took our studies seriously.'

'You and Andrew were an item all through uni?'

'Yes. He drove by my house each morning to pick me up in his mother's old Mayflower. We lunched together beside the Arts building and met up again around five for the peak hour traffic journey home.'

'No other boyfriends?'

'None. I was very young to be at university, only sixteen, adrift in a sea of hundreds of men. After years of all-girl schooling, it frightened me to be a student in a faculty with so few women you could count them on the fingers of one hand. Andrew was my security blanket, I guess.'

'And you've stuck together ever since. The happy-ever-after ending. Just like one of my romance novels.' Jenny huffed out a smiling sigh of satisfaction.

'Yep.' Sarah swallowed nervously, her reasons for 'sticking' not so convincing now. 'What about you and Jack?' She redirected their conversation to a safer topic.

'Similar story. Both of us very young, but not as young as you. Unlike you, we were both country kids, so we were living away from home as university students. We were in different faculties. I studied Arts. I met him at a campus party.'

'Lucky you.'

Oops. A Freudian slip. Sarah wished she'd been that girl meeting Jack. She rushed to explain herself. 'I never got involved in the social life at uni. No drunken binges, no law-breaking incidents, no rebellion against the rules of parents. Plenty of study. More fool me!'

'Sensible. I came unstuck with it. We quickly became a couple and starting fooling around. It was easy to do, away from the strictures of home rule, even the relatively lax boundaries set for me.'

'Heady stuff, eh?'

'I found Jack totally irresistible. But I can be pretty absent-minded and I confess to being careless about contraception, despite promising him otherwise. The pill was new—that's why we thought ourselves free of worries—but I forgot to take my pill for a few days at the crucial time. Next moment I was pregnant.' She gave a rueful grin.

'Oh, boy.' Sarah eyes widened as she did a double-take. First, how on earth do you forget to take the pill? Second—Jack's marriage had been a 'shotgun' affair?

She hastily rearranged her impression of him as totally competent and in calm control. She envisaged her boss as a twenty-ish man, panicking over what to do next.

Jenny shrugged. 'Jack was just as responsible then as he is now. It's what attracted me to him. He accepted the consequences of our actions. Abortion was never a consideration for us. We married within months.'

Sarah compared their parallel experiences of sharing their university days with a boyfriend. No roller-coaster rides of exploring the opposite sex for her and Andrew. They'd started out as the girl-and-boy-next-door friends. Sure, they'd tiptoed nervously into the sexual arena, but spectacular feelings had never developed from their matey relationship, only comfortable ones.

'We struggled as impoverished students.' Jenny gave another nonchalant shrug. 'But we managed.'

'Quite an achievement, especially given all the

ribbing and tut-tutting you must have endured from different quarters.'

Jenny nodded her thanks for Sarah's understanding comment. 'It got better once we left uni and Jack started work.' She smiled. 'Then we decided Tom shouldn't grow up as an only child and needed a sibling.' She paused. 'That decision meant that, unlike you, I've never used my qualifications in the workforce.' Her voice trailed away, her shoulders sagged and she stared at her lap.

'Does that bother you?' Sarah felt a tug of sympathy for Jenny, who might be equally as despondent about having her kids at the *wrong* time as *she* was at being unable to have them at all.

'Not while two babies needed looking after. What alternative did I have?'

An ah-hah moment hit Sarah. She and Jenny had so much in common, with both being married so young and both trapped in lives not of their choosing. Jenny with her kids, she with Andrew.

Jenny flipped her head up and burst out with, 'Child care centres only exist in other countries, not ours, so I try to ignore the man's world we live in.' Jenny's moment of defiance faded, and her face brightened. 'With me not working we were very poor, but Jack has a good job now, and there's no need for me to work while the children are small.'

She sighed as she spotted the men coming back with Tom and Lottie. 'Jack would like to have more kids. He has a tribe of brothers and sisters but, personally-speaking, it's too much hard work for me. Two's enough.' She shrugged. 'I can't wait for them both to be at school. Meanwhile, I'm living vicariously, through my romance novels.' She gave an embarrassed little laugh as Lottie plonked herself down on the picnic rug and demanded her mother's admiration for the handful of treasures she'd collected on her walk.

At home, Sarah thought about Jenny's story. No wonder Jack differed so strongly from the men she knew. His siblings had taught him to defend his position while mastering the arts of co-operation and compromise, and he'd learned early to stand on his own two feet in young adulthood. Rich parents had not bought him a house, or a fancy car, or found him a cushy job in the family company to prop him up. He'd taken full responsibility for himself and his actions and had come out on top in the end.

That must explain his inner confidence, she thought. He's learned that the answers lie inside your own head, and the way you think about a problem dictates how and where to find a solution.

Her new experiences were building her levels of trust in herself, too. Moving to another country, changing careers, and facing the problems of infertility, she was learning to notice the ways of other people, reflect on her actions, examine choices, make decisions.

It felt good to engage with her expanded mental framework and gain this inner strength. She didn't want to be a helpless female, drifting through life within her comfort zone.

Life had turned into a grand adventure.

CHAPTER FIFTEEN

When socialising with their friends, the Robinsons never mentioned their child-free status, but after many months of watching them both, Jack drew his own conclusions. He'd noticed that Andrew often looked fleetingly as sad as Sarah. Could he be the problem? It happened. He knew all about the birds and the bees—he was an agriculturalist, after all.

He sat contentedly on the picnic rugs, amidst the leftovers and debris of their Sunday lunch.

Tom, who had disappeared with Andrew to find a clearing where they could kick a ball, was now yowling in the distance because he had whacked his leg on a tree stump. Jenny had gone to check on him.

Lottie sat on Sarah's lap, her legs wrapped round Sarah's hips and her arms draped lovingly around Sarah's neck. Sarah was cuddling her back, rocking backwards and forwards, her eyes half-closed, blissful in her instinctive response to Lottie, unaware of his steady gaze.

His heart bled for her. Jenny had two children that she hadn't really wanted, and here was a very special woman who plainly ached with longing for a baby.

Lottie soon tired of cuddling and scrambled to her feet, running off to join Tom and shrieking with delight at having two adults to serve as fieldsmen for their wild kicks at the ball.

He took his chance to speak up. 'Sarah, there's something I've been meaning to ask you. Please forgive me if I'm taking liberties.'

'Liberties, Jack?'

'I want you to stop me if I tread on dangerous ground.'

'Okay.' Her nervous voice faded as she watched him shift his position to gain eye-to-eye contact.

'We've known each other for nearly two years, and I believe we've become good friends.' Bloody hell, she represented much more than that to him.

'That's true.' She raised her eyebrows, as if wondering what might be coming next.

'To me it seems fairly obvious that you'd welcome children of your own.'

Sarah blinked and stared at him with astonishment.

She hadn't said 'mind your own business' so he continued. 'But—there's a problem. Am I right?'

Relief was her first reaction. Relief that someone didn't pretend about important topics. She was overwhelmed with gratitude for him raising what was culturally an unmentionable subject—the absence of children in a marriage.

Infertility was not a topic for conversation. Society accepted the arrival or non-arrival of babies fatalistically, as either mother nature's blessings or curses, or the failings of a woman's body. Women could be particularly scathing about childless women. 'Oh, she's barren,' they'd sneer.

Andrew was miserable with his own pain, his own sense of failure as a man, and he was hiding behind a wall of pretence that none of this was happening to him. She'd been protecting his feelings by keeping his secret and helping him come to terms with it, with the passage of time, all the while attempting to conceal her own intense disappointment at being denied the birth of children.

She drew her knees up towards her chest and hugged them, as if in self-protection. 'Is it so obvious, or is your penetrating insight hitting the bullseye again?' She sighed heavily.

'I can read the signs. Anyone married as long as you two, wanting children as you clearly do, would have at least one by now. It's about five years, isn't it?' He paused for a moment, as if choosing his next words carefully. 'I figured that there must be a physical cause.'

Her face crumpled. He sounded so kind and understanding.

He reached across the rug and squeezed her hand, concern swimming in his eyes. 'Don't forget I grew up in a grazing world. Lots of discussions about whether the cows were on heat and whether the bull had done the deed or not.'

She gave him a puzzled look.

'With that as my background, I figured it was more likely to be Andrew than you.'

She gasped. How had he guessed her burdensome secret? 'What makes you say that?'

'You show flashes of sadness, but he's subdued rather than sad, as if he's carrying a burden. You don't need to be Einstein to work that out. He's said nothing to me.'

She groped around for a tissue. She was drowning in her sorrow but it was only smart and intuitive people like Jack who realised. 'So the doctor tells us, but he can't, or won't, say anything to me either.'

Jack said, 'I'm sorry.' He handed across a square of paper towel for her to dab her nose.

With the others coming into view as they returned with the ball, he said quietly, 'Have you thought about adoption?'

'Constantly. But talking with Andrew is difficult. His masculine pride is damaged.'

'Understood. A challenge for any bloke.'

'Adoption has crossed my mind, but my phone at work has an ISD bar on it and I can't ring the officials in Sydney to make enquiries.'

'You just want basic information, right? Some brochures sent to you? Would you like me to ring that number? I make international calls from my office constantly.'

'Oh, would you?'

'Consider it done. Easy.' He paused. 'Relatively easy.'

As if responding to a question mark on her face, he broke the tension with a wry smile and said, 'Mostly the switchboard operator at reception plugs the right telephone cord into the right jack but sometimes I have to go over and ring the bell to rouse her from an after-lunch snooze.'

She gave him a watery smile. 'Okay. Thanks.' She brushed away a tear. 'My misery has paralysed me. I should have tried harder to organise this myself.'

She envisaged leaving the brochures lying around at home, giving Andrew the chance to process the material at his own pace, without feeling pressure from her. It would leave him free to decide whether to express some interest.

On the way home, Sarah sidled into it. 'Don't you love our Sunday activities with Tom and Lottie?'

'They're okay.' He smothered a bored yawn.

His half-hearted response wasn't a good sign. She gathered her courage. 'I find them so enjoyable that,' she paused and twisted in her seat to look at him, 'I've been considering adoption as a possibility for us.'

Silence.

'How do you feel about that idea?'

'I haven't ever given it a moment's thought,' he muttered.

'Our personal issues are irrelevant here, with so few doctors and all of them run off their feet with basic health issues. If I research the details of how to adopt, would you be willing to consider the idea?'

'I suppose so,' he said, grudgingly. 'It's worth thinking about, anyway.'

He took his eyes off the road for a second and glanced her way. 'I told you before, last year, I understand why having your own baby is important to you. I can't completely deny you your chance at motherhood.' His voice sank with dejection.

She leaned across and kissed him on the cheek. 'Thank you. I know this is hard for you. I'll see what I can find out.'

She breathed a sigh of relief. There was no sense in labouring the point.

Jack walked past and nonchalantly dropped a bulky envelope on her desk, which he'd marked 'Personal'. When she saw her name in his handwriting, and not his secretary's, she knew what the packet must contain. She watched the clock all day, anxious to leave work and reach the privacy of her own home.

Hands trembling, she ripped open the envelope and yanked out a wad of general information sheets prepared by a government agency in Sydney. She read the introductory details and the application guidelines with increasing excitement.

She and Andrew fitted perfectly the profile of desirable parents. The only negative aspect was the long wait involved. But they were young. Surely, within a few years, they would be lucky enough to be offered a child.

She placed the papers prominently on Andrew's desk, on top of his other unopened mail, awaiting his return. She tore up the incriminating envelope containing Jack's handwriting and tossed it into the kitchen bin. Her husband wouldn't thank her for involving an outsider in business he avoided facing, even with her.

When he walked in the door on Friday afternoon, she greeted him with a hug and warned him in advance about the special mail sitting on his desk. Their childlessness was a touchy subject so she left him alone and stayed in the kitchen, preparing the evening meal, giving him space to peruse the material in private.

Half an hour later he sauntered in and propped himself against the kitchen bench. 'I've read all that stuff about adoption procedures.'

'And?'

'I've been thinking it over since the day of that picnic when you suggested the idea. I needed to know the implications before I said yes.'

'Are you reassured?'

'So-so. We have to have a legal domicile in New South Wales and by that they mean that the husband has to have been born in New South Wales. So we qualify.' He sounded less than enthusiastic. 'I'd be doing it for you, not for me.'

'We'd be doing this together. You can't be half-hearted. It wouldn't be fair to the child.'

'Agreed. I've decided. We might as well make an application.'

'Thank you. It means so much to me.' She flung her arms around him and squeezed him tight. 'I'll ring the local contact number and arrange an appointment for an interview. Someone from the local Child Welfare Agency will visit the house to conduct the assessment, so you might have to defer one of your trips for a day.'

'Go right ahead. I'll manage my travel arrangements,' he said gruffly.

Two weeks later the Moresby-based representative of the agency in Sydney, social worker Stephanie Cooper, arrived at their home to evaluate their credentials as prospective parents.

She was enthusiastic in her assessment. Andrew and Sarah were young, healthy, well-educated and financially secure. Their home provided suitable accommodation and was clean and tidy. She recommended them as the ideal recipients of a newborn relinquished by its biological mother and posted the glowing report off to the authorities in distant Sydney.

CHAPTER SIXTEEN

While Sarah waited impatiently for news from the adoption agency, Andrew became even more distant. His trips away became more frequent and more prolonged, as a few days at a time stretched into the entire week. Sometimes he stayed away on the weekend as well.

She recognised his life as tiring and stressful, because he arrived home exhausted and needing sleep. Both were wary of travel in small planes, but he knew one of the chaps killed in the latest plane crash, and these crashes were getting just too commonplace for comfort. The pilot had ignored the bad weather and flown in cloud all the way, against the rules, until he hit the side of the mountain at a crash site above 10,000 feet.

It was stressful in Moresby too, with a tribal war being waged in the streets between the incoming flood of young, single Highlanders from New Guinea and the Goilalas, the main group of unskilled local Papuans, both groups of men competing for the same unskilled jobs. Men were running around town with axes and spears. Scores of people took up temporary residence under the houses of expat policemen, as protection.

Andrew's Highlander line gangs usually travelled about Moresby on eight different trucks but one morning the supervisor came out and found everyone hanging off one truck. There's strength in numbers, they said. All of her night school students were Highlanders, and one Wednesday night several young men asked her to drive them home, fearing the Goilalas would get them otherwise. The law of the jungle ruled—the random payback of an eye for an eye.

It was a relief for everyone living in Moresby when, after weeks of input from skilled negotiators, both sides agreed to a meeting to swear friendship and end the feud. The final score was three dead and three injured, while ten men were detained in gaol on murder charges.

But the divide between the relative affluence of the employed and the poverty of the urban unemployed, coupled with the divide between the physically smaller Highlanders and the taller Papuans, remained a permanent feature of life in the town. Local politicians began to call for Highlanders to be sent home to their villages and requested bans on the sale of any more one-way air tickets to Moresby.

She lived as an expat among these pressing social issues, but as an interested observer, not as a participant. Her primary focus was closer to home.

She wore a path to the mailbox, but the longed-for letter from the adoption agency in Australia did not appear. Babies placed for adoption were scarce, she knew, and she expected to endure a long wait. Rather than add another unnecessary layer of anxiety into her daily life, she avoided discussing the matter with Andrew.

On her more despondent days she acknowledged that infertility problems must cause many problems in marriages. She gave herself a pep talk. 'That woman who interviewed us said we'll need to go to Sydney to collect the baby from the authorities, so I'll arrange for us to see a specialist counsellor there.'

September passed into October, and the weeks dragged into November, the doldrums—repeating the annual weather pattern, sultry, building up to a thunderstorm every afternoon, a storm which never delivered its promised load of rain. The dry landscape turned brown, the trees drooped, the parched grass crunched underfoot. People were irritable and cranky. Fans ran at full bore. Top sheets were discarded in bed at night. Water restrictions came into force.

For Sarah, the doldrums were more bearable than last year, but was she just getting used to the cycle of weather in the tropics? You acclimatise to everything, eventually.

Or did Jack's presence make it more bearable? She felt a pang of guilt whenever she realised how much she looked forward to going to work, and how little she looked forward to Andrew's arrival home for the weekends. Andrew no longer showed interest in her wellbeing, and sex before he turned over to go to sleep had become a routine physical release for him, without preliminaries, without words. He took her for granted.

Andrew could not be more different from Jack if he tried. Jack didn't take her existence for granted. He communicated with her, engaged in eye contact, often showed interest in her life, in her interests—but he was just being friendly, wasn't he? He was no different with his other staff, just as interested in them too, wasn't he?

She knew one thing for sure. Sparks zapped her nerves when she was around Jack. He gave off an aura.

Andrew was a damp squib by comparison. Why hadn't she listened to her own inner voice before she married? After five teenage years with him, she'd known there was no sizzle, but until Jack dropped into her world, she'd never seen a real-life example of someone with sizzle—except for movie stars, in their on-screen world of make-believe.

The doldrums broke into the steady downpour of the wet season. Andrew's project work was 'on hold' because of the weather, so he'd not been away this week. She'd been home for barely five minutes when he walked in from work, his face set in the stern lines of a public statue.

He dumped his briefcase and stated abruptly, 'Sarah, I have something to tell you.'

She'd sensed for weeks now that something new troubled his mind. He'd lost interest in her as a sexual partner many months back, beyond his basic urges, and she'd long abandoned the idea that he would ever unburden himself over his damaged self-image. Their marriage had become a daily habit, a routine you took for granted without feeling the need to pay attention.

She grabbed onto the slim reed of hope that he was ready to share his fresh troubles, whatever they were.

Moving straight into the lounge room, he tossed a surprise over his shoulder to where she stood in the kitchen. 'I applied for another job a few weeks ago and the news came through today. I've been accepted.'

'What?' She rushed to follow him, find out more.

'A promotion.' He stared at her triumphantly for a few moments.

'Congratulations. Where? Why didn't you tell

135

me?' She wrinkled her nose in astonishment.

'I've been mulling it over in my mind, trying to decide what I wanted, without pressure from you.' He stuck out a defiant chin.

What was going on? 'Do we have to leave here?'

'Not you. Just me. *I'm* leaving.'

He sank abruptly into his chair and leaned back expansively, hands gripped behind his head, elbows wide, watching her.

Her jaw dropped. 'Leaving for where?'

'Going back to headquarters in Sydney. Back to the surf. Some weekend tennis. My old mates.' He shifted position and gave an obstinate toss of his head.

Her eyes rounded. 'You've broken your contract of employment with Posts and Telegraphs?'

'Yes, the top brass in Sydney have done a deal with the government here and are sending someone to replace me.' He looked very pleased with himself, just like he had on graduation day at uni.

'But why have you done this?' She collapsed into the chair opposite him, staring at this sudden stranger hiding inside the familiar body of her husband, struggling to adjust to his news.

'Why not? I can't take this stress.' He glared at her, as if it was all her fault.

'With me, you mean?' Her newfound self-confidence took a nosedive.

'We're both unhappy and you know it. I'm stuffed.' His rebellious tone brooked no disagreement.

She couldn't believe he was acknowledging this. He'd uncannily duplicated the relationship between her parents, bottling things up and then letting fly without warning, with drastic consequences.

He gave an offhand shrug, 'We've grown apart. I've been thinking about it a lot lately, in my hotel rooms, on those flights, up on those mountain tops.'

She couldn't deny that particular unhappy truth, it being a relief to have it out in the open, but his decision suddenly hit home. 'Where will I live, if you're leaving?' Had he considered this obvious practicality? What did he expect would happen to her?

Stubbornly he said, 'You'd better sort out your own contract, decide your own future.'

She recoiled in shock at his matter-of-fact attitude, until something more important set her body trembling with icy fear. 'What about the adoption?' she whispered.

'You'll have to cancel the application.' He spoke as if it was no different to cancelling a reservation in a restaurant.

'But we only applied a few months ago!' Her heartbeat raced in panic.

'Changed my mind after that interview.' At the shocked look on her face he added, almost as an afterthought, 'I decided I was making too much of a personal sacrifice to please you.'

'But you give every sign of enjoying being with children. Kevin's older kids. Jack's son Tom.' She scrambled to comprehend what he was saying. And why.

'They're boys, not babies, and I understand boys from growing up with my brothers and my mates. I know the parents of the Mitchell boys and Tom, where those boys came from. I've decided if I can't have my own, then I don't want kids at all.'

'You mean you don't want to raise someone else's baby?' His reasons were starting to come clear to her.

'That's right. Too much of a lottery dip. We'll likely get the kid of a heroin addict or a dope pedlar. My mates in head office tell me recreational drugs are swamping Sydney.'

'I don't get you. Why have you kept these thoughts to yourself?'

'Because you're too stressed out. Your need for a baby is too much for me to handle.' His voice rose, as if he was angry with her.

She skewered him with a sharp look. 'You're saying it's *my* fault you're leaving?'

'No, but I need less stress in my life. We got married too young. Family expectations placed me under as much pressure to marry you as you to marry me.'

Who was this man, suddenly so willing to open up and talk? Was this the start of a more honest relationship with him, just when he was about to walk out the door?

She should grab this chance to explore his true feelings. 'You've never said that before. Does it mean you're sorry you married me?' She kept her tone neutral, desperate for a genuine response from him.

'Not exactly. But I'm ready to move on. You still have the chance to find someone else. Someone who can give you the baby you want.'

How typical of his engineer's 'critical path' approach to life. 'But that's why we planned to adopt.' She leaned towards him, wringing her hands, imploring him to see her point of view.

He ignored her. 'Maybe someone like Jack. He's more your type. You and he get along pretty well together. You could look for a bloke like him.'

'What a thing to say.' She shook her head in disbelief and glared at him. He didn't sound in the least bit jealous, just pragmatic, as if the process of choosing the right mate was like working through a decision tree.

'You haven't noticed that being an expat in the tropics is a graveyard for marriages? Half the blokes I work with are having it off with someone else's wife. Plenty of wife-swapping parties happening. Your sleazy colleague John Bartlett enjoyed that lifestyle when he lived here.'

It was the first she knew of it. How could she be so naïve? So that explained John's slothful behaviour at work and Jack's failure to extend that lazy man's contract when it came up for renewal. John had been up partying half the night? 'Surely you don't think that's what I'm doing.'

'Nope. But you might want to. There's no action between us, is there!' His bitterness resounded in his voice.

'Expat life in the tropics has always carried risks and this year the doldrums broke up our marriage,' she said sadly.

'You know damn well that's not the reason. It goes much deeper, goes back longer. We've disappointed each other.' A cynical smile accompanied his careless shrug.

He was correct. He had disappointed her. Each other, he'd said. Maybe she was about to learn how she'd disappointed him.

'Can you deny we *are* another statistic, another example of the reasons expat couples should stay away from the tropics if they want to stay married?' Stubbornly she hung onto a rationale she could grasp, struggling to come to terms with this new Andrew.

'If you want to see it that way, go ahead. I've let you down, sure, on what you wanted, but I've finally worked out that *I* don't want what *you* want. I've stopped worrying about what you might think. Truth is, I'm damned tired of worrying about your needs. I realise I had enough of that when we were teenagers.'

Her jaw dropped at these home truths, pouring out of his mouth. She needed to know more. 'And that's how I've disappointed you, is it?'

'Yes. I'd like someone more like my mates' wives. Less challenging.' He sounded as matter-of-fact as someone picking the likely winner in a horse race.

'More fun and flirty, you mean.' She was aware that socially she gravitated to the men, not the women, but the attraction was their topics of conversation and not the chance to bat her eyelids at them.

'Exactly. You don't fit in.'

That comment hit home and it hurt. She knew it. She'd always known it.

At school, she was an outsider, scorned by the girls using every available trick to win their man-hunting competition. She'd concentrated on her schoolwork and socialised with those similarly 'bookish' and naïve about the rules of being a proper female. No giggling with her friends over clothes, makeup, hairstyles and boys.

He'd known her through her teenage years and knew she was well-trained in how not to be a 'real' girl. In his eyes she wasn't a real woman.

Her mind shifted gear as she began to process Andrew's unexpected outbursts. His capacity to reject her as a woman and turn his back on her just like that, putting his own needs first, devastated her.

He was even leaving her to do the dirty work and cancel the adoption application. He was abandoning her, but he didn't want to front the child welfare authorities and confess to his behaviour.

As her shocked paralysis abated, her anger rose to the surface. He wasn't a man—he was showing his true colours as a mouse. Good riddance.

But not good riddance to the baby she'd been longing for.

What would she do now?

Her world had upended. Because her husband had a low sperm count. Not just low—practically non-existent and not motile. Life was so unfair.

Like an owl she stared unblinking at Andrew, sitting in his usual easy chair, calmly expecting her to serve up his dinner as if the last hour hadn't happened.

A tear trickled out but she didn't respond to his words.

What was the point? Every instinct in her body confirmed their marriage was dead and buried.

She withdrew to the kitchen to distance herself from him. It's not as if he could duck out and buy his dinner elsewhere. Apart from a couple of hotel restaurants, it was home cooking or nothing in this place.

She crashed and banged a few saucepans to release her stress. A worrying little voice intruded insistently, telling her that Andrew was uncannily right about Jack.

He had banged that nail squarely on its head. The idea of a man like Jack had always interested her, but as she didn't conceive that the phantom stranger of her dreams could be a reality, she'd settled for what she had, the familiar boy next door.

Her conscious realisation shocked her to the core. *Jack has a wife who is my friend. He has children. I couldn't possibly be interested in him.* More destabilising thoughts raced through her brain and she pushed them back, scrambling for safe ground. *I'm deadset not interested in Jack. Not like that, anyway.*

She indignantly recalled Andrew's wife-swapping carp. She'd read that some women have no qualms about running off with someone else's husband. *Not me.* She sternly reset her moral compass to true north.

She took his meal out to her now-estranged husband and dumped it on the dining table, still silent, before retreating to eat her meal standing up in the kitchen. *Now I know people like Jack do exist, I'll know what kind of man to look for in the future. Definitely not one like Andrew. No sirree.*

Another tear escaped her lids. Another sniff. She needed another tissue. Her future looked black.

CHAPTER SEVENTEEN

Next day at the office she asked to speak with Jack. Overnight she had lain rigid in the bed beside Andrew, her stomach tied in knots, considering her options.

She had elected not to break her contract of employment with the government and leave, thwarting the plans so blithely taken for granted by Andrew. She'd found a job she loved and she'd do her best to hang on to it.

Jack stared at her across the desk, dumbfounded. 'Didn't expect this, Sarah. I've always thought of you two as a solid couple, facing a cruel fate together.'

'I've decided to stay in Moresby, if I can, on my own.'

'A brave decision.'

'No, cowardly really. I don't feel like coping with a move back to Sydney, my family, finding a new job, all in one go. Losing the adoption option is enough for me to deal with at present. Things might change later, when my contract expires. For the time being I enjoy my work here, and the company of my friends.'

'We'd love to keep you on the staff.'

'Andrew's packed his bags and moved out, this morning, to the Gateway Hotel. He's leaving Moresby in a few days. Can I hold on to the house, do you think? In my own right, I mean.' Fingers crossed, Andrew wouldn't force her to lose her home, as well as her baby. She hoped to continue taking solace from her garden.

'I'll speak to the bigwigs. I'm sure they'll arrange something. They won't want a well-trained analyst like you to leave, especially with self-government and independence coming up. There's a lot of nation-building to do here, and with Australia phasing out its role as administrators, there's been a marked decline in enquiries from people seeking employment here.'

At the morning tea break she told her colleagues, 'Andrew's been promoted to a new position back in Sydney.'

Charles whistled his disbelief. 'What a bummer.' He glanced at the shocked faces of their colleagues. 'For us, I mean. When are you leaving?'

'I'm not.' A tone of defiance overcame her instincts to burst into tears in front of them. 'I'm staying here.'

She let the implication sink in, that she and

Andrew were splitting. A stunned silence filled the room.

'You mean Christmas on your own?' Charles was the first to speak. 'No way. Come to our place on Christmas Day.'

She smiled her relief at him. He was a good friend without stirring carnal thoughts in her brain, as Jack did.

Having somewhere to go at Christmas in a few weeks' time would help to fill the current void in her life. She had a phone call pre-booked to her parents on Christmas Day, at ten to eleven, and was looking forward to hearing their voices, but steeling herself against feeling quite homesick. The three minutes of allocated time on these calls just wasn't long enough, as the clock ticked down and the pressure mounted to condense everything you'd like to say into a few short sentences.

Otherwise it didn't feel very Christmassy, with no decorations in the shops and most of the expats 'gone south' on leave. She'd already received many cards from old friends back in Sydney but she'd decided that those who barely said 'Happy Christmas' and wrote no news at all would be instantly crossed off her Christmas card list. Why should she keep them informed of her new direction in life?

Charles quickly added, 'It'll be a quiet day. Just us and the baby.' His rueful laugh reminded her

147

of Andrew at his long-suffering-husband best. 'Carolyn needs a distraction. She's struggling with her second pregnancy. Again, she reckons she got the timing all wrong. The school age timing's right this time, but she doesn't enjoy being heavily pregnant through the wet season.' He raised an eyebrow, as if the foibles of women were beyond him.

'Right. I'm warned. I'll give her a ring. See what I can do to help her with the food.' She struggled to sound matter-of-fact, as if her separation from Andrew was an everyday occurrence. It wasn't. Married couples in their world never split up.

'No need. You know Carolyn. She loves to cook. With you coming, she'll spend a few happy days preparing festive fare.'

Sarah appreciated his look of concern and offered a sad smile.

'I won't have to put up with her complaints about the unfairness of being a female. Payoffs all round.' He cautiously returned her smile. 'I might round up a few others to join us.'

'More strays, like me?'

'Don't be like that, madam. You're never a stray. You're a friend.'

Andrew's departure for Sydney brought into sharp relief the role he'd played as her security blanket, the obvious foundation upon which she'd built her circle of friends with whom she could relax.

Now that she was on her own, the perennial problem of 'two's company, three's a crowd' brought unexpected changes in her lifestyle. Her social life slowed to a crawl and she wondered if it was due to the other wives worrying about including an unattached female in their dinner parties.

Maria and Kevin Mitchell were different from the average married couple. They continued to invite her for the occasional Sunday barbecue with their tribe of children. Originally Andrew's friends, after his defection they sympathised with her as an abandoned wife.

'What's wrong with that bloke?' Kevin asked, as they relaxed on the verandah. 'I don't get it. Engineers are rusted-on conservatives. They don't leave their wives.' He frowned, visibly shocked that his fellow engineer had abandoned Sarah. It spoiled his image of his profession.

Sarah shrugged without commenting, and Maria prodded him. 'Shut up Kevin, it's none of our business.' She glared at her husband. 'It's getting late. The kids are hungry. Let's get lunch underway.' She turned to Sarah. 'Would you mind feeding Isabella if I plonk her into her high chair?'

'I'd love to. Come here, poppet.' She held out her arms and Isabella toddler-tottered across to her, squealing with enjoyment. Sarah picked her up and gave her a hug before handing her over to Maria, who strapped her into the battered high chair.

'I'm feeding her before the others because she's overdue for her daily nap.' Maria handed over two spoons and a bowl of mushy food. 'One spoon for her. She has to learn to feed herself. One spoon for you, to ensure some of that nourishment gets into her mouth.'

Sarah couldn't resist a grin. 'Should I try the "open wide, here comes the choo-choo train into the tunnel" treatment?'

'Got it. You've got the magic touch with kids, Isabella especially. She loves it when you come round.'

Sarah heaved a sigh of relief that Maria always stayed clear of asking why she had no kids herself. Maria was a smart woman. It comforted her to have a friend like this.

Like the Mitchells, Charles and Carolyn Williams were also willing to risk her presence in their lives. They regularly invited her for a drink at their place after work, followed by an early meal together at the town's newly opened bistro. Their elder child Ricky, a month younger than Isabella, squirmed on his mother's lap as she fed him titbits. The new baby lay fast asleep in a carry basket on the floor. The arrangement made for an early night, but Carolyn said she enjoyed the opportunity for an outing.

Her friends, other than Jack, had never realised that she and Andrew had a fertility problem, because she'd shouldered the burden of hiding their secret to salvage his masculine pride. She was not emotionally ready to divulge it now.

She didn't explain to anyone, beyond Jack, the details of why Andrew left, leaving her behind. People could draw their own conclusions, behind her back. Better that the outside world imagined that Andrew's career ambition most likely hid his desire to run off with another woman. A proper woman, not like his career-oriented wife.

Her sense of loss was profound. It was not so much that she missed Andrew, as they'd been drifting apart for so long that his absence left a small hole rather than a gigantic canyon in her heart. No, she mourned the dream of what could have been, the babies she would not have, the lonely days coming her way.

She became the great pretender as she soldiered on, with her chin held high in public, even if it wobbled in private.

Time had never moved so sluggishly.

Music became her constant night-time companion, such was its power to match her moods and console her. On constant replay, the languorous guitars of the Los Indios Tabajaras brothers wove their magic with 'Maria Elena', soothing her soul.

Watering duties at the end of each day, holding the hose in her right hand and a vermouth and soda in the other, marked her wind-down time, before the early nightfall of the tropics. The soil, foliage and flowers gratefully responded to their drink and released a delicious combination of garden smells, as good as aromatherapy. She limited herself to one vermouth and soda, choosing this mild form of alcohol as her daily refresher. Despite having good reason to drown her sorrows, it wouldn't do to emulate the B4s she'd met on her travels.

On weekends, her work in the garden kept her going. A vigorous morning of digging was the perfect start to a Saturday, Kirua being such cheerful company. His broad grins lifted her spirits.

Step by painful step, she regrouped and dreamed of a future for herself—what it might look like and how she might take control of it.

CHAPTER EIGHTEEN

Jack continued to invite her to departmental social activities, but the happy weekends she'd spent with the Martin family unit faded into the past.

She understood that Jack, a kind man and the only person aware of her adoption dreams, wouldn't want to rub salt into her painful wounds by exposing her to an overdose of ongoing interaction with his children.

Jenny must have noticed the change in their routine, but was unlikely to think twice about it. According to the social mores of the time, Andrew had been invited to the family picnics as male company for Jack. Andrew was no longer around. No man would invite a young female member of staff to attend on her own.

If her weekends were mostly quiet and lonely, filled with yearning for the Jack-inspired Sunday fields of gold, suddenly stripped to barren paddocks, she could treasure her weekdays spent working with him. They shared the same sense of humour, laughed together, giggled over small jokes. Her days at the office kept her motivated and preserved the structural framework in her life.

Like a guardian angel, he noticed her moods and unobtrusively did little things to bring her comfort. Dermatitis under her engagement and wedding rings, heat rash and fungal infections had plagued her fair skin in the tropics. One morning she complained at work about her new problem with tinea, caused by the humid conditions and compressing her toes into sandals with straps which were too tight across the toe-line. The following day she found a new tube of Tineaderm on her desk, still in its chemist's bag, with a note tucked inside: 'Once you have cured the problem, remember to dry between your toes. J.'

Next time he passed by she made eye contact with him and pointed to the packet. 'Thanks.' Enough said.

She was grateful that he acknowledged her caution with a nod and a wry smile and walked on. Unnecessary office speculation about his potential reasons for such a thoughtful gesture was the last thing she needed.

He kept her busy too. Jack sent her to report on the economic activity in the remote area of Milne Bay, where brave coastguard watchers had helped change the course of the Second World War. The journey involved a long air trip to Alotau and then a three-hour launch journey to Sideia Island. She couldn't believe her good fortune in being handed this assignment. 'Half your luck,' said Charles, green with envy. 'I'd give my eyeteeth to get down there.'

Sarah doubted her luck on the return flight, delayed for four hours by a torrential downpour. The airport terminal comprised a modest tin shed, with overhead fans and a few hard benches where a cluster of men with straggly beards and women with long, lank hair sat, smoking and chatting, surrounded by containers and cardboard boxes. From time to time they passed around an object and discussed its features.

Across the shed, she watched their activities with interest, concluding they were anthropologists from unis down south in Australia. The villages in this region had long provided fertile research fields for many anthropologists.

Meanwhile, ground staff weighed the intending passengers and their assorted luggage, and made their calculations. Due to fear of over-loading the plane for the dangerous trip over mountainous terrain, they consigned the precious anthropological artefacts to the next day's flight.

While the hours ticked by, and the attention of ground staff was otherwise engaged, the owners of these objects surreptitiously reclaimed selected treasures from the 'tomorrow heap', intending to smuggle them on board as cabin luggage.

She was hungry and thirsty by the time their plane appeared through a break in the rain clouds. Soon the passengers surged aboard with their reclaimed items, and they took off.

Sarah recalled the enormous escarpment over which they'd flown on the way to Alotau. One minute they'd almost touched the treetops, and seconds later the valley was thousands of feet below them. 'Crikey,' she thought, remembering the weight of the illicit cabin items, 'if ever my time is up, it's now.'

Resigned to crashing in the overloaded aeroplane, she folded her arms and shut her eyes, preparing for the big bang as they slammed into that fearsome cliff.

The engines droned, twenty minutes passed, and they were still flying.

Gingerly she opened her eyes, relieved to see bright blue sky out the window. They'd passed the danger point. 'I live for another day,' she sighed in relief.

Long before her inner self had stabilised, and much sooner than expected, a letter arrived from a government department whose return address was 'Department of Child Welfare & Social Welfare' in Sydney.

She slit the envelope open with a sinking heart.

Dear Mr & Mrs Robinson,

We are pleased to confirm that your application for adoption has been successful. We invite you both to contact our office for a final interview, as you will be in the group of parents to be considered as candidates for the next baby becoming available.

The words blurred before she could finish reading, and she burst into tears. She and Andrew had reached the top of the waiting list for an adopted child. The officials had always said they completely matched the desired profile of would-be parents. Had they been fast-tracked?

Only married couples were eligible, deemed officialdom, so she no longer qualified. She'd been meaning to write to the adoption agency to cancel their application but, in the stress of recent months, she'd prevaricated, hoping to regain some inner strength before the inevitable trauma of that process.

The letter reactivated the emotional pressure on her, forcing her once again to face her childless future.

And it revived her anger at Andrew. He hadn't opened the correspondence, addressed to them both but forwarded on to him in Sydney from his old work address in Moresby. It was typical of him to redirect this confronting item of mail straight back to her.

He must have known its likely content, but instead of contacting the department to save her feelings, once again he'd avoided facing his painful self-image issues.

She rang the local contact for the agency on Monday morning and made an appointment to meet Stephanie Cooper at her office.

At first Stephanie exuded the routine sympathy of professional counsellors. But after hearing Sarah's story, her words of comfort sounded more genuine. 'I've heard this story before. Too much stress. It's so sad.' She slid the box of tissues across her desk towards her client. 'The baby will be placed elsewhere. But you'll have to provide a letter for the file.'

The tears rolled in a steady stream down Sarah's cheeks and dripped onto the page where she was writing, blotching the ink.

Dear Ms Cooper,

I write to advise that unexpected marital difficulties have arisen since my husband and I first made approaches to the department, and we will have to withdraw our application.

Naturally, this cancellation comes with the most profound regrets.

Thank you for recommending us for this rare privilege, but it would not be fair to the child concerned to proceed under the current circumstances of our marriage.

Yours sincerely,

Sarah Robinson.

Stephanie took the letter. 'If circumstances change, please let us know,' she murmured in her most soothing tones as she accompanied Sarah to the exit.

The weeping woman at her side knew she would never be back. If she still wanted a baby, she'd have to find herself another husband.

Sarah drifted out of the building in a daze. She wandered along on automatic pilot, scarcely noticing where she was, and somehow found herself seated at her desk, where she sat all afternoon, intermittently gouging a hole in it, not doing much else. Her white face and puffy eyes told its own story, and her colleagues left her alone with her misery. They knew she'd recently separated, and she let them assume she was having a bad day.

She compared Andrew's world with hers. No-one had forced him to give up anything he valued, someone he loved, the chance for a baby. He wasn't fussy about the company he kept, as long as it was companionship of sorts, and wouldn't be facing a lonely future, like her.

Another tear trickled past her nose and, out of pride, she dabbed it away as fast as she could. No need to blubber in front of her workmates. There was no possibility of salvaging her marriage. To feel better, she must take action herself to change her prospects.

CHAPTER NINETEEN

Sarah had been feeling off-colour all weekend, slightly spaced-out. Strapping into her seat on the plane on Monday morning, minor difficulties in focusing her eyes warned her of an impending headache. Damn, she hadn't suffered from a vascular headache for months.

She fished two paracetamol tablets out of her bag, ready to swallow them with the drink to be offered by the cabin crew. This was a longer flight, and she was traveling on a regular service, not a single-engine charter aircraft.

Closing her eyes, she tried to rest as best she could. Normally, lying down with a cold washer across her eyelids and forehead averted the development of a full-blown headache and its associated nausea. Today, no pre-emptive treatment was possible because she had yet to endure a second flight to reach her destination.

Her head still hurt as her small plane approached one of the world's most dangerously exhilarating airstrips. Wau airfield, on a hillside with a twelve-degree slope and a mountain at the end, required the pilot to land uphill and take off downhill, no matter which way the wind blew. She tried to relax and not think about her nerves as they landed, or her mounting level of pain, which refused to budge.

Not one to give in to ailments easily, she swallowed more pills, Panadeine this time, and continued with her assignment for the day, a tour of a small demonstration farm run by her department. Her job was to write up its activities as a management report for others to use when deciding its future level of funding.

When she returned to her hotel room, she attempted to assemble her notes but could only manage to clip them together in the right order before the pain behind her eyes and pounding in her brain made her abandon the struggle.

The headache was not improving. If anything, it was getting worse. Hoping it would fade by the morning, she grabbed two more Panadeines and forced them down her throat with a mouthful of water, trying not to gag. Dinner was out of the question. Too bad about her sweaty clothes—she collapsed on top of her bed.

She woke early from sleep with excruciating pain, unable to lift her head from the pillow. Or turn it. A thousand hammers were attacking her brain. She felt hot with fever. And her eyes were impossible to focus. There was absolutely no way she could get out of bed.

Hours later, she heard a knock at the door. The hotel manager called out to her, 'Are you alright in there?'

'No, not really.' It was an effort to talk.

'I'll send someone in,' he replied.

This being a bush town, the only other female to hand was the hotel's cook. Fresh from her duties preparing breakfast for the other few guests and still wearing her apron, she knocked, unlocked the door and bustled in.

'What's the matter, love? Your driver came to collect you and, when you didn't turn up at the desk, he asked my boss where you'd got to. Are you sick, luvvie?'

'It's my head,' whimpered Sarah.

The cook took one look at her pain-wracked face. 'You need to get out of here. Fast. There's no doctor here, and no flights today. We'll send you with the driver straight back to Lae.'

She called out to the manager, and between them they manhandled Sarah out of bed and carried her to the office vehicle, where they reclined the front passenger seat and deposited her as gently as they could, with a pillow under her head and a wet washer over her eyes and forehead.

The cook had grabbed her belongings and

stuffed them into her bag, which was stashed in the back of the jeep.

'Take her straight to the doctor,' said the manager to the local driver.

Over one hundred and forty kilometres of ill-formed dirt road in a bone-rattler with no air-conditioning was the nearest Sarah had yet been to hell. With the windows wound down because of the heat, dust swirled in and settled on every square inch of her. She endured part of the journey partially unconscious, her body's defence against the pain.

A medico examined her. He'd come out of his surgery to the vehicle, summonsed by the driver. The doctor pressed around her neck and peered into her eyes with a bright torch. He asked her to rotate her head as far to each side as she could. She could barely move it one inch. 'How long have you been unwell?'

'My headache started yesterday morning, but I felt off for a few days before that,' she croaked. Her throat felt sore, too.

'Go straight to emergency,' he said to the driver. 'I'll phone them.'

Sarah didn't remember her transition to the hospital bed, but she was certainly glad to get there.

It was 24 hours before she was next aware of the time. Had they knocked her out with medication, or had the pain in her head stopped her body clock?

She reckoned it must be afternoon, judging by the temperature and stillness of the atmosphere, the standard measures of time of day and seasons in the tropics.

Her sudden wakefulness held another dimension—something strange in the air. She heard a distant rumbling noise. The room swayed. Loose items crashed to the ground. It was an earthquake, normal for these parts, but this was a big one. Frightened nurses in the corridor beyond her door yelled 'outside, outside.' Doors banged as they raced off, abandoning those patients like Sarah who were helpless and quaking in their beds.

The quake ran its course, inflicting no damage on the low-rise timber and galvanised iron buildings, and the hospital returned to normal.

The word 'normal' in a developing country was relative, though, and did not equate to Sydney standards. Care was of the most basic standard, encompassing the administration of medicines according to instructions by a doctor, the offering of food at intervals and the bringing and disposing of bedpans when needed.

Sarah's headache remained, but was less intense. She couldn't eat and was barely drinking enough to need a bedpan. Her body was sweating out its excess moisture.

After the quake, she drank a few sips of water from the covered glass on her bedside table and drifted off to sleep again.

Morning. Struggling to orient herself, she

worked out it must be Thursday. Since her admittance to hospital on Tuesday afternoon, no-one had come near her to wash her. Feeling quite putrid, she recalled that her last shower had been early on Monday, before she left home to travel to the airport. She was still dusty from the road trip, the dust now overlaid with stale perspiration and general body odour.

Her head felt heaps better, as if she could safely lift it off the pillow. She had to clean herself up.

Gingerly, she sat up on the bed and swung her legs over the side, sitting like that for a few minutes to check her sense of balance. She slid to the ground and stood beside the bed, holding on again to make sure she could stay upright. Her thighs felt shaky, but the pounding in her head had stopped and her eyes stayed in focus. Carefully, she bent to open her bedside locker, thankful to find it contained the small overnight bag she'd brought on her trip. She extracted her bag of toiletries, clean undies, a crumpled T-shirt and a skirt.

Clutching these items, she took the threadbare towel hanging on the rail beside her bed, slipped on her sandals and shuffled out of her room. Sliding along the corridor against the wall to give herself extra support, she soon found the bathroom. Using this mouldy facility worried her, but she had little choice about whose germs she might be sharing. She balanced on her heels and on the outer edge of her feet, keeping her toes off the shower base. No need to offer a safe haven to any more invading bugs, she thought, wondering where her current troubles had originated.

The spray of water was cold, as usual, but refreshing. Ah, that soap felt good. So did her shampoo. She dried herself with the skimpy hospital towel, applied deodorant and towel-dried her hair, running her hands through the thick mass to pat it into shape. She brushed her teeth. Fresh breath at last.

Wearing her cleaned body and her change of clothes, she felt like a new woman. She could escape from this place now. If she could only find a doctor to discharge her.

When she returned to her room, she nearly fell down, but not because her illness had flared. There stood a very concerned looking Jack. She gasped, 'What on earth are you doing here?'

He rushed over to take her arm. 'Sarah, thank god, are you alright? I thought something terrible must have happened when I found your bed empty.'

'I wasn't okay a few days ago, but I'm a lot better now.' *Especially now that I've seen you.*

'You still look very pale and washed out. I worried when the local office told me you were in hospital with viral meningitis. I came on the first available flight to take you home. You shouldn't be traveling by yourself in this condition, and I'm your boss, responsible for your welfare on the job.'

'That's what gave me that excruciating headache? I was too ill to hear what anyone said to me on Tuesday, and the level of care since I regained full awareness of my surroundings hasn't exactly been first-class.' She spoke tongue-in-cheek, with an ironic smile, recalling her smelly state and that bathroom. He'd understand. They weren't here to complain but to help improve conditions for the local people. There were only two doctors in this town, both of them run off their feet.

'The doctor who examined you gave instructions to the sister-in-charge. She told me medicine can do little for viral meningitis. It just has to run its course.'

'I'm glad you didn't arrive an hour ago. After days without a shower I stank, and was not very nice to be near.'

'You're always nice to be near,' muttered Jack.

Her ears pricked up. Had she heard him correctly? Her lonely, longing heart fluttered like a flag stirred to life by a puff of wind.

He clamped his jaw and hastily changed the subject. 'We're booked on the return flight this afternoon. Do you think you can make it, if the doc gives you the green light?'

'That sounds like a wonderful plan. I can't wait to leave this place. Remind me to stay out of hospitals in the future, won't you?'

'Will do.' He picked up her bag and took her

arm. 'We'll find somewhere air-conditioned while we wait for the plane. Grab a bite to eat.'

'I'm rather bedraggled and creased—not looking my restaurant best.' She tried to smooth her crumpled top.

'Who cares? I bet you've barely eaten in the last few days. I saw the lunch trolleys being prepared, while I was waiting at reception to find out which bed you were in. The meal preparation area was opposite the desk. Don't think there's been much training of the kitchen staff in hygiene standards. I wouldn't touch the food here with a forty-foot barge pole, even if I was fit and healthy.'

'I was too sick to eat but, now you mention it, I *am* starving, and dying for a cup of tea.'

'So what's new,' laughed Jack.

They waited fifteen minutes for the doctor to arrive for his hospital rounds. 'Glad to see you're up and about. I checked on you each day,' came his reassuring words, 'but you were out to it most of the time.'

He read her temperature chart, asked her a few questions and gave the all clear. 'The blood tests are fine. We took samples while you slept and sent them to the lab. You were lucky,' he said. 'Young adults fit the profile for this illness, but you're healthy and you had viral meningitis, not the pneumococcal variety, so you've suffered no complications. It's a pretty common infection of the fluid surrounding the spinal cord and the brain. Babies and children get it too. With your serious symptoms, we had to check you out, and look after you, but there was nothing much we could do, other than administer strong pain killers and let you sleep it off.'

'How did I get sick? What caused this?'

'You don't have kids, do you? You're not changing dirty nappies?' She shook her head.

'Or kissing too many strangers?' His eyes twinkled a little as he looked at her and Jack. Did he think they were a married couple?

'Definitely no kissing.' She wished otherwise.

'In that case, I'd say that personal hygiene was not a problem. It was probably a mosquito bite. That form of viral meningitis is not contagious. Are you often outside around dusk?'

'Yes,' said Sarah, 'that's when I water my garden.'

'Then you'd better switch to watering in the mornings, before you go to work. You'll feel tired for a few more days, and you may suffer a few more headaches, but less severe ones. By Monday you should be back to normal.'

Jack hooked the strap of her overnight bag over one shoulder so that both his hands were free to steady her as they descended the few steps in front of the hospital. Jack's touch aroused too many disturbing emotions, forbidden to her. Better to keep him at a distance.

Reaching level ground, she walked unaided to the taxi which had ferried Jack from the airport and which he had ordered to wait.

He took her into the only tourist hotel in town. No-one would rate it with five stars, but it was air-conditioned, and it featured a bistro. Sarah selected a light meal—a toasted ham, cheese and tomato sandwich. Jack chose the same, and he poured himself a cup from her pot of tea, so they requested extra boiling water. How companionable, she thought, sharing tastes in food.

Another short taxi ride saw them at the airport. Jack had pre-arranged with the airline for her return ticket, booked for a later date, to be transferred. He checked them in as travelling companions. The flight would take an hour, and she felt strangely exhilarated at the looming prospect of sitting so close beside Jack for that length of time.

Once on board, jammed together into the narrow seating, she steeled herself against the dangerous urge to snuggle in to him. Heat radiated from him with magnetic force and his after-shave tempted her to lean closer and breathe it in more fully. Her arms felt like jelly as she fumbled with fastening her seatbelt. It hit her like a freight train that he overwhelmed her every sense.

To distract herself, she keenly watched everything happening outside her window. The busy activity on the tarmac, the ground falling away as they took off, the cloud formations.

She gazed at the magnificence of the Owen Stanley Range, at the rows of mountain peaks towering above the valleys, and her eyes grew heavy from the glare. Her ears absorbed the low-pitched pink noise generated by the droning engines and lulling her into her lethargic state of the past few days. She dozed off.

She returned to consciousness when the engines idled back, changing the sound inside the cabin and signalling their approach to their destination. Her head was resting comfortably on Jack's broad shoulder and she sat bolt upright in startled confusion. 'Sorry Jack, why didn't you push me off?'

'Because you needed the rest,' he responded gruffly, but Sarah could sense guardedness in that answer. He seemed reluctant for her to move away, then he shifted his own position and sat up straighter. Had he been leaning towards her too?

Jack had parked his car at the airport, and he ushered her into the front seat to drive her home. It was an unnerving experience to sit in Jenny's customary place. Sarah fought a crazy urge to reach out and claim as hers that muscle-bound left thigh of his as he worked the clutch.

She craved physical intimacy with him, just being close to him, being held and comforted by him, the human contact missing from her life. What she'd unwittingly found when she fell asleep on the plane and woke against his shoulder. Instead, she sat in silence, staring ahead as he drove. Jack was taken. Not hers.

He too was silent. There was tension in the air.

He escorted her to her back door and, once she'd unlocked it, he leaned in to deposit her bag. It suddenly became extremely important that he not come any further.

Sarah hastily stepped past him, being careful to avoid any inadvertent physical contact, and stood holding the door in a half-open position, using it as a partial defence barrier as she turned to face Jack, still standing on the mat.

The man she fervently wished had his arms around her, with his lips against hers.

'Thank you so much for coming to my rescue,' she said. 'I really appreciate what you've done for me today, but I'll be fine now.'

'Are you sure, Sarah?'

She detected a note of longing in that question, a kind of misery, and glanced at Jack's expression, relieved to see no hint of a crass proposition by a man seeking to take advantage of an unexpected opportunity. He looked sad and tense, not lascivious.

Trying to stay strong herself, she replied, 'But of course. See you on Monday.'

'If you need anything over the weekend, call me at home. Look after yourself, Sarah.' Jack's wistful words of farewell were almost a whisper.

He turned and strode back to his car, as she waited at her door to wave him goodbye.

She struggled for the rest of the day to overcome her uneasy sense of disorientation and disquiet over Jack's appearance as her rescuer, his puzzling behaviour and her yearning to be physically close to him.

CHAPTER TWENTY

She'd agreed with Jack that she should take Friday off, but she managed over the weekend to write up her report of the day spent at the demonstration farm. It surprised Jack to find it sitting on his desk on Monday morning.

'There's no doubt about you, Sarah, you're a very observant interviewer, even when you're on your last legs. I take it you're back to feeling 100%. There's good ammunition in these pages. We should be able to get more funds for that trial project, to help subsistence farmers more widely adopt better techniques.' He was firmly re-establishing a purely professional relationship with her.

His praise of her work pleased her. 'But I'm sorry I didn't get to complete the remainder of my assignment last week.'

'No worries, I'll deal with that problem. Someone else can take over. I have a bigger job in mind for you, a major project related to potential sources of fresh food for the workforce for the giant open-cut copper mining project on Bougainville Island.'

Her pride swelled that he'd given her this assignment. The mine's construction phase at Panguna was newly underway. Ten thousand men needed to be fed over the next twelve months, offering a golden opportunity to entice the local population, many opposed to the mine being built on their traditional land, into a market-based economy instead of subsistence-based production.

Two weeks later she thrilled as the plane approached the island. The pilot's voice crackled over the intercom. 'Passengers on the left of the aircraft will have an excellent view today of Mount Balbi, the highest point on Bougainville.'

She pressed her forehead to the window and spotted volcanic craters and several crater lakes. Wisps of steam drifted upwards into the sky. As they flew south towards the airport at Aropa, the pilot spoke again. 'Mount Bagana to our left. Don't want to frighten you, but it's very active. Beyond you can just see the Billy Mitchell crater lake, filling the caldera. Two kilometres wide.'

She craned her neck and spotted the signs of lava flows from the top of the classic volcanic cone extending down all sides of the mountain, shaking her head in disbelief at this amazing country.

The company constructing the open-pit mine at

Panguna hauled every piece of equipment over the mountain on a single slippery strip of mud track, with no hint of a safety barrier in sight. Checkpoints at either end alerted the traffic controllers, should any vehicle slip off the edge of this road. A D9 bulldozer attached at the front of each haulage truck, with a D9 dozer at the back, pulled and pushed the loads at ten miles per hour up the steep slopes from the coast before abandoning the trucks to career down the hill into Panguna, virtually out of control. The valley floor lay hundreds of feet below the road, a cliff on the other side.

Her driver kept a careful eye on oncoming traffic, judging the timing needed to reach the intermittent passing bays, while Sarah braced her feet, gripped the overhead handrail, and took deep breaths to calm her jittery nerves. The alternative to racing towards a passing bay was to back the vehicle until there was room to pass, a terrifying prospect. In one section of the road there was a constant danger of landslide but, as they passed that section, no boulders came crashing down, just the soft and steady plop-plopping of mud and gravel onto the road.

In the mine pit, massive dump trucks with wheels twice Sarah's height churned through the mud generated by four hundred inches of annual rainfall, steadily recontouring the valley.

She worked pretty hard in her three days at

Panguna, talking to people all day, every day, concentrating on what they were saying and scribbling down a few jottings in between interviews as a summary, remaining at the office until 10pm to write up her notes, facts and figures.

She was accommodated for several nights at the dirty, untidy, dingy and depressing single girls' mess at Panguna. What a misnomer. It explained why the men she had interviewed during the day were so interested in her marital status and whether she lived with her husband. All night long men banged on windows and tramped up and down the corridors in their heavy boots. She kept her door and windows firmly locked!

Staying there made her feel pretty much out of her depth and ill at ease, especially in the morning when she went for a shower and found the smelly bathroom full of men shaving, one being an executive she had interviewed in his office. Tolerance might be easy in theory, but not so easy in practice, and she wished she was a bit more sophisticated, able to take this in her stride.

At breakfast in the cafeteria one of the 'single girls' took pity on the married ingenue in their midst and confessed how bored were the secretaries at Panguna. Too many office staff with not enough to do, and she'd filled one afternoon typing five envelopes. She and her mates swapped books every morning at the breakfast table to ensure their supply of reading material for the long day at work. 'You're lucky doing the interesting work you do,' she said.

By an amazing coincidence, friends of Sarah's from Sydney were based on the island, the husband working for a major accounting firm auditing the massive project. His wife worked as a secretary for a construction company at Arawa, a new town being built on the east coast. The couple lived on Kieta Beach, in a large caravan with a bedroom at each end and living quarters in the middle, and they offered her a place to stay once her meetings at Panguna concluded.

For the remainder of her two weeks on Bougainville it was like stepping into the film set for 'South Pacific'. The coconuts clunked on the roof at night, and the waves swished gently up to the front door when they stepped outside in the morning for a stroll along the tropical foreshore. Spraying themselves with insect repellent kept the sand flies at bay.

A pontoon was moored about 20 yards off shore. On Saturday night a party developed in the next-but-one caravan and everyone bee-bopped in the shallow water on the beach, there being nowhere else to dance. They swam out to the pontoon at midnight, quite an eerie sensation in the dark. People paid a packet to savour these experiences as tourists, whilst she had the privilege of being paid for her good fortune.

She visited distant villages, greeting some of the blackest people on earth, their skins much darker than in other parts of Papua New Guinea, Australia, the Pacific and Asia. They disdainfully referred to the mine labour imported from other parts of Papua New Guinea as red-skins and did not welcome them.

Bougainvilleans, men, women and children alike, seemed addicted to chewing betel nut for its nicotine-like effect, heedless of the mouth cancers suffered by long-term users. Their ear-to-ear smiles, revealing whatever white teeth still survived in their betel-nut-stained mouths, topped by the whites of their eyes, were a study in red, white and black. Walking tracks were splattered with red spittle.

The island's cash economy relied on copra and cocoa, sometimes interplanted, and grown on plantations by the international trading company Burns Philp and expatriate owner-occupiers. Smallholders also grew coconuts and cocoa for cash, plus a wide range of tropical fruits and vegetables in the non-cash economy. Their staples were kaukau, taro, yam and pumpkin, with some dry-land rice.

The inevitable pigs roamed freely under the gigantic kapok trees and the areca palms, whose fruit yielded the seed bonanza known as betel nut. The fruits in plentiful supply included bananas, pineapple, papaya, mangoes, guava and the mango-like golden apple.

Coastal vegetable markets already operated.

Clearly, the opportunities for the island's residents to feed more people abounded.

Her two weeks of work on the island convinced her that the road network, or rather, the lack of roads, was the major constraint on sourcing fresh foods for the mineworkers. The locals had little incentive to sell their wares if the sale involved a day's walk each way, through the steep country she'd observed from the plane, carrying their bananas and papaya in *bilum* bags slung over their heads.

She recommended building roads linked to the current walking tracks. Local growers could then catch a ride into a central point suitably located as a market place.

Jack congratulated her. 'With those tables of statistical analysis and display of original thinking, you're a full-fledged economist now, my friend.' His touch of extra emphasis on *my* warmed her heart.

Earning his praise was becoming the highlight of any day, exceptionally important to her, because through his assignments she was discovering her niche in the workforce, the work that brought her meaning and joy.

But since the day he'd retrieved her from the hospital, she'd become uneasily aware that his proximity triggered disturbing bodily responses in her. Jack's striking physical presence, his dynamic energy, and his zest for life had always aroused her interest. Gradually, she'd become aware of how much his daily behaviour at the office consistently proved he recognised her needs and cared about her as a person.

Today, she looked back over the past year and realised how much she'd missed Jack when he was absent for a few days on field trips. Yet she didn't miss Andrew, at least the essence of him, although she missed the companionship of living with someone. Instead, Jack was taking centre stage. She'd grown to trust him implicitly, remaining perfectly correct in her conversations and actions, even if less proper thoughts infested her dreams at night.

Her reactions to being physically close to him frightened her with their implications. She must push away such thoughts the moment they impinged on her consciousness. To minimise their frequency, she must stay well clear of him by keeping her physical distance.

It helped that Jack's long leave was due. He and his family would spend the six weeks leading up to Christmas on a family farm in the central west district of New South Wales, helping with the wheat harvest.

'Too bad if it's stinking hot. At least it'll be a dry heat. And we're escaping the doldrums.' His voice lifted in relief.

'Lucky you!' Her voice sagged in contrast.

His face clouded with concern. 'Christmas is looming. Why don't you take a few weeks off over Christmas yourself? You could use the opportunity to return home to Sydney, to spend Christmas with your family. I'm worried you'll be too lonely here by yourself.'

'No need to worry. *Samting nating*, as the locals say.' She shrugged away his concern. 'The Port Moresby Choral Society is performing Handel's Messiah at St Mary's Cathedral. The Hallelujah chorus will lift my pre-Christmas spirits and my friends Maria and Kevin Mitchell have invited me round for Christmas lunch with their brood. Kevin was Andrew's mate at work, remember?'

Jack nodded.

'It suits me to stay here. Andrew's back in Sydney, so I know he won't be calling in at Kevin's at an embarrassing moment and we can all relax. I'll have fun playing with their youngest, Isabella. She's a favourite of mine.'

'In that case, I hope we'll see you when we return just after Christmas. Will you be going to the New Year's Eve party at the Williams' place?'

'Yes, that sounds like fun. It's been too long since I put on my dancing shoes.'

She flashed back to the last time, again at Charles and Carolyn's. It had been before Andrew left, with Jack and Jenny and other ag couples, fourteen in total for dinner and then madcap dancing to shake it all down. A limbo competition. A can-can dance. One wife was nine months pregnant but nonetheless she did a fabulous mimicry of a rock'n'roll singer on stage, singing the Beatles song 'I Want You (She's So Heavy)'. She had all the right actions, swivel hips, soft shoe steps, the works, plus the enormous stomach, convulsing everyone in laughter. It was impossible to get even slightly tipsy at these dancing-till-the-wee-small-hours parties, with the energy expended on such hi-jinks.

'Come on, Miss Blue Eyes,' Jack had said to her, 'get up and dance with me, why don't you.' Both had marital partners inclined to be couch potatoes in a social setting, so their dancing was a way to discharge excess energy, and it was fun to be whirled and twirled, smiling and laughing.

She and Andrew had left that party around four fifteen, she being absolutely soaked with perspiration from dancing, and she got to bed at a quarter to five after having a cold shower. Brrr, at that hour. The climate did not suit such energetic activities but being sweaty was a vast improvement on the boring old ballet lessons of her childhood. Ballet may encourage shapely legs, but it didn't stir her spirit. Her face lit up with sheer joy at the whole physical sensation of letting go to the rhythm of the music. A sure-fire directive for happiness was 'Go dancing'.

She'd do her best to avoid him this time. There were plenty of other men amongst her colleagues with whom she could dance. Even Charles occasionally graced the dance floor, given the right dose of insistent persuasion.

As if able to read her thoughts, Jack said, 'I'm not sure we'll be there. We have a few family commitments. Jenny's widowed mother is returning with us after Christmas. She's not as young as she used to be, and we may keep her company at home.'

Sarah thought that Jack staying at home on New Year's Eve, away from her, was an excellent idea.

CHAPTER TWENTY-ONE

New Year's Eve gripped Port Moresby in a special air of festivity this year because the country had just become a self-governing nation. Full independence was coming. Big changes lay ahead.

Sarah's reflections on the past were done, and her New Year resolution was a foregone conclusion. It was to stay well clear of Jack for a little longer. Her contract would end soon and she'd soon have to face leaving to find other employment, even if it could never rival the many undoubted attractions of her present position.

Only for a limited time need she sustain her vigilance concerning Jack. She'd soon be somewhere else, gone from this place.

Meanwhile, party fever gripped her and the age-old problem—what to wear? New Year celebrations invited a creative approach, the opportunity to be different, to shake off the blues and go dancing without a care in the world.

Yet no smart little fashion boutiques lurked

around the corner.

The time was long overdue for her to brush up her dressmaking skills. She was out of practice since the 'Night on the Nile' party months before Andrew left, when she'd made a heavy yoke collar with rows of braid around it, and draped the rest of herself in white evening-y material, tied at the waist with yellow ribbon tie.

A special piece of material had taken her eye before she left Sydney. The royal blue, almost purple, colour was perfect for her skin and hair tones and, with its large swirls of teal and white, the design evoked completely her pre-conceived idea of the tropics. It had cluttered up her sewing basket for years now, waiting for the right occasion.

Importantly, the fabric suited the atmospheric conditions, being pure polished cotton with no artificial fibre. She was confident she wouldn't dissolve in a lather of perspiration the minute she donned her new creation, even if later exertions on the dance floor induced unladylike sweat.

In Sydney, she'd also picked up a stunning pattern. The skirt was full-length, a fitted bodice at the front tapered in a V to the waistline at the back, and the halter neck tied with a bow, making the dress backless. It would show off the graceful line of her shoulders and disguise her major figure-fault, her short waist combined with long legs. The easy-sew design meant that there were no zips or buttons, only a hook and eye fastening at the waistline.

Her sewing machine was a little rusty from lack of use, but the pattern was so basic that even a novice seamstress like her could succeed. It gave her spirits a lift just thinking about a special new party outfit. Her high-heeled sandals were the right colour match and, with her long drop earrings and a clean pair of knickers, she had all she needed. Women more daring than her might saucily dispense with undies in this climate, as the skirt swished at her ankles and was opaque, but that state of devil-may-care abandonment was a step too far. For Sarah, it was enough to embrace the spirit of New Year, get festive and go backless and bra-less to a party amongst her friends.

Kneeling on the mat in the living room, she laid out the length of fabric and pinned the pattern to it. Just a few simple shapes to cut out. Easy. The sewing machine whirred away. In no time, the dress was ready. She tried it on and twirled before the mirror. A success. It made a daring new woman of her.

She smiled with relief. For once she could present herself as womanly, confident in her selection of the right attire for the occasion. If he could see her now, Andrew might even take back what he'd said about her before he left, that she wasn't a real woman.

It was true, she'd never paid much attention to her own looks. In a family of four girls, she'd learned that drawing attention to the respective beauty endowments of siblings led to the unhappiness of any sister being compared less favourably to another.

The whole subject was best avoided in the interests of family unity. That's what her family did best. Avoided the issues.

That was then, and this was now. She'd love the chance to draw admiring glances from the opposite sex. Including Jack.

A little shiver of excitement raised goosebumps on her arms. Part of her hoped that Jack would be there tonight, to see her in her Cinderella finery.

Festivities were well underway when she arrived around nine pm. Charles and Carolyn greeted her in unison: 'We're so glad you came.' They'd gone to considerable trouble, even setting up special lighting, and its ultra-violet component had a dramatic impact on her dress, highlighting the white and intensifying the blue into deep purple. She and her swirls glowed in the dark, as did the men who'd worn white shirts.

'Sarah, that dress is fantastic. Oh boy.' Charles let out a quiet wolf-whistle.

Carolyn laughed good-naturedly. 'Husbands! No need to rub it in. Just because I'm still losing my baby fat!' She patted her waist and hips. Her second son was now two months old.

'Sorry, sweet Caro,' said Charles. You look gorgeous tonight too.' He gave his wife a quick cuddle and planted a peck on her cheek.

Mollified, Carolyn smiled at her guest. 'I agree with Charles. You'll be the hit of the night in that dress. It's got fabulous style.'

'Too bad we can't offer any foot-loose and fancy-free bachelors, eager to be swept off their feet.' He grinned cheekily as he ushered her further into the room. 'Come and talk to Jack, he's on his lonesome over here. See if he recognises you in your party attire.'

Sarah's heart missed a beat. So Jack and Jenny *were* here. At work, she hadn't wanted to ask Charles if the Martins would attend, in case she seemed too interested in his answer. She'd wondered if they'd stay home, minding Tom and Lottie *and* Jenny's mother. Jack must have deemed his mother-in-law able to cope unaided with babysitting her two grandchildren tonight.

Sarah's suppressed emotions rose to consciousness in a whoosh.

For months, she had determinedly denied her feelings for Jack, a married man obviously committed to his wife and family. But as Carolyn steered her towards the man staring out the window at the view, his back to her, his legs askance, confidently relaxed, she trembled, dead scared to be near him tonight.

189

She'd known that fear since her trip with him on that plane from Lae. He felt right to be with. She trusted him and felt at ease with him. She admired his qualities at work and at home—being competent was so sexy. He challenged her intellectually and an intelligent man was so seductive. His energy invigorated her. She loved catching his eye and laughing with him at the same amusing quirk of human nature. They were on the same wavelength. And now she faced the irresistible force of the sexual attraction to him she had long repressed. Her body flooded with uncontrollable warmth of desire.

Sarah nervously licked her lips. The prospect of facing up to Jack in merrymaking mode was altogether different from their daily dealings in a professional office relationship. Or their banter and focus on the children at a family picnic. Now that she'd received, and accepted, the flash of insight that he meant far too much to her, how was she going to hide this new awareness from him?

Carolyn tapped Jack on the shoulder. 'Look who's with me. Doesn't she look stunning? Will you get her a drink while I rush off to check why the baby's crying?'

He turned round. His face lit with pleasure. And something more than that. The same depth of longing she felt for him.

'Sarah!' He narrowed his eyes as he absorbed her attire. 'I'd better stand guard over you, to protect your virtue, looking like that,' he teased. But there was an edge to his voice.

'Thanks for your gallant offer, Jack, I appreciate it, but I can look after myself, surrounded as I am by my friends.' Her nervous smile betrayed the butterflies fluttering in her stomach. *There's only one man in this room I need protection from—and he's standing right in front of me.*

Quickly moving onto safer ground, she asked, 'How was your Christmas? I suppose Tom and Lottie woke you with the pre-dawn chorus of the kookaburras.'

'They did that alright. It was great. The smell of the eucalypts and those cackling laughing birds were unmistakeable signs of being back home.' His wry grin told the story. 'I wondered how you fared. Were you okay?'

'Oh yes, fine thanks,' she replied. 'The Mitchells invited me to join them, as you know. Their kids had a ball. It was the first Christmas where Isabella comprehended what it was all about, but scrunching the cellophane wrapping paper offered more fun than the gifts inside.'

Sarah's face threatened to crumble at the recollection of the painful gap in her own life, but she was an expert at suppressing the dull ache in her heart. 'Where has Jenny got to? I didn't see her as I came in?' She suspected Jack had noticed her quick change of subject. He was no fool.

'She ducked off to the loo and on her way back I saw Charles waylay her and inveigle her to dance. He's just loaded 'A Hard Day's Night' on the turntable. My request. She needs a bit of persuading to relinquish her chair, so it's good she's succumbed to my favourite group of mop tops and embraced the festive mood.'

Sarah watched Jenny shuffling around with Charles. At their occasional office get-togethers, neither had ever indulged in much dancing. Jenny was her usual languorous self, but tonight she'd dressed up too, minimising her plumpness and enhancing her features with careful makeup. She was smiling at Charles, her calm, relaxed smile and, in that moment, Sarah understood how Jack fell for her back in their uni days. She epitomised the 'You can't tell a book by its cover' idiom. Those few quiet chats at family picnics had revealed an interesting woman, once you opened the Jenny story book.

Her own book cover this evening was nice and shiny—but inside her cover she was anything but tranquil, a mass of tattered dog-eared pages. No matter how good is your packaging, it doesn't mean you'll end up with the right man. *How I envy Jenny*.

Sarah refocused her attention. 'Charles is being a very attentive host, dancing for a change, so I'm glad Jenny's enjoying herself. Making the most of New Year's Eve! It's pretty hard not to respond to that Beatles album.'

'I know *you* love to dance. So before I get you that drink, will you join me?' He swished his arm towards the dance space, but his voice sounded tense, as if apprehensive she might make an excuse. She should say 'no'. It had always been her intention to avoid any dancing with him, if he was present.

She looked at him, and overwhelming desire swept over her. 'Yes, I'd love to.' Would her treacherous body give the game away, like Maria's when she and Captain von Trapp danced the Laendler in her favourite film, 'The Sound of Music'?

Before Andrew left, when Sarah had gyrated with Jack to rock-and-roll, sometimes till three in the morning, it had energised her and left her wishing that the fun with him would never end.

This time dancing to The Beatles was an electrifying experience, now that she'd finally, belatedly, consciously recognised Jack as a very sexual being. And that she responded to him the same way. Ignoring those bopping around them and making the floor vibrate, he held her close to him, firm in his embrace, choosing to dance half-time to the slower underlying rhythm of 'I Should Have Known Better' and not the song's upbeat tempo.

His aftershave was subtle but distinctively his and she resisted an overwhelming urge to lean against him, to be wrapped in his powerful arms.

His right hand was on her back, just above the

waist, where his thumb found bare skin. It felt like a branding machine, marking her as his, but his thumb did not wander. He maintained propriety. It wasn't his fault that she'd worn a backless dress. His voice too close for comfort, he murmured, 'You look absolutely stunning, Sarah. Tonight you've excelled yourself.'

'Thank you. Your compliment means a lot.' More than he realised, she thought. It meant everything to her. Did she do this all for him, hoping he'd notice her as a woman and not just as a colleague and friend?

'Got your New Year resolutions ready?' He exhaled his soft words into her ear.

'Yes,' she sighed, trying to ignore the thrills invading her. *Stay away from you was at the top of my list, and I've broken that resolution before the year has even begun.* 'Have you?' She struggled to regain rational thought. 'I hope the year ahead brings you good fortune and fulfils every one of your dreams.' There, she sounded perfectly polite and in control, mouthing the right words for the occasion.

'One is coming true right now.' His left hand increased its pressure on her right hand.

'Which one, exactly?' Her knees went weak at the thought that they might share the same dream and she almost stumbled.

'The dream of having you in my arms,' he whispered.

Taken off guard by a flood of dopamine through her body, she almost surrendered her iron self-discipline in favour of seeking refuge in his warm embrace. She'd been craving his touch for months.

The fingers of his right hand pressed into the small of her back, the increased pressure hinting at his wish to possess her. His thumb unobtrusively began to caress her, suggesting forbidden sensual possibilities. 'From the instant we met, I was smitten.'

The shock of his simple acknowledgement of her physical attractiveness to him, and her jolting realisation that this was the man who felt 'right' in every way, numbed her mind. She said nothing but prayed the music would never stop.

'For these past few years I've tried and tried to resist the irresistible. You. You're a very desirable woman.'

The music didn't stop, and she regained partial equilibrium, despite the overwhelming and alarming escalation of intensity as her body rushed headlong into a state of fever.

Jack's arousal pressed against her. 'Andrew was a fool not to realise what you offer, and what a gem he possessed.'

As sexual desire mounted, she fought her reckless urge to dance cheek to cheek with him. She prayed that those jiving around them were so exuberantly singing the chorus line of 'I Should Have Known Better', raising the roof, that they'd fail to notice Jack's close hold on her and their escape into their own world.

He whispered hastily, 'I know you, Sarah. Like the back of my hand. You feel things deeply. So vulnerable, but so resilient.'

Her heart gave a leap of joy. He understood her. Her fingers tightened on his.

'I shouldn't say this to you but, like the words in this song, I can't help myself. I love you.' His voice trembled.

She gasped. Three magic words, little words, short words, conveyed huge meaning. But he sounded so sad.

'I've tried to hide it.' He sighed.

Her guarded tongue sprang free, releasing her own repressed feelings. 'Why was I kidding myself? Why didn't I realise before tonight that I love you too?'

'I think I knew that, deep down, instinctively.' He pressed her closer to him.

'What are we going to do, Jack?'

'I'm gutted. I can't do *anything* about it.'

'I know that. Jenny. The kids.'

With John Lennon's final insistent 'you love me too' and his burst of breath into his harmonica, the last bars of the song faded away, and reluctantly she relinquished Jack's enveloping arms.

He turned back towards the window to screen his arousal from public view.

She hastily retreated to the bathroom to give herself time to regroup.

How could she have been so stupid? She'd moved unwittingly—but willingly—into dangerous territory. She had to do something before someone got hurt.

Their mutual declarations of love had engulfed her in panic. She wanted to run away, but on the thirty-first day of December no-one left an event before midnight. She could sneak away, but her friends would think that very odd. Jenny might become suspicious if she disappeared immediately after slow dancing with Jack. On the other hand, saying polite goodbyes would draw attention to her leaving—and the tension in her.

She'd have to stay. Put on a brave face. Call on her full array of acting skills, already honed to perfection from hiding Andrew's secret. Ignore her inner turmoil.

She summoned enough courage to emerge from the bathroom and rejoin the throng of revellers. Avoiding eye contact with Jack, she made a superhuman effort to chat to other guests, hiding her alarm at the realisation she was in love with a man who was someone else's husband, with young dependent children.

She grabbed a glass of bubbly, getting ready

for the toasts to come, but stayed right away from Jack and Jenny when the clock chimed twelve. She placed perfunctory pecks on the cheeks of those standing close to her, occupying the awkward moment when others might have expected her to be celebrating with her boss and his wife. From across the room, as the first of January arrived, she watched them exchange the affectionate hug of a long-married couple.

Afterwards, a smiling Jenny came over and kissed her cheek. 'Happy New Year, Sarah.'

Sarah responded with a guilty kiss of her own, and Jenny said, 'You look great tonight, by the way.'

'Thank you, so do you.' What else could she say?

'It's been fun. Sorry I've been a tad antisocial this evening. Too busy dancing to do much talking.' She laughed. 'Jack'll be happy that I got off my bum, for once.'

'An auspicious start to the year, then.' Sarah dragged out a smile for Jenny, putting on the supreme acting performance of her life. The year 1974 had started disastrously for her.

Pleading the need to leave while plenty of people were out and about, making her drive home alone safer, she escaped into her living nightmare.

The bottom had fallen out of her world. She didn't see herself as a marriage breaker, especially one involving young children. He'd indicated his intentions to stay with Jenny and the kids, but they worked together and opportunities for an illicit liaison would arise. She was no Eve, proffering the tempting apple. What should she do?

On New Year's Day she lay on the living room floor and stared at the ceiling, trance-like, listening to Mozart's third violin concerto on repeat. The underlying gentle but frenzied pace in the music suited her agitated mood perfectly. She remembered that scholars believed this genius composer had written music designed to calm himself. *Thank you, Mr Mozart.*

Part of the tenth commandment of her Sunday School days played over and over in her mind, suddenly making sense: 'You shall not covet your neighbour's wife'. She'd failed the test. She coveted her neighbour's husband. Intensely.

The holiday period ended, and it was time to face Jack at the office again. Unable to concentrate on the work at hand, she distractedly doodled on a sheet of paper.

Jack appeared similarly agitated. Normally he attacked his paperwork with his customary vigour. Not today. She overheard him instructing his secretary to fill his diary with activities taking him outside the office.

Circulating past her desk *en route* to a lunch appointment, he acknowledged their mutual longing for a relationship with a few quiet words—'It's tough, isn't it!'—but otherwise they didn't speak of it.

In the evenings, that day and for the rest of the week, she returned to her prone position at home, playing her music constantly, weighing up her options, sleeping fitfully when she went to bed.

She knew one decision was a given. She did not intend to have an affair. It wasn't right. It wasn't her. All that sneaking around. Lying. Guilt. The taunts of her schooldays flooded back. She was too strait-laced. Too proper. Too much a goody two shoes.

It never occurred to her to demand that their mutual feelings be made public, that he come with her, or that he ask Jenny to leave. She respected Jenny's confessions about her shotgun marriage, had always borne witness to his loyalty to his existing family unit, and herself was keenly aware of the needs of trusting dependent children. She simply could not take her happiness at someone else's expense, especially when that meant Tom and Lottie. The type of man who'd walk out on his family held no appeal, as she'd always fear he might abandon her one day. She wanted a husband she could trust, who kept his word.

The forces which had always made Jack so attractive overwhelmed her now, with the physical enticements out in the open and so powerful. She was not strong enough to withstand the sexual impulses flooding her body. She wanted him and shivered with desire if he walked anywhere near her desk, craving to explore his nakedness.

She needed a plan to resist him and remain professional. It was not a plan she could discuss with Jack. She had to step up independently of him, take personal responsibility for doing the right thing.

Once again, she'd have to take charge of the situation, just like with Andrew and the adoption plan. As she had with her mother, too, now that she thought about it. Think of others first.

After a week of inner turmoil, she reached her decision. Giving up her career and removing herself from Jack's presence and the temptation he represented was going to take a mighty effort of her willpower but flight, not fight, was the only option. She must walk away, leave Port Moresby.

CHAPTER TWENTY-TWO

She drove to work with a heavy heart. Jack always met with the Departmental Head first thing on Monday mornings. When he strode briskly into her building an hour later, she summonsed up her failing courage and waylaid him. 'Jack, could I see you, please?'

Their eyes met, burning with unrequited passion, but bearing in mind the close presence of their colleagues, he replied, 'Of course. Come to my office.'

She followed him and sat in his visitor's chair, pointedly keeping her distance from him, determined to maintain her professionalism. He closed the door and, with a longing glance at her, he followed her lead and sank into his spot on the other side of the desk. Sarah gave him no chance to speak and launched straight into announcing her decision.

'I'm requesting formal leave of absence with immediate effect, and early termination of my contract of employment, to date from the end of that leave period. I think you know the reasons.' Her bottom lip trembled but she held her body rigid, to bolster herself against changing her mind under the influence of his magnetic presence.

His heavy sigh reverberated in the room. 'Hell, I've been thinking too. Endlessly. It's the only way out for us, isn't it? Remove ourselves from the possibility of bloody temptation. For sure, resisting you any longer will be impossible.' His voice choked up. 'And I can't just pack up my family and move on, not without awkward explanations to Jenny—lies they'd be—and great upheaval for the kids.'

A look of supreme misery plastered his face. His tortured eyes locked into gear with hers. 'But what will you do? Where will you go?'

'Jack, you've said it yourself. I'm resilient. I plan to return to Sydney for a while. It'll be easier to think more clearly there.'

He inclined his head, signalling his agreement.

'I'll book a seat on Friday's plane south.' Her hands clenched and her eyes filled with tears. In trying to do the honourable thing, she was making the ultimate sacrifice for the man she loved. There was no self-respect in any other course of action.

The door to his office was closed, always the warning to his colleagues that a private meeting was in progress. No-one would barge in. Jack stood up, came round his desk, lifted her out of her chair and took her in his arms.

'Come here, my darling. Let me hold you close for a moment.'

As if he was a lifejacket to a drowning man, she flung her arms around his shoulders and squeezed herself so close it almost took her breath away.

He whispered, 'It's inevitable that we'll succumb to temptation if you stay. But we can say a proper goodbye now, without fear of the consequences.'

He kissed her for the first time. A kiss to die for. The passion ignited like a bushfire, a spark one minute, a conflagration the next, flaring up and out of control. He braced his legs slightly apart and she curved in towards his lower body and his rock-hard arousal.

She surrendered to the heat invading her. This was the man for her, absolutely no doubt about it. He suited her perfectly in every way.

'Jack, oh Jack, I love you—and I want you so much.'

'And I adore you, my darling. Always have. Always will.'

He kissed her again. His fingers roamed over her body as he caressed her through her thin cotton frock. She couldn't get close enough to him. She pressed harder, pulling with her hands on the back of his neck to make sure his lips could not escape hers. Her breasts swelled to explosion point. She was so wet she was dripping. She'd never had an orgasm at the mere thought of sex, but it was about to happen, here in Jack's office. Miracles of sensation were rippling through her, from head to toe.

Her brain snapped back into gear. To yield would be so easy, but life would be too emotionally fraught afterwards, for too many people. She pushed him away with the same hands which a second before had been inciting him to make love.

'No Jack, no. We mustn't, we mustn't. We have to stay strong. We have to. You know that as well as I do.' She stepped back from him, sucking in deep gulps of air as if she'd just run the marathon.

''I'm in agony. You are everything I always wanted, but I can't have.' He groaned his despair.

'I keep remembering little Tom and Lottie. They adore you. They trust you. You'd miss them terribly if you and Jenny broke up. It would break your heart not having them in your daily life. You'd blame me in the end. It's only natural.'

She moved towards the door. 'I'm leaving in a few days. The thousands of kilometres of ocean between us will sever our link, kill off this uncontrollable desire. Until I leave, please help me be strong. Please Jack.' She held up her hand in a warning signal for him not to come near her again.

His strangled voice barely registered across the few feet separating them. 'Once you leave, we must have a surgically clean break. I won't be able to cope otherwise. Since New Year I've been struggling to hold my own at home. I can't bear the thought of constantly hanging out for news of you.'

The lump in her throat threatened to cut off her airway. 'You mean 'miss me, but let me go' is our best form of mutual self-preservation.' It wasn't a question. She knew it was their only option.

He nodded sadly. 'We have to save ourselves from each other. No letters. No phone calls.' He folded his arms tightly against his chest, as if resisting the urge to embrace her again, as if warding off emotional danger, his eyes pleading with her.

She greedily sucked into her memory bank her final image of the man she loved, her soulmate, and reached for the door handle. 'Starting now, we must remove every avenue for temptation. I'm doing my bit by leaving. Please, will you invent an urgent reason for an out-of-town business trip this week?'

Not giving him time to answer, she rushed out of his office without a final goodbye. Tears plucked at her eyes. She dabbed them away. For once she appreciated working in a department full of men, busy with their post-mortems of their weekend and oblivious to her emotional state. Just in case, she muttered something to her nearest workmate that she had a family emergency in Sydney. She hoped they'd attribute any lingering tears to that excuse.

She dealt with the files on her desk by putting them into her 'out' tray with stickers marking them for Jack's attention, to re-assign her workload once she'd gone. Meanwhile, she heard his secretary telling Charles that Jack had been called away unexpectedly, and he'd be in charge for the rest of the week.

She left the office within the hour, farewelled by the good-natured banter of her colleagues. 'Bye Sarah. Hope everything's alright when you get home.' They assumed this was a temporary departure. 'Don't do anything we wouldn't do. See you soon. Take care!' The wrench to her life hit home and the tears spilled down her cheeks, unchecked, as she waved them goodbye, knowing she'd never see them, or Jack, again.

She crawled home in her car, forcing her blurry eyes to focus on the road. Pack up her life and move on, that's what she must do next.

Kirua had cried last Saturday when she told him she was leaving. *Mi sori tumas, Misis*. She'd cried too. At least his job was guaranteed, as the garden needed ongoing attention and the next tenant would likely have children, with washing, ironing, and cleaning to be done.

She didn't have to worry about removing her basic household furniture, all of it government-issue, and there was little else to pack. All she had to do was book her flight, purchase several extra suitcases for her clothes, and organise a company to come on Wednesday and collect her kitchen items, hi-fi gear and other personal effects for shipment back to Sydney. She took pains to clean the house thoroughly on Thursday and leave it immaculate. The physical effort of the housework diluted some of her heart pain.

A young unattached female couldn't rely on taxi drivers in Moresby to convey her safely, without fear of molestation. She asked Charles, as her trusted colleague and mutual friend of Jack's, to drive her to the airport to catch her flight next day. Her platonic relationship with him was unusual, but she'd long since worked with her male colleagues as 'sexless' creatures. Except for Jack.

Charles sounded surprised to receive her call. 'I thought you'd left days ago.'

'It's an upsetting story. Please don't ask.'

'Okay, Sarah. I'll be there in time to pick you up.'

When he arrived, she tossed him her car keys. 'Will you do me another big favour?'

He switched his puzzled stare from the keys in his hand to her face.

'Dispose of my car. Keep it, sell it, give it away, I don't care. I can't take it with me. I've attached a tag with my parents' address, if you need to get in touch with me.'

'What! You mean over these past few days you've been preparing to leave here for good?' His voice reverberated with shock.

She nodded at him and burst into tears. He fished for his handkerchief and handed it over. She mopped her eyes and blew her nose, grateful for his years of uncomplicated friendship.

'You know, Sarah, I've known Jack for a long time. Having observed events in the office since our New Year's party—the tension between you, his sudden trip away, your absence this week—I've got a pretty fair idea of why you're leaving.'

Her chin wobbled again as she nodded her wordless agreement.

Charles hoisted her suitcases into his boot and they set off. At the airport terminal, he stood with his arm around her shoulders, hugging her to him as she continued to struggle with her tears.

He surprised her with his final, open acknowledgment of her predicament. 'Jack's eyes have followed you everywhere for weeks. Months. It's plain to me he's crazy about you. You're two of a kind.'

Too distraught to prevaricate, she beseeched him: 'Is it so obvious? Do you think anyone else has noticed?' He shook his head.

She'd implied that she and Jack had done more than exchange a few passionate kisses in a heated embrace. 'As soon as I realised myself that I'm besotted with Jack, I decided to leave.' Her jaw trembled, and she sniffed away a tear.

'You can relax, matey. The penny didn't drop

for me until today, seeing you so distressed. You two have obviously conducted yourselves properly and discreetly. Your secret is safe with me. I know from our uni days that Jack never loved Jenny with a passion. They were teenagers fooling around with sex, and it back-fired on both of them.' He sighed. 'But he's a good man, and he's tried his best to make it work, for the sake of the kids. They're happy little ones, and Jenny loves Jack, I'm sure, in her own laid-back way. When he married her, there was always the risk that he might later meet his soulmate. He has. You.'

His comment provoked a fresh welling of tears from Sarah. She found the last dry patch of the cloth clenched in her hand and wiped them away. 'Your hanky's a sodden mess. Sorry,' she muttered.

'No worries. I heard them call your flight.' Charles embraced her sadly, worry in his eyes. 'You're doing the right thing, even though it's painful. One day it might all work out. I sure hope so. You might meet someone else or Jack might leave Jenny. You deserve to be happy.'

CHAPTER TWENTY-THREE

As the plane droned its way towards Sydney, a flash of foresight brought Sarah's future life into focus. In a lifeless daze, she passively accepted offers of food and drink from the cabin crew but left them untouched as her anguished mind faced the likely prospect of years of real personal loneliness.

She stared sightlessly at the azure blue infinity beyond the small window pane beside her. A vast emptiness. No more Jack. A tear trickled down her cheek and she brushed it away. Another tear followed. In a battle to focus her thoughts and fight off the tears, she blew her nose, clenched her jaw, and sat bolt upright in her seat. What she wanted for herself, a strong and loving family unit, was unattainable with Jack because he was taken.

She was doing the decent thing. She would survive.

A westerly was blowing over Sydney, so the plane winged in from the east towards Kingsford Smith Airport. Off to her right, as the sea met the coastline, she spotted a patch of the world's most desirable real estate. Thousands of headstones at Waverley Cemetery glittered white in the afternoon sunshine, rising in their serried ranks up the cliff from the Pacific Ocean. *I'll probably end up down there at that permanent address one day. What family will I have to mourn my passing?*

She stayed with her parents for a few days while she re-oriented herself in her old hometown. She gave no explanations, and didn't mention her lost love, or even hint at his existence.

They assumed she'd finally cracked under the strain of Andrew's abandonment of her and lamented her bereft state. Much hand-wringing ensued. 'How could Andrew do this to you?' asked her mother. 'How *could* he?' It was doubly distressing, for them, that he'd crashed from his pride of place on the family's pedestal.

Disoriented by the events in her life, with no obvious opportunities to continue her current role in the workforce, she made an appointment with a careers counselling service. She spent three hours of one Saturday morning doing a battery of aptitude tests.

When she returned a week later for the follow-up interview, the counsellor stared at her as if she was an object in a freak show. 'First time I've seen this. Top 1% of adults—for verbal intelligence—*and* for numerical intelligence—*and* for abstract knowledge. Top 1% of adult females for speed and accuracy. Excellent scores for mechanical comprehension and spatial relations.'

Sarah took a few moments to absorb those surprising statements. *Maybe that's why I've never fitted in. Except with Jack.* 'No-one's ever told me that before. What do those results mean, for me?'

'They prove that in all areas of reasoning, you far exceed the average to be found amongst university graduates and senior executives in industry. You're a highly flexible and versatile thinker.'

That comment hit home. Offered her a pathway to finding happiness again. Her emotions might be in tatters, but *thinking* her way out of being stuck on Jack might work. Using her brainpower could improve her life, give herself renewed hope.

A weight lifted off her shoulders. The world suddenly made more sense to her. Not that she'd admit her yearnings to this career adviser. She'd keep it professional. 'I've always felt like a visitor from space with my colleagues.' *And with most others, except Jack.*

'You're still young. No doubt the men you've worked with have patronised you and it's hard for women at the best of times. With your innate skills, you must have been very lonely.'

Yes, lonely, that was the word, now this

stranger had articulated it. 'One man treated me as if I had a brain in my head.' She kept Jack's name out of it. Then she remembered Charles, who'd also been respectful, as a colleague and a friend. 'Two, actually.'

'Then you were lucky. But you need more. Only an especially challenging position will offer you full satisfaction in the workplace because otherwise you have untapped and unused intellectual ability.'

'Sounds like an impossible dream.' *Except it wasn't, in my old job. I engaged fully and enjoyed great workforce satisfaction. Oh boy, how I wish I could return there.*

'Agreed. Women are treated as second-class citizens in the workforce, but a few are breaking through the barriers. Men won't always have it their way.' The counsellor's voice rose in an air of defiance.

'You mean we'll move beyond the typing pool and the boss's secretary in an office setting, like I did in PNG.'

'You were fortunate to get that job, under the UN umbrella. Australia is incredibly chauvinistic. Blame it on our country's convict history, when males outnumbered females by six to one. What hope did we ever have?' She quirked an eyebrow.

'Good point. We live in macho land. You've broken free though, here I mean.'

'I chose social work as my course at uni. A woman's field. And I operate alone, as an independent consultant.'

'I can't do that. Work independently, I mean. With my economics and maths background. That's a man's world.'

'True. Becoming a secondary teacher is an option for you—a qualified one, I mean, not like your first stint as a teacher. Or, you could study for a higher degree and become a university lecturer. An actuary perhaps. But with your current qualifications and experience, I suggest you start in the finance sector. There are many interesting jobs there, with global perspectives and impact.'

'You suggest I take on the challenge of beating the men at their own game?'

'The path won't be easy, but some women have done it, in America and England. I hear several have worked their way into senior positions as managers at Barclays Bank. None on the Board yet, of course. Another woman led a project linking individual Barclay branches together via a mainframe computer. Amazing technology. Pioneering stuff.'

'My field of interest is more international in scope. But I have to make a start somewhere and the world of finance is a good suggestion.'

'I'm glad you agree. Meanwhile, why not join Mensa? You might find congenial company there, while you look for a suitable job.'

Sarah took the woman's advice to heart. Within a week, she found herself a temporary clerical position in the foreign exchange settlements office of a major bank. Not ready for socialising, especially if it involved one-upmanship over who was smarter than who, she put the Mensa idea on hold. She rented a tiny flat at Cremorne, overlooking Mosman Bay, and a short walk from a ferry wharf. She haunted bookstores at lunchtime and devoured her purchases in the evenings.

After an absence from Sydney of almost five years, her return to a culture offering plentiful consumer choice unsettled her. It gave her a headache every time she entered a supermarket and was confronted by dozens of different breakfast cereals, after living in a country where tinned tuna, a packet of rice and a bag of sugar were luxuries.

It made a mockery of her supposed thinking skills. She should be able to rationalise the discrepancy between the first and third worlds, but sadness descended on her, a mild sense of guilt for stepping back into the relatively easy lifestyle of her own cultural milieu.

She craved a daily life not requiring continuous decision-making about everyday activities. Not much chance here of 'set and forget' habits, freeing up her brain for other thoughts. She became paralysed by indecision when asked whether she'd like her espresso coffee as a long black, a short black or a white coffee served 'flat', when a week before her only choice had been Nescafé, in the one place in town serving coffee. PNG might grow that crop, but that didn't mean it served the beverage. She realised just how much she'd learned and changed, even in a few short years.

As she readjusted to a consumer-driven society, her flat at Cremorne saved her sanity. The joy of her walk along the harbourside path to the wharf each morning, to catch the ferry to Circular Quay, eased her troubled emotions. The flash of a rosella's red and blue plumage, and the song of a hundred birds chattering in the treetops, distracted her from her sense of isolation. Sydney was so lucky to have a thin strip of national park surrounding much of its spectacular harbour.

She enjoyed watching her ferry chugging in to collect its next load of commuters, its white, creaming wake fading away like a memory. The turbulence of the threshing water as the ferry reversed its engine thrust and approached its mooring reminded her of her own inner turmoil. The clang of the metal gangplank became a time-marker of her day.

Like a mother's heartbeat to an unborn baby, the ferry's throbbing engines soothed her as they propelled the craft across the magnificent harbour towards the landmark bridge and then left past the spectacular new Opera House, throttling back to glide in to the Quay.

She walked up Pitt Street towards Martin Place, and the tall buildings squashed by topography into a small central business district towered over her. In one of those was her temporary office.

Her job was just a fill-in, while she regained her equilibrium, a state of mind she found hard to achieve. Despite the many years she'd spent in Sydney with Andrew, it was as if those times had never been. Her current experience of her home town opened a new world to her.

Sarah's duties at the bank involved long, busy days, allowing little time to mope. She was glad to get home in the evening, make herself a light meal, catch up on the day's events by watching the late ABC news telecast, and fall into bed with her latest book.

Fridays ended with 'raging' night for younger staff employed in the banking, accounting and legal offices around town, but Sarah's depressed mood left her unwilling to join her workmates as they tripped off to the nearest bar.

She trotted out the convenient excuse of meeting a friend at the movies but, if she attended a film session, she usually emerged from the theatre more dejected than ever. It was hard to find a program not focusing on the perennial themes of sex and love, both missing from her life. A re-run of 'South Pacific' enticed Sarah to spend another solitary Friday night in front of a screen. She cried her eyes out at the happy ending, comparing her own experiences in a different tropical outpost. How could she survive without Jack?

On Sundays she visited her parents for lunch, for a family visit and to collect her mail, as she used their home as her forwarding address.

'You've got so thin. Are you eating?' This was the predictable anxious enquiry from her mother.

'Yes, Mum, I eat quite well. I do a lot of walking these days. It was too hot to walk much in the tropics.' Excuses, excuses. No need to admit that she tossed and turned many nights.

'Your letters are on my desk,' said her father, 'don't forget them when you leave.'

'No Dad, I won't forget.'

It pleased her to see how comfortable they were together, like they'd each slipped into a pair of old shoes. They'd put their problems of twenty years ago behind them, but kept the secrets of their successful reconciliation to themselves.

All parents, she supposed, felt invested in the lives of their adult children, but hers were not nosy about her affairs. They didn't ask outright questions. Nor did they leave room for her to open up in conversations, and she skimmed over the details of how she spent her time. She and Andrew had never confided the reason for their childlessness or their hopes to adopt a baby and she wasn't ready to cope with too many more of her mother's 'it's just not fair' remarks. Chatter about the various doings of her younger sisters, their husbands and boyfriends and two precious grandchildren filled every visit home. She wondered what version of her life would reach her siblings.

As soon as the lunch timetable and good manners permitted, she liked to gather up her pile of letters, kiss her goodbyes and head off for Cremorne.

This week, when she reached home and slid the elastic band off her father's neat bundle of correspondence, her heart kicked up when she saw a PNG stamp. Her bubble of elation popped when she recognised the handwriting on the envelope. It was Charles who had written. She wanted only to hear from Jack, who did not write. He'd said he wouldn't. She knew he wouldn't. They'd agreed on a clean break. She trusted him to stick to his word.

Still, she hungered for any scrap of news about him. She tore the covering off this first letter from Charles, ignoring his news about his disposal of her old car and his general chat, soaking up his closing remarks: 'Jack is coping with your absence, but he looks very tired around the eyes. But for the kids, I think the outcome would have been altogether different.'

Charles, who knew why she'd left PNG, had used carefully chosen words to reassure her, while pointing out the hopelessness of her cause. Sarah read that letter over and over. It was her only tangible, independent evidence she *had* been important to Jack, and that he might be missing her. Not that she wished him to suffer, but she craved proof beyond that last day in his office that he'd genuinely cared, that her sacrifice had not been for nothing. That he had loved her.

The letter convinced her she needed to 'do something'. Deal with the emotional baggage she dragged behind her each day. Face a future on her own.

Next morning she rang a solicitor and instructed him to begin the legal proceedings for divorce.

Divorce. What a horrible word. She'd never enjoyed the non-stop titillation in the daily press reporting the scandalous affairs of divorcing couples and never expected to become a player in this form of theatre. It was a relief to learn that new 'no fault' divorce laws were wending their way through endless debates in Federal Parliament. She told the solicitor to go slow and wait for the legislation to be passed, making her eligible to terminate her marriage on the grounds of a twelve-month separation.

Her divorce would prove to the outside world that she'd failed as a human being, but part of her held on tenaciously to one positive thought. Now that she knew what the word soulmate meant, she wouldn't fall for less in the future. Andrew had been her friend as a husband but, in Jack, she'd found her ideal partner. Her world made sense with him in it—work, family, friends, chemistry, communication styles, value systems. He'd made her feel good. Not so alone. He was kind and loyal. He understood her. Life had sparkled.

But he was so far away. With Jenny. Who had become her friend. Life was so unfair. This was the lesson she struggled to learn and accept.

Would he ever write to her? They'd agreed to make no further contact, but nevertheless she rushed home from work to delve anxiously into her mailbox. Her parents were now redirecting her mail. His handwriting never graced an envelope. The lingering hope slowly faded.

She wrote to him many times, expressing herself as if he were there to comfort her, as in the past, but she crumpled every letter and tossed it into the bin, stamping resolutely on the urge. 'No letters,' she commanded herself each time. 'I made my decision. He's not for me. His commitment was elsewhere when I met him, and still is. He's probably forgotten me already.'

CHAPTER TWENTY-FOUR

Five long months had passed since her return to Sydney, forlorn months filled with the endless, aching need for Jack. At any unexpected time of the day or night, someone's word or expression or action triggered an image of him. She couldn't escape his hold on her.

Sunny autumn days and crisp nights were fading into the start of winter. Not cold by the standards of someone from Vienna, or Chicago, but cool enough for a recent resident of the topics. She sat inside on her daily ferry rides, rather than outside on the deck in the fresh air, wishing she didn't have to put up with the cigarette smoke puffed out by fellow passengers.

The phone rang. 'Hi, Sarah. How's things?' It was her old friend Maria Mitchell, who sometimes called on a Saturday afternoon.

'Great to hear from you. Doing my weekly household chores, as usual.' She gave a wry laugh.

'The worst part is the several hours spent at the ironing board, but at least I don't need the fan on me full blast, like in Moresby. What about you? No more babies on the way, are there?'

'No way. Isabella was the last. And that gets me straight to the point of my call. We've been feeling very guilty that she's never been christened, while her older brothers and sister have.'

Puzzled, Sarah recalled that screaming child in Dr Chadwick's surgery and did a quick mental calculation. 'But her third birthday's coming up. Isn't she too old now?'

'Nope. Never too late, says the church.' Maria laughed. 'Don't forget, we're in a different mob to you. Hence our brood. One almost every year, until I put my foot down.'

'Half your luck.'

'Sorry, this must be a touchy subject for you.'

Was Maria thinking of her marital status or her childless status? 'Yep, we weren't fortunate enough to have kids.' There, she'd voiced aloud her private sadness.

Maria did not pick up the cue but rushed on with her own concerns. 'The ceremony will be here, because we're still not sure when we'll ever get home to the parish where the others were baptised.'

Sarah heaved a sigh of relief. Her childless state was not something she wished to discuss on an international phone call. Even with a friend. Why had she even gone there? 'Fair enough. I'll be glad to see you back in Sydney, but you can't defer such an important event forever.'

'True, and here's the thing. We'd both be so happy, indeed honoured, if you'd agree to be the godmother for Isabella.'

Sarah's jaw dropped. 'Even after all this time away from her? With me not being religious?'

'You're a fine, upstanding person and so good with children. We'll be in regular contact once we eventually reject this expatriate existence. Will you accept, and come back for the christening?'

'Umm, when will it be?' Sarah stalled for time. Going back would re-open the Jack wound in her heart. But, as he and Jenny barely knew the Mitchells, the risk of socialising with them should be low.

'Next month. Sunday the fifteenth. Please stay with us. It would give us a chance to say goodbye, as you left in such a hurry. And we'll return to Sydney in a few years, fingers crossed, so you'll be able to see a lot more of Isabella then.'

'What about Andrew? He's Kevin's friend. Is he invited too? Won't this be awkward for everyone?'

'Nope. The way he dumped you, we've dropped that friendship.'

'In that case, peace and harmony should reign on the day. As long as Isabella behaves herself, that is. No more screaming sessions, like that episode in the waiting room.'

'That was just so embarrassing. Thank God you were there. She's been remarkably placid in the last month or so. Hopefully getting past the terrible twos.'

'If you say so. You're the expert on babies. You've had years of practical experience.' Sarah wished the same applied to her.

With a catch in her voice, and to divert attention from this, she asked, 'Who else will be there?' The question was at the front of her mind since Maria called. 'Quite a few of the old crowd must have moved on by now.'

She needed to check, definitively but surreptitiously, whether the Mitchells had become friendly with the Martins. Engineers hadn't fraternised with the agriculturalists in her day, but it was a small town and social patterns changed. It would be supremely awkward to face Jack again. Shattering. The prospect was unbearable.

'You'll know Kevin's workmates, and a few of my girlfriends from the neighbourhood. With the demands of our tribe of mini-Mitchells, we don't get to meet many new people in this place. All the kids, of course. It'll be a Sunday lunchtime event.'

'The regulars. Perfect.'

Maria's voice took on a thoughtful tone. 'Hey, what about those old friends of yours? The ones who live on the other side of town from us. The husband was to die for. Was his name Jack? And his wife was Jean—no, I mean Jenny. I could ask them as company for you, if you like.'

'Oh, please don't, Maria, you've enough people to worry about without adding my friends to the guest list. I'll catch up with them separately.' That was a gigantic white lie. She had no intention of going anywhere near Jack and Jenny.

'Okay, whatever you say. But do say "yes" to being Isabella's godmother.'

'Maria, I'm honoured. Thank you. She's a sweetie. Can I confirm it tomorrow? I'll have to check with work, as I'll need to take a few days off.'

Sarah agonised over the prospect of returning. Having so recently given up the chance for her own baby, adopted or not, could she hold this toddler in her arms in the church without bursting into tears? Yes. Because it was Isabella, with whom she had a special bond, she'd manage somehow.

On a flying visit, it was unlikely she'd bump into Jack, living as he did in a distant suburb. If she departed Sydney on Friday and returned on Monday, on Saturday she'd help with preparations, and on Sunday with the all-important ceremony and christening party. She'd have no spare time even to contemplate the temptation of seeing him.

It would be re-assuring to return for a weekend and might close a painful chapter in her life. They say you have to go back to a place you miss to set it in perspective.

She cleared the leave with her boss, rang Maria, and booked her flights in time for the baptism ceremony the following month.

As the plane flew in over the coral reefs and lined up for the runway, she absorbed the sight of tiers of mountains rising into the distance, topped by fluffy white balls of vapour which built by day's end, in the wet season, to cumulous clouds bursting to dump their heavy load of precious water. *God, this is such a beautiful place. And my beautiful Jack is down there somewhere, but he can't be mine.*

Maria and Kevin, with their family of four excited children including youngest member Isabella, were waiting to greet her at Jackson's Airport. Kevin had taken Friday afternoon off work to be part of the reception committee.

'How wonderful to see you, Sarah. We've all missed you. But you've lost so much weight. Are you eating?' Maria kissed her on both cheeks before issuing a command to her troops. 'Say hello to Aunty Sarah, kids. She's not really your aunty, but she's close enough that it doesn't matter.'

Kevin gave her a friendly peck on the cheek. 'I'll get your bag. I suppose you travel light. Not like us. We need a camel train to cart our luggage.'

Maria continued in Mother Duck mode. 'I hope

you remembered to take your chloroquine tablet a week ago. The malaria problem doesn't get any better here.'

'Relax, Maria, I did remember. Old habits die hard.'

'Don't forget to keep taking them for a few weeks after you return to Sydney.'

'Yes, Mum.' Sarah joshed her friend, basking happily in the genuine warmth and care of this family.

She dawdled through the terminal, looking around her with interest. 'You know, something did strike me when my plane landed today. Clear signs of a transformed economy. I never noticed it when I lived here.'

Kevin pricked up his ears. 'And what's that?'

'The first time I landed at Jackson's the ground staff wore lap-laps and bare feet. Today they were all attired in white shirts, shorts, long socks and lace-up shoes.'

'And they're driving the latest model Datsuns,' laughed Kevin. 'Be warned. Take care on the roads – these new drivers are still learning about road safety and traffic rules. I nearly had a prang the other day, on a blind corner. A large truck came tearing out on my left and I stopped so hard I could smell burning rubber and saw smoke out the rear vision mirror.'

'It's all happened so quickly. In a few short

years. A colonial town has been transformed into a Melanesian city.' A small thrill of achievement warmed her heart. Thanks to Jack's supervision, she'd made her own minor contribution to helping set the economic future for this magnificent country, agriculture-wise.

'But maybe not fast enough to be ready for independence? Our techies certainly aren't skilled-up yet.' Kevin frowned.

She sighed. 'I miss the meaning and significance of the work I did in this country.' *And I miss Jack.*

Maria interjected. 'Hey, you two, enough of that serious work talk. Sarah is here for a celebration.'

They piled into the car and Maria's cheerful chatter continued all the way to the Mitchell household.

'Take a seat. And can you watch this jack-in-the-box for me? She gets into too much mischief when my back's turned.' Maria thrust her daughter into Sarah's hungry arms. 'I'll find everyone a cool drink. It's hot work meeting people at the airport.'

Isabella was not at all perturbed at being plonked in a strange lap. Playfully, she pulled at Sarah's earrings and, failing to pull them off into her grasping hand, she scrambled down and ran over to her pile of toys. Selecting her favourite doll, she held it up by the arm for Sarah's inspection.

'What a pretty baby, sweetheart. Are you her mummy? She looks just like you.'

Isabella nodded her head, examined the doll's features for proof, and responded with a coy smile of satisfaction.

Maria handed Sarah a drink. 'Now you see why we picked you. You haven't seen this kid for months, but she remembers you.'

'Thanks Maria, it's my pleasure to be her godmother, she's a little cutie.'

'You're so maternal in your instincts, I think it's cruel you don't have any of your own.'

So Maria hadn't forgotten her 'we weren't fortunate enough' remark on the phone. It warmed her heart to have a supportive friend who also spoke her mind.

'It won't happen now. I lead a nun's life these days, as far as eligible males are concerned.'

'Rubbish,' said Maria, 'things will change. Someone in Sydney will snap you up. They'd better. Can't let *you* go to waste.'

'Hear, hear!' Kevin raised his can of beer in salute.

What with the banter and the attempts to cheer her up, it was some time before Sarah escaped to her room to unpack her few belongings. Damn, she always forgot something. Today, her hairbrush.

'Maria, I need to duck into town. I left my hairbrush behind and, with my hair, what a disaster that is. Can I borrow your car for an hour? I remember that Steamies used to be the only store which sold what I need—a hard plastic brush with rounded tips on the end of each stiff nylon bristle.'

'By all means. Here's hoping they have one in stock. Mine would be a waste of effort dealing with your mop. I've never seen hair as thick as yours. On Caucasian heads I mean. It's fabulous. You'll never go bald.'

———

Sarah parked the car and walked down the hill towards the store. The first person she saw was Jack, talking in the street to Charles. For a split second her heart missed a beat and she struggled against fainting.

He noticed her coming, his eyes widened for an instant, and he abruptly stopped speaking. Deliberately, unbelievably, he turned and strode away without speaking to her, not even stopping briefly to look back before getting into his vehicle and driving off. She thought she saw the flash of his eyes reflected in his rear-vision mirror, the only hint of a backward glance in her direction.

She stood anchored to the spot, staring in disbelief at the disappearing car. How it hurt, this pain of rejection.

Charles turned around and spotted her, astonishment written all over his face. 'Sarah! Mystery explained. Jack must have seen you coming towards us. I couldn't work out why he took off like that.'

'I can't either,' she whispered.

'Strange. It wouldn't have killed him to at least say hello. Not like him to be so rude.'

'It was a shock for me too, seeing him.'

'How long will you be here? Where are you staying?'

'Just a few days, Charles. I'm here for the christening of a friend's child. I'm the godmother.'

'But why didn't you tell us you were coming? Carolyn would love to catch up. So would I.'

'I think the answer is crystal clear, don't you?'

'What? Oh, yes, I suppose it is.'

'It would be awkward to explain seeing you, but not the Martins, especially when I was so close to Jack and Jenny.' Sarah's lip trembled. Her eyes grew watery.

'I understand. Of course. I'm sorry. It must be hard for you. Perhaps I shouldn't say so, but I suspect it's been pretty tough on Jack too.'

'It doesn't seem that way to me, Charles. Not a word have I heard, although we agreed on that, but he just made a point of turning his back on me. His decision has the hallmark of finality, don't you agree?'

'The decision may be. I'm not so sure about the feelings. Not that we discuss this. You know what men are like. But I can tell that he hasn't been the same bloke since you left.'

'How is he, Charles? I miss him dreadfully. I hope he's alright.'

'At work, he continues to function normally. He hides things well, behind his aura of professionalism, but I'm sure he's felt your absence deeply. All your old workmates are sorry you've gone, as you provided a much-needed feminine touch in our male enclave, so I can imagine how he feels. As I said in my letter, he looks very strained around the eyes.'

'Ah, the strain of pretence. Tell me about it! It's my specialty, in public at least, most of the time.'

'I have to say, your discreet behaviour, and his, must have been faultless. Your sudden departure mystified everyone, Jenny included. Jack told our group you had a family emergency and probably wouldn't be back. He passed on your apologies.'

She nodded.

He said, 'Several people who saw us at the airport, with you crying and my arm around your shoulders, assumed that we'd been 'having it off,' to use their crude vernacular. But Carolyn and I have a strong marriage, as you well know, and those whispers soon died down, leaving only the notion that you must finally have cracked.'

She gasped.

He shrugged. 'Some speculated that your family emergency might have been a polite euphemism for you breaking down over losing Andrew. Especially as you never made contact with anyone, not even us.' He looked disappointed.

Her blood boiled. 'And isn't that just fine and dandy! I'm the one doing the right thing here, but added to my other troubles, I get saddled with the reputation of having a nervous breakdown.' She directed her bitter remark at the world in general, not at him in particular.

Her defiant streak rose to the surface. 'Make sure you tell my former colleagues that I dropped briefly into town, squeezing in a weekend around my busy new job, and I'm looking fit and well.'

'I will. Even if you're skinny as.' His face creased with worry. 'You're certainly having a hard time of it.'

'Before I get even more upset, Charles, I'd better go. Apart from my friends and their children, I didn't intend to meet with anyone from my old life on this trip, especially Jack. But you and Carolyn must look me up if you are ever in Sydney. You've got my parents' address.'

'Yes, we'll do that. Goodbye for now. Take care. And good luck.'

White faced, she stumbled into the store, found her replacement hair brush and returned to the Mitchell's.

'My God, are you alright? You look as if

you've seen a ghost.' Maria gasped as Sarah came through the door.

'It's nothing, it must be the heat. I'm not used to it any more. I might go to my room for a while and flop.' This was a polite fib. She needed time alone to process and digest Jack's reaction to her.

'Good idea. I'll bring you some tea. You always liked a hot cuppa, even on a sweltering day.'

Sarah retreated to her room on legs like lead weights, flopped onto her bed and stared at the ceiling. She hadn't expected to bump into Jack on this trip. *Stop right there. Be honest with yourself. I did long to see him, if only in the distance.* A big reunion was out of the question, but at least he could have maintained the appearance of normality.

Maria bustled in with the tea. 'This'll revive you. Stay here and rest for a while. Dinner will be ready in half an hour.' She set the cup beside Sarah's bed. 'We need you to be fighting fit on Sunday.'

'I'm fine Maria, really I am. I'll be out soon.' She dredged up a smile. 'What do they say—a cup of tea, a Bex and a good lie down?' She fished a powder out of her purse to keep up the pretence of mild heat stroke.

Maria left the room and she revisited that dramatic moment in the street. Her selfless departure, to protect Jack's interests as much as hers, and her suffering since, was wasted effort. Despite what Charles said, she doubted she'd ever been significant for him. No letters from him confirmed it. He'd never wavered from his clean break.

She'd misinterpreted Charles' letter and his attempt to offer reassurance. She was no longer a source of daily temptation for a man out of love with his wife. Today had proved how guilty Jack felt that he'd almost strayed. Having her out of his sight and out of his mind suited him.

If he was back on an even keel and well able to do without her, then she'd fight to achieve *her* equilibrium. Her emotions might be raw, but she'd get through tomorrow, Saturday. And on Sunday she'd hold Isabella in her arms at the christening service and chat brightly to guests at the party afterwards.

She succeeded, although she functioned on automatic with her heart and mind elsewhere. If the priest only knew what a heathen was standing before him, holding Isabella. When she was introduced as the godmother he said 'Do I know you?' He would have been even more horrified to know that she wasn't 'one of them'.

Isabella was perfectly behaved and beamed at everyone the whole time, although she did get a bit heavy and mighty clammy to hold.

In the late afternoon Maria said with concern, 'Sarah, I'm concerned that you haven't had time for your friends Jack and Jenny. Why don't you call them? See if they're home. You could go round and visit them after dinner.'

'Thanks for your suggestion, but I'll give it a miss. Today has been a long day and I'm pooped by this weather. Don't forget I'm here straight from Sydney, where it's winter. Would you believe the idea of an early night sounds good to me? I'll catch up with them another time. I came to spend this weekend with you.'

Retreating to her bedroom, she suffered a second sleepless night. Her sense of self-worth was over-turned. Up to that point, no matter what happened, no matter how discouraged, she'd kept going in the belief that someone, Jack, understood her and cared for her. She'd been mistaken. The most profound personal communication experience of her life had meant little to him. He'd rejected her. She internalised his rejection as confirming there was something wrong with her, that she meant nothing.

She concluded she was unlovable. Or a poor judge of character—Jack's in particular. Both, most likely.

Next morning Maria looked at the white face and dark circles under Sarah's eyes. 'Hmm, there's more to this than you're admitting. Want to talk about it. What ghosts have you confronted during these past few days?'

Prevaricating, Sarah replied, 'Just the ghosts of returning to a place where I was contented and happy. It was more painful than I expected. Nothing to do with you two, and your lovely kids, of course. You've been kindness itself. I'll be better once I get back to the new life I'm trying to create for myself.'

'Okay, if you say so, but I'm worried about you and I'm taking you to the airport without the Mitchell tribe in tow. Less stress. I can give you better attention. Our neighbour can mind them. We often help each other out that way.'

After Sarah checked in, Maria hugged her and said, 'Look after yourself. Just remember, you're special. Andrew was a fool. Someone else will care one day.'

Sarah shrugged listlessly. 'Maybe. Maybe not.'

She boarded her return flight to Sydney, a second journey of quiet suffering. She should never have come. It was a big mistake.

She set her intellect to work. By the time the plane landed, she valued the trip as an unexpected turning point. It had taught her a lesson. She must banish her thoughts of Jack, learn to function again, properly, and stop drifting in the limbo of the last six months.

She closed the door on her feelings, locked it, and threw the key into the deepest recesses of her mind.

CHAPTER TWENTY-FIVE

Jack stared glumly out his grimy office window, reliving last Friday afternoon.

He'd watched her reflection in the plate-glass window of the shopfront as he strode away from Charles. He'd studied her in his side mirrors as he drove off. Her puzzled, hurt expression was like a dagger in his heart.

I don't know why I did that.

It was an enormous shock to see her. When she suddenly floated into his line of vision, like a mirage, his breath stuck in his throat.

He'd panicked. His sense of duty to his family, his inner resolution, might falter if he got close to her again. His natural defence mechanism, his self-preservation instinct, had kicked in.

These days he didn't like himself much.

He recalled a comment made by Jenny after Andrew left: 'It's all very well for you to deal with her at work, but she makes me feel inadequate just by being Sarah.'

Since he was finding it increasingly difficult to hide his growing desire, he'd taken Jenny's early warning signal seriously and cut down on their pattern of weekend social engagements.

Jenny hadn't twigged to his reasons, but six months ago, just after that fateful New Year party, she'd made another telling remark: 'I was sorry that Sarah had to leave town, because I like her, but I'm rather glad she's gone. She's too much competition for me and the other stay-at-home wives.'

If only Jenny knew the truth. Sarah wasn't trying to catch her man. She'd caught him by mistake and let him go. *She and I truly loved each other, but still she walked away with honour, betraying no-one.*

Charles barged into his office. He swivelled his chair to face his friend. 'G'day mate.' What a joke. He felt anything but good.

Charles braced his arms and leaned over the back of the visitor's chair. 'It's none of my business, I know, but what the heck was going on in your head last Friday? With Sarah, I mean. She was pretty upset.'

He sighed heavily. 'A rude shock, that's what. I wish I could undo it but I don't have any way of contacting her.'

'Well *I* do, mate. She gave me her parents' address when she left. You know, I told you, that I had to dispose of her car for her.'

Jack's heart rate soared. 'Have you got it on you?'

'Yep, I came prepared for this conversation.' He handed over a slip of paper containing the details.

'Thanks.' Jack shoved the note into his desk's top drawer.

Charles nodded, turned on his heel and returned to the main office.

Jack spent lunchtime after lunchtime composing a letter of apology and then ripping it to shreds. What exactly could he say, other than *I'm sorry I did that to you* and *it's killing me that you're not here*? He couldn't promise her anything.

It took him two weeks to be satisfied with his final draft, copy it out and get it into the mail. The only 'farewell my love' letter he'd ever written. He'd poured his heart and soul into it.

Guiltily, he craved her reply.

CHAPTER TWENTY-SIX

The several propositions made by new work colleagues in Sydney shakily confirmed Jack's New Year's affirmation that she was desirable—but that was not the same as lovable.

Jack had always felt like someone with whom she could be herself. They'd interacted honestly. She hadn't felt like an invisible person around him. He'd aroused her physically, like no-one else. She'd believed he knew her, on the inside. That he 'got' her. That she could be lovable just for being herself. Until he'd shown otherwise and turned his back on her. Not lovable after all.

How could she ever explain to anyone else that sense of connection she'd had to Jack? They would disapprove. 'You mean he was married?' they'd tut-tut. 'What did you expect? Just another man looking for a bit on the side.'

To avoid any more disasters like Jack, she must endeavour to keep her distance from people, and not let anyone know who she really was. Revealing oneself was too risky, and led to too much pain. She suppressed his importance to her, even though her experience with him was the key to understanding herself and for others to understand her. She shut down many of her feelings and began building invisible walls to protect her personal secret, Jack, outwardly involved in the world but freezing people out if they took any liberties with her personal space.

It was easier to talk about subjects outside herself. She stepped forward using her intellect, determined to make a completely new life with different people, as far away as possible from anything reminding her of what she was missing.

Recalling the career adviser's words, she made a snap decision to head for expanded career opportunities in London. She'd always wanted to visit this legendary city. It would challenge her. She was young enough to qualify for the age restrictions on working holiday visas. She could lose herself in London.

She preferred to ignore her inner voice telling her she was running away from her real problem, just like she'd run away from Port Moresby. Her problem of being scared to let the world see her real self.

Her parents wrung their hands. 'Do you have to go? Why the rush? You don't know anyone in London. We'll be worried about you.'

'I'll be fine. I'll write to you the minute I get myself a permanent address.'

Two weeks later she was on the plane, down the back in economy class, saving her money for London in case it proved difficult to find a job. Economy class seats on the long flight from Australia, renowned worldwide as an endurance test, still provided an armchair ride by comparison with her memorable flying experiences in light aircraft, a helicopter and Fokker Friendships in PNG. Jack had instigated those adventurous flights. She brushed a tear from her eye.

But wait. This was a new adventure. Her 707 stopped at Darwin for refuelling, then again Manila, before reaching Hong Kong, where the aircraft made a sharp right turn on approach and quickly landed at Kai Tak Airport. She could almost reach out and touch the washing suspended from the balconies as they screeched past the residential apartment buildings sitting right beside the runway.

After they took off and flew over North Vietnam, she watched bursts of light on the ground, anti-aircraft fire from Viet Cong troops. 'We're not the targets and we fly too high for them to do us any damage,' came the reassuring captain's voice from the cockpit of the 707.

At Delhi they sweltered on board while the plane refuelled again and headed for Tehran. Her eyes popped at the high, snow-capped mountain range north of that city.

After another brief stop in Vienna, she finally

reached London over thirty hours after leaving Sydney.

She whispered to herself, 'Jack, is there no end to the unexpected adventures I'm having because of you?'

At Heathrow, exhausted and disoriented from her minimal sleep, she encountered the usual battle with immigration officers processing the 'aliens' lined up in their never-ending queues, officials ever suspicious of the motives of incoming passengers. 'No, I'm on a working holiday. Yes, I have a return ticket.'

Staggering under the weight of her awkward suitcase, she followed the signs and caught the Piccadilly Line to Kings Cross, north of the City of London. Close to the station, places offering short-term accommodation were plentiful.

Over the next few days she contacted employment agencies, and with her previous experience as a selling point, she soon found temporary work in the settlements area of a major bank.

It thrilled her to walk down Threadneedle St, past the Bank of England, where her grandmother had said that a forebear had worked. She felt she was walking in his footsteps.

Her new office was close to Moorgate tube station, on the Northern Line, so she found a cheap basement flat within walking distance of Angel tube station and more convenient for her new place of work.

The flat comprised a living area sectioned off from the bedroom area, a small kitchenette, and a bathroom. Bath, basin, toilet. No shower. It proved difficult to adjust to the English tradition of bathing, rather than showering. She took to rinsing off with the handheld showering nozzle attached to the bath tap, trying to minimise the splashing of water onto the floor. Neither the bathroom nor the kitchen had windows, but the living space looked out onto a tiny courtyard, from which a staircase led up to street level.

Her isolated, self-imposed exile in London at first entailed a struggle to survive. Being the keen gardener that she was, she visited the local market and purchased a few potted flowering plants for her courtyard. This late into autumn the choice was not wide, but her instant garden at her front door helped to soothe the soul each time she left for work, and returned home in the evenings.

Tending these few pots took up very little time, leaving her with many hours of solitude. *Maybe it wasn't a wise move to isolate myself so dramatically.* The mood took firm hold with the northern hemisphere's season of long, wintry nights and short, dingy days. The lack of bright Australian sunshine dampened her spirits.

For the first few months, she found it difficult

to cope, both mentally and physically, with nothing and no-one to live for. Surrounded by people, she suffered from acute loneliness. She picked up the razor beside her London bathtub and held it to her wrists but did not initiate the fatal slash marks. Although she felt she meant nothing to anybody, the urge to stay alive triumphed. When stepping on and off the Underground train carriages, she was careful to 'Mind the Gap'. She never again sank so low that she could contemplate throwing herself off the platform onto the live electric rail into the path of an oncoming train. The occasional sad notice at the entrance to her tube station: 'TODAY - Delays on Northern Line, due to a person under a train' reminded her that others were far worse off than her.

Regular letters from her mother proved that someone cared. One of the early ones contained an apology. 'Dad sends his love, but also a *mea culpa*. A couple of letters and cards which arrived after you left got caught up in the rubbish on his desk and were thrown out by mistake. He says sorry and hopes nothing important.'

She shrugged it off. Why worry? If necessary, those correspondents would contact her again.

Having to turn up at a regular job each day saved her from abandoning all hope for her future. The City of London held its own unique charm. Gradually she found some kind of reason to live again, just by existing in a large, culturally vibrant city. She revived herself spiritually by attending orchestral concert performances at the Festival Hall and the Royal Albert Hall.

Sarah was a temporary employee and did not expect inclusion in the annual performance reviews for the permanent staff, but as they got underway her boss called her in for an interview. Holding her CV in his hand, he asked why she was working in settlements when her other skills were very saleable.

She didn't wish to elaborate on her reasons. 'Um, er, I came to London to see the world. I'm here on a working holiday visa.' *Not good enough. Speak up for yourself, girl.* 'As I'd worked for a short period in settlements in Sydney, that area seemed a good place to start when I arrived here, since all the advertisements for jobs in the City contained the words 'experience required'. I needed the money when I arrived, so I applied. Since then I've learned a lot about the markets.'

'That strategy paid off, then. You got your foot in the door. And you've made a good impression on the powers that be. You shouldn't be working in the back-office, Sarah. It's time you moved into an area which will reward you for your qualifications. We need people with your academic background.'

A small flicker of hope rose in her chest. Women were not put down here. That counsellor back in Sydney was right.

'I'm going to recommend that we hire you on

a permanent contract, and that you move into the risk assessment area,' her boss continued. 'It's all beyond me, but they all sound as if they understand what they are doing. Take a holiday to France while the authorities process your new visa and then re-enter as a contract employee with a different immigration status.'

The song 'April in Paris' by Doris Day sprang into her mind and became an instant earworm. What a perfect suggestion from her boss. She might not have gone to Europe on her own without an incentive like this. Without Jack at her side, she might never have gone to a city like Paris, with such a reputation for romance.

Saving her pennies to spend there, she booked a second-class ticket on the Night Ferry from Victoria Station. The prospect of an uncomfortable three-stage journey, sitting up all the way, did not bother her. *Australians are world famous as intrepid travellers. That's going to be me too. Intrepid.*

As she disembarked the train in Dover, she watched the sleeping cars being shunted onto the ferry. *One day I'll do this trip as a first-class passenger, in luxury, like that.* She stood on the outside deck of the ferry, watching the white chalk cliffs fade into the night as they sailed out into the English Channel for the three-hour sea crossing. *I'm coming alive. Life is beautiful.*

France would be different. Nothing could dampen her excitement at this unexpected challenge of surviving as a solo tourist in a foreign country where English was not the national language. She hadn't felt like a tourist in London where, everywhere she turned, there was a street name familiar to her from her childhood games of Monopoly, and those addresses on the Monopoly board slowly became part of her lived experience.

As her train from Dunkirk pulled into the Gare du Nord, a few butterflies fluttered in her stomach. Would she survive using her schoolgirl French? The French spoke so quickly. Strains of their stirring but bloodthirsty 'La Marseillaise' anthem echoed in her head. *Marchons, marchons*! She didn't need to march, literally, but she needed to press on with courage.

Paris was everything she'd imagined, starting with the Art Nouveau entrances to the Métro. After she'd worked out that the *Poussez ici* sign on the barrier door meant exactly what it said, to push on the hand sign displayed and nowhere else, she entered the platform to board her first train in Paris. Her nerves fizzed with excitement.

Her initial port of call was the Visa Application Centre at the British Embassy. Over the next ten days she rushed to explore the sights. Notre Dame. The Eiffel Tower. The Champs-Élysées and Arc de Triomphe. Moulin Rouge. Montmartre. The cruise along the Seine on the bateau-mouche with *'Sous les ponts de Paris'* by Eartha Kitt wafting out as background music. The Louvre and the Mona Lisa. The Tuileries Gardens and the Musée de l'Orangerie. The train to Versailles.

She absorbed the jaunty strains of the accordion on every street corner in these touristy areas. So distinctively French. *'La vie en rose'* by Edith Piaf was on high rotation in every café. Mournful. A wave of longing for Jack sometimes washed over her, pushed back by Piaf's equally famous song *'Non, je ne regrette rien'*. If only Jack could be with her now, humming along to these songs. By the time she boarded the train to return to London, she was more in the mood for the slow version of 'I Love Paris' by the sultry contralto Ella Fitzgerald than the swinging, exuberant version by Frank Sinatra.

It wasn't difficult for an Australian with a modicum of ability to do well in the City of London. That career counsellor had informed her she had much more than a modicum of ability, and she worked conscientiously through many long days at the office. Her sound training allowed her to think through a problem and set out the issues logically.

In her brief sorties at lunchtime, seeking sandwich outlets, she explored the historic and cultural treasures surrounding her at every turn. The back alleys of the City still contained remnants of the old coffee houses where the banking and insurance business of the City flourished from the end of the eighteenth century.

On weekends she explored the West End. She especially loved to swish amongst the autumn leaves in St James Park and to walk through Regent's Park on a summer's day, when all the families emerged from their 'shoeboxes' to enjoy the space, the sunshine and their ice creams. These were simple freedoms and pleasures which she'd always taken for granted as an Australian.

Her favourite sight in all of London was the dome of St Paul's Cathedral, triumphant over the city. It was a miraculous survivor of the fire storm deliberately created by enemy bombing during the Second World War blitz, a fire storm intended to destroy that priceless cultural icon. At night many vantage points in London offered a view of the floodlit dome and Sarah often sat on top of Primrose Hill, or leaned on a balustrade along the Thames, gazing towards St Paul's and gaining inspiration from the victorious history of this massive building.

Nearly a year had passed in her new place of residence. It was a Saturday morning. Sarah sat in her local café at Angel, her cappuccino getting cold as she studied the mail she'd brought with her to read as she drank her coffee. Half an hour earlier it had fluttered to her floor through the mail slot in her front door. London's mail service was fabulous, she thought. The postman even delivers on a Saturday.

One envelope contained an Australian stamp and the return address of her solicitor in Sydney. Eighteen months had passed since she'd consulted him, so she knew what the letter inside would contain. She was right. He was writing to confirm that the new Family Law Act had passed Parliament and received Royal Assent. He would file her application early in the New Year, when uncontested divorce after a twelve-month separation officially became law. Her imminent status as a divorced woman aroused fresh feelings of personal failure.

That night, alone in her flat in London, Sarah watched a programme on television, an American programme about divorce, filmed in front of a live audience. The panel included a woman psychologist who advocated staying together and another woman, a Doctor of Philosophy, who was into all the trendy aims of self-realisation, moving on, etc, etc. The panel also comprised a couple who had married and divorced each other three times, due to the husband's alcohol abuse and violence. They were currently married to each other for the fourth time. It was an interesting mix.

Most of the contributions from the audience supported the views of the first woman, the psychologist. Many people got up and spoke about the traumas in their marriages but were happy that they did not feel personally destroyed, with the inescapable sense of personal failure that haunts many divorced people, even those who remarry. They praised the much re-married couple for the wife's tough love for her husband, displayed by her insistence that he look inside and heal himself, and for his strenuous efforts to overcome his problems to win back the prize of her presence in his daily life. The emotional bond they shared was quite obvious. They had clearly won a great personal victory.

Sarah was pleased to see that community opinion seemed to support the idea of marital commitment. She and Jack were not so strange and old-fashioned after all.

With the perspective of distance, Sarah contemplated the marriages of her closest group of friends back at home. Jack, obviously committed to his wife and family. Charles and Carolyn, happily settled in domestic harmony, their second son turning three soon. Kevin and Maria, with their brood. Her friends proved that negotiating the pathway to a successful marriage was possible. She wished she knew their secret.

CHAPTER TWENTY-SEVEN

London was a magnet for international bankers. Sarah met plenty of men during her working days, but she continued to wear her rings so they'd assume she was married. Her heart was taken. Jack and she had shared something special, a meeting of minds, a fusion of spirits, another body calling to her physically. Once you've learned something in the school of hard knocks, it burns its own indelible image, knowledge not easily forgotten.

The men who crossed her path in London came nowhere near supplanting him. She was never tempted to obtain a prescription for the pill, a contraceptive precaution she'd not had to worry about for years.

You can carry on with your life even if the outside world would never guess that a key ingredient is missing.

Her training in economics and her on-the-ground experience in an underdeveloped country became known to her superiors, who moved her into another section of the risk management area. She wrote papers on country risk analysis, occasionally quoted in London's *Financial Times*, and slowly developed her reputation as an independent thinker. She was achieving career success and making her mark, just like Jack.

But he wouldn't know. In his line of work, he wouldn't be reading the *Financial Times*, or turning up among the tourists crowding into London from every corner of the globe.

London was a particular mecca for Australians. Not a month went by without a phone call from a visitor Sarah had known back home. 'Is there anyone left in Australia?' asked her secretary, as the latest caller with an Australian accent rang to speak to her.

Sarah picked up the intercom. Beth was on the line, a friend since childhood. In London for a conference, she had a few hours to spare. 'I want to see you, of course I do, but can we kill two birds with one stone? I'd like to visit a specialist knitting shop at Angel, near where you live.'

Sarah smiled. Beth was a social worker, working in palliative care, but her creative passion was knitting. 'Of course. I know the place. It's open until 8pm. I'll meet you there.'

When Sarah walked into the shop with Beth a strange sadness overcame her. The jumpers on display, knitted by craftspeople, were very creative and beautiful. It reminded her of the brief years with

Jack, creative and beautiful in a different way, helping to shape her as the woman she might have been. Without Jack to free her spirit, she'd become so buttoned up here in London that she wondered whether she'd ever again be able to behave as she wanted to, revealing her true self.

Sarah and Beth left the shop and headed for a little Italian restaurant in Upper St, Islington. Sarah sometimes had a plate of pasta and a glass of wine here, on her way home after work, as a change from eating alone at her flat. She loved its crisp white tablecloths, shiny glasses, candles in straw-wrapped Chianti bottles and bread baskets lined with red and white checked cloths.

They sat down and agreed to place Sarah's regular order. 'It's wonderful to have your company, Beth, to share a meal. Just like old times. We have so much to catch up on.'

'Work talk is banned, even if your job here is fascinating. I want to know how you're doing.'

Sarah shrugged. 'You know me. A woman of few words.'

'Then let's start with the latest news of Andrew,' said Beth, rushing in where angels might fear to tread.

In a supportive gesture, she reached across the table and gave Sarah a comforting pat on the arm. 'I think I have the friend's right to tell you what I think of him.'

Sarah nodded. Beth had known Andrew for nearly as long as she had. 'Did I tell you the divorce came through a few months ago? It was one of the first processed under the new laws.' Sarah went quiet. She was on her own, and likely to remain so, but Beth wouldn't understand how divorce felt, having never married.

Beth knew the moods of her long-time friend, even if they hardly saw each other these days. 'Something's troubling you. What is it? It's more than Andrew, I can tell.'

Old friends can sometimes trigger an honest exchange, especially when one is a trained social worker. 'You seem to be happily single, and a contented professional, not yearning for a husband and babies. How do you do it?'

'I don't know. It's true, I've had my opportunities, but I don't seem to be very interested in the notion of husbands and babies. My brother and I grew up in a pretty bland household. Not much drama or passion. Not like yours.'

'Tell me about it!' Sarah thought back to those times. Maybe she could open up to Beth. She'd known her since primary school. 'You know, there was one specific dramatic episode that really upset me, when I was about ten.'

'That far back? I knew you then. What happened?'

'Family violence. Dad attacking Mum. I've got

it into better perspective in the last few years.'

The waiter deposited their drinks on the table. She took hold of the stem of her wine glass to give herself courage, something to hold onto. Her only confidante to date had been Andrew. And he'd gone. She dared to risk repeating the story to Beth.

'Oh my God, you've been carrying that personal load all this time. No wonder you feel so burdened.'

'It *has* weighed me down. In my heart of hearts, that episode shaped my life for years, but I never articulated it. I kept dreaming of an "all things bright and beautiful" world, like the words of that hymn we learned in Sunday School.'

Beth was silent for a few minutes. 'Do you mind if I say something?'

'Not at all. Your feedback might be helpful. If not, you'll be back on the plane to Australia in a few days.' She gave her friend a rueful grin. 'We'll have months to forget any injured feelings and our friendship will continue as before.' She'd finally worked out that nothing scary need necessarily flow from discussing her bottled up feelings with someone she trusted, like Beth.

'If you'll pardon me getting straight to the point, you need to repair the damage of your childhood.'

'What do you mean? Repair? How do I do that?' She stared uneasily at her friend.

'By creating your own family, but a family with a different focus to the family in which you grew up. No offence intended.' Beth spoke cautiously, as if choosing her words carefully.

Sarah gave a huge sigh of relief and smiled. 'First time I've thought of it in that way.' She picked up her glass of wine and clinked it with Beth's. 'Thank you. Come to think of it, my search to find the honest, loving world I craved began when I was ten, without me knowing what, exactly, that meant in reality. I simply knew it wasn't the pretend world of my parents.'

'The drive to have children is strong in most women, but that special need of yours adds an extra dimension to your craving.' Beth paused, took a sip of her wine, then admitted, 'To be honest, I'm not terribly fussed about having a family. There were no babies to cuddle in my family, or younger siblings and a dozen small cousins to look after, as in yours.'

'We were so rowdy in our family, so exuberant. Four giggling girls.'

'I remember Dad's favourite saying to you.'

'So do I. "A little decorum, please"!' Sarah laughed. 'But your dad surprised me in a big way one day.'

'Eh! How?'

'Remember that day he was driving us to ballet and he wound down the car window and yelled out to all the passers-by, "I'm fifty today," as he bipped the horn madly?'

Beth laughed at the memory. 'Just as well Mum wasn't in the car.'

'Your dad must be at least fifteen years older than mine.'

'Yep, he's getting on. Yours was always so young and energetic. I grew up looking after the needs of older people, the path I've followed in my adult life. My job requires me, usually, to look after people older than myself, but not all palliative care patients are elderly.'

'Interesting. You could be right about me hankering to repair the damage of long ago. It makes good sense when you put it that way. I'll have to give it some thought.'

'The key point is this. You're probably looking for someone who doesn't pretend or dissemble about important issues, someone who notices what's happening in your life.'

'That's certainly true. I already knew that.' She'd found such a person. Jack. He'd noticed what was happening in her life and spoken plainly and directly to her, not in a roundabout way. He acknowledged problems and took action accordingly. But she couldn't have him.

The tempting aroma wafting from her ravioli reminded her to pick up her fork and eat something. And gave her a few moments for quiet reflection. She wondered if Beth's theory explained why Jack's ghost still pervaded her days and nights. Was he really so special, or did she miss him so much because all those characteristics meant he'd been helping to heal a trauma from her childhood?

Beth's professional point of view generated a new 'aha' moment for Sarah, a new way to view Jack. She could never deny the physical elation of being with Jack. No-one had ever aroused those feelings, before or since. No-one else had seen her as the passionate woman she tried to keep hidden from general view. But, in a way, he'd been pretending too. On the surface, a committed husband and loving father, but under the surface lusting after another woman. *And that was me.*

She rolled that idea around in her mind, weighing it up. That's how some might view the situation. Was Jack another pretender? Did he hold power over her simply because he'd verbalised the things she wanted to hear, bolstering her self-esteem and confidence? Yet she was wired to pick up pretence directed at her, and Jack had never triggered that alarm bell.

Beth's plate was already scraped clean but the crusty bread demanded her attention. She nibbled at a piece while Sarah ate her meal. Finally, she spoke. 'Watching this play of emotions across your face, I think you're speaking from sad experience.'

'There was someone, but it didn't work out.' Sarah dropped her gaze and focused on the breadcrumbs strewn on the tablecloth, an unlikely shield for a secret she'd never admitted to anyone until now. Jack was buried so deep she would struggle to find the words to explain him, even to Beth.

'That remark couldn't possibly refer to Andrew. I never saw him as the right man for you.'

'Why ever not? You never said anything.' Her head shot up and she leaned forward, keen for this unexpected truth-telling to continue.

'I suppose I let you down, through fear of causing offence. We were a lot younger, don't forget. But you two didn't seem to be "in love". And you're clever, much cleverer than Andrew, even if he did coach you in chemistry. We had a boring chemistry teacher at school, and it's a wonder anyone learnt anything from that woman. Wanting to master the subject despite our poor teacher was typical of you.'

'You remember a lot about our school days.'

'Andrew seemed to struggle with the effort of keeping up with you. I just didn't feel that you'd met your match.'

'I kind of knew that myself, but I wasn't strong enough to call the whole thing off.' She had a sudden flash of insight. Beth was yet another person who hadn't been direct with her.

'Let's face it. You were under a fair bit of family pressure, with Andrew being everyone's favourite. He was like a son to your parents and a brother for your sisters. He drove your sisters around and he taught you to drive in his mother's old car. I don't think your family was very fair to you. It was fairly obvious he answered their needs, but not yours. You were very young when you married. Someone older and wiser should have said something.'

'Well, they didn't.'

'I know. My parents used to say it was all a big mistake. As we said before, they are much older than your parents, so I suppose they had more experience in assessing suitable marriage partners. They said you were too young to get married, and too smart for most men to cope with, especially Andrew.'

'Really? That makes me feel a little better, in some ways, and worse in others. Better because someone saw my needs, for a change. Worse because with a bit of guidance my life might have taken a different course, with a different husband by my side and several children to love.'

An inner rage smouldered. People had avoided the issue with her all her life. Or said things to suit. Very few honest interactions. A steely determination fuelled her rage. Things were going to be different in the future.

She would look inside people instead of taking their statements at face value. Ask more directly for opinions and compare words with actions so she'd become a better judge of people. Take more responsibility for herself. Not bad as a resolution when she wasn't yet thirty. She planned to make certain that the next decade would be radically different from her twenties.

She gulped down a large mouthful of her wine. She'd start now. 'What did your parents say about Andrew? Specifically.' The tone of her voice demanded a straight answer.

Beth gave her a wary look. 'They thought Andrew was a sympathetic type, but too much so. He listened and soaked up whatever you said, like a sponge, but gave no feedback. There was nothing terribly firm and resilient for you to bounce off. He was a "yes love, no love, anything you say, love" type of fellow, who always followed the easiest path for him.'

'That's what they said to you, even before I married him? Why didn't you tell me? Tactfully, of course.'

'Would you have listened? Your family conditioned you to look at life a certain way.'

'What else have they said? Recently, I mean.'

'They said it was a completely predictable outcome when they heard about you splitting up.'

'Wow.' Her heavy sigh nearly blew out the candle flickering between them.

'So now the inevitable has happened, you shouldn't take all the responsibility of divorce onto your shoulders and blame yourself.'

'Thanks Beth. For trying to cheer me up.'

Sarah's shoulders drooped, and her bottom lip trembled.

Beth grimaced. 'My efforts have met with limited success because you look as if you might burst into tears at any moment. Can't tell if they're tears of rage or sorrow.'

'Both, I think.'

'I've touched a few raw nerves. Want to tell me about the mystery man?'

'Not really. He was my old boss. He's married. With young children. The old story.' She watched her friend's jaw drop slightly and she added, 'We never became involved in an affair, although the physical attraction was overwhelming. So was the mental bond.' Sarah felt her tears prick and she clenched her jaw to control herself. She'd said enough. There was no need to open herself up to judgment, even from her oldest friend. For several years she'd kept Jack locked in his own compartment in her mind and there he should stay, for safekeeping.

'And the mental bond is what you need more than anything else.'

'I've never found it before or since.'

'You never know what might happen in life. What was that old song? *Que sera, sera.* If the bond was that strong, he'll surely come looking for you one day.'

Sarah's heartbeat gave a little flutter of surprise at Beth's sympathetic response. Not even the hint of disapproval in her voice. But she had to face the facts. Jack was in her past. 'I doubt it Beth, as much as I might wish that to happen.' A tear welled and sneakily rolled down her cheek. 'Come on, let's get the bill and make our farewells.'

She dabbed at her eyes and signalled the waiter. 'I'm trying to take a leaf out of your book these days, by concentrating on my career. We career girls need our beauty sleep, so we can function at the required 110% level expected of us at work.' She spoke with false gaiety.

'You're right there. You know, it's been a real pleasure to have this conversation tonight. It feels as if we have suddenly got closer. You've always been such a bottler, keeping your feelings to yourself. You should have told me long ago about all these burdens you've been carrying. That's what friends are for.'

She was part of the way towards reclaiming an important bit of herself. At a business function, she met a banker whose physique reminded her of Jack. This physical similarity unblocked a choke point in Sarah's brain. For the first time since they'd parted, a vivid dream about Jack woke her in the middle of the night.

In the dream, she'd been leaning up against him physically, something she'd not been willing to do with anyone in real life since her experience with him. Their heads faced forwards, his face pressed against hers, cheeks squashed flat together. Although the rest of their bodies touched, they angled away from each other at the shoulders, indicating they'd taken opposite directions, different courses in life.

Half awake, half asleep, she tried to focus. Was the dream telling her she didn't want to turn the clock back to those days? Fuzzily she recalled more of her dream, and remembered them talking easily about their new lives, but not of the experiences they'd once shared, which were not acknowledged. It symbolised a failure to discuss important issues, but was that her fault or his?

The dream probably signified her frustration at not knowing what she'd meant to him and that he'd be unable or unwilling to tell her. In all this time, he'd never attempted to contact her. Although they'd agreed on a clean break, she reluctantly had to assume she'd meant nothing to him. She suspected they might have little in common now.

Fully awake from her dream, a strange peace of mind enveloped her like a blanket, leaving her much happier, relieved that she hadn't lost him after all. There had been a lot of unresolved grief about losing him. After the dream she felt that she'd regained a part of herself, the feeling part, the part that she'd given away to him and had never got back. She hadn't lost that part of herself after all.

Through the dream mechanism, she regained for herself what he'd meant to her. She went to bed the next night wishing he'd come back to her again, so she'd feel good like this again, re-united with this lost part of herself, but he didn't return. The dream had done its work.

What with Beth's insights and that stray banker, from that moment onwards she lost many of her long-standing anxieties about not having a family of her own. She became more willing to reveal her feelings again. She expressed herself physically a little more warmly with the people in her life, without fear it would lead her into the 'Sea of Heartbreak' described so perfectly in Don Gibson's earworm of a song.

CHAPTER TWENTY-EIGHT

Life in London was intellectually a challenge, and culturally a rich experience, but the call of home was strong. After three years in London, Sarah returned to Sydney for a five-week break before she moved to Washington to take up a new position.

Back in her hometown, she slotted missing pieces of her life into place. She visited her parents. She visited her sisters. They were younger, but each had husbands and babies and she was the only career girl in the family. She visited Beth.

She had abandoned all contact with anyone who knew about her life in PNG, which was her way of suppressing Jack's importance to her. With so much unresolved grief about losing him, she'd feared the pain of reviving her memories in actual conversation with her old Moresby friends.

Now she felt stronger. Ashamed of her poor performance as a godmother, she rang the Mitchells who were back in Sydney, visited them and fell in love all over again with little Isabella. She didn't ask directly about Jack but eventually his name came up in conversation as they gossiped about this and that. 'On the grapevine I hear Jack and Jenny Martin have shares in a family property out Dubbo way,' said Kevin.

'It's dry territory out in that part of New South Wales,' she said, trying to keep the small talk going while she processed this further proof of Jack's determination to make his marriage work.

'Definitely a change from the tropics. Like us, he's probably had enough of that weather,' said Maria, wrinkling her nose.

'I've lost touch. Does he live there?'

'No, in Sydney somewhere. He operates a consultancy to the state and federal governments and international agencies. His name crops up in the paper from time to time.'

Jack was nearby? Resettled? He'd created an interesting new life for himself?

It jolted her into an awareness that he had moved on and it was time to put down some roots of her own, a permanent base to call home no matter where she lived in the world.

She forced herself to pay attention to the traffic as she drove home from the Mitchells but her thoughts stubbornly strayed to Jack. If he had a property in the central west of the state, Jack would likely choose to live in Sydney's western suburbs for the sake of travel convenience. In such a large city, she mused, she'd be unlikely to bump into him if she stuck to the area of her hometown she knew well, the Lower North Shore.

It was just a matter of deciding her price bracket and trekking round the agents. Location, location, location were the three golden rules in buying real estate, but Sarah was also looking for sunshine, light and the magical ingredient of ambience. It was necessary to be patient, but eventually she settled on an appealing property in McMahons Point, quite close to the hotel where she was staying. The final legal documents for the transaction would have to be couriered to her overseas, and the agent promised to find her good tenants until she returned to Sydney.

By chance, on the last Friday of her holiday, she bumped into her old colleague Charles Williams in Macquarie St. She hadn't sought him out because she'd heard he lived overseas.

'Where have you been, Sarah? We've missed you.'

'London. For three years. I hear you haven't been around here much yourself.'

'True. I've had a posting in the Philippines for the last eighteen months. Just got back, in fact. Glad to be back, to be honest. This city sure takes some beating. It beats Manila, that's for sure. A lot safer too.'

'I agree it's good to be back. I've been on leave

for the last five weeks, catching up with old friends. And I've been investigating the real estate scene. Am buying a property at McMahons Point.'

'Coming home to live, at last?'

'Not yet, but I need a home base. To feel that somewhere is mine, when I'm home on leave.'

'We'd love to catch up. Carolyn will be excited to hear that I bumped into you. She'll be even happier to think that you'll ultimately settle in Sydney again. Can you come to lunch on Sunday?'

'That would be delightful. I'd love to come.'

'Is there anyone you'd like to bring?'

Rather flippantly, Sarah replied she would come to lunch alone. 'Footloose and fancy free, Charles. Despite all the years I've spent at work, surrounded by men.'

She was well-used to going places on her own. Her days in London had been one long round of seminars, lunches, dinners and cocktail parties, meeting various visitors to the financial capital of the world.

Charles gave her a peculiar look but said nothing except 'See you then, Sarah, around twelve thirty. The address is 15 Glover St, Neutral Bay. Don't bring anything, just yourself. At our place it's casual. Australian-style casual, not the English-style casual you must be used to by now.'

She knew what he meant. No sports jackets and ties for the men. Everyone on first-name terms.

People offering to help. Not that this mattered for an impromptu lunch with her old friends and their two boys.

She found suitable gifts for Ricky and his younger brother, no longer babies. It would be nice and relaxing to sit outside in the sunshine with a glass of wine and catch up on old times, but it would probably not do much for the slight headache which was trying to worm its way into her skull with some insistency. She blamed it on an allergic response to the wattle blossom of this spring season, took some antihistamine and hoped that she was not coming down with one of her migraine-type headaches.

Her pollen-induced headache lingered as a low-grade discomfort but rapidly intensified when she arrived at Glover St and discovered that the lunch was a large reunion gathering for all those with whom she'd worked in Moresby. It was purely coincidental that she could attend, and Charles hadn't enlightened her about its nature.

She looked around her with a rising feeling of panic. Was Jack here amongst the crowd?

It confirmed her worst fears when she saw Jack standing at the end of the verandah outside, a beer in hand, his back to the railing and the spectacular harbour view, looking back into the room where she stood. He was alone.

Where was Jenny? Jenny would have been a shield, making it easier to talk to Jack. Sarah hadn't realised the pain could still be so strong until she saw him there. Three years had gone by since that incident in Moresby's main street, yet it seemed like it happened yesterday.

Jack came straight over to her. 'Hello Sarah.' Today a man of few words, a step up from last time, when he was a man of no words.

She kept her wary distance. No polite kiss on the cheek. 'Hello Jack. Fancy meeting you here.'

Why didn't Charles warn her? She was psychologically unprepared for this surprise face-to-face meeting.

He spoke cautiously. 'I was hoping you'd be able to come. Can I get you a drink?'

The deeply etched pain of his back-turning episode and of her heart-breaking loss, of him and the family life she'd craved, memories resurrected without warning, suddenly overwhelmed her. 'No drink, thanks, I can't stay long.'

He gasped.

'In fact, I really only dropped in to tell Charles that I can't stay at all. I didn't have his phone number, only his address, so I thought it'd be easier just to call in and tell him. Besides, I wanted to drop off these gifts for the children.'

She babbled, hastily inventing the story as she went along.

He paled. 'Are you sure you can't stay, even for a short time?'

Completely rejecting Jack's overtures of friendship, she said, 'No, I really must fly. I double-booked, and I'm meant to be at lunch at Mosman right now.' This was an outright lie. 'Nice to see you again. Give my love to Jenny and the kids.' Turning on her heel, she didn't see the look of pain which passed across Jack's face.

She rushed over to Carolyn, gave her a hug and a kiss, and said 'I can't stay Carolyn, I'm truly sorry to miss your lovely party. Hope the boys have some fun with these small offerings. I'll call you tomorrow to explain.' She thrust the gifts into Carolyn's hands and flew out the door, towards her hire car. Eyes misting over with tears, she drove off.

Astounded, Carolyn watched Sarah's car disappear round the corner. Charles came over to her. 'What was that all about, Caro?'

'I'm not sure. I noticed her entrance a few minutes ago. Who wouldn't, with her looks? Next time I noticed, she was talking to Jack, only for a minute or so, but she looked quite upset when she spoke to me, and she left in a hurry, saying she'd ring and explain tomorrow. She didn't even speak to the others. It's all very odd.'

'Jeez,' said Charles, 'I'd better ask Jack what's going on. He looks pretty upset too.'

Jack turned his back on the other guests and leaned on the verandah rail, head sunk towards his chest, beer can gripped tightly. Every part of his body ached with emotional pain. His thoughts spiralled around in his head. 'Her reaction to me today must have been fate. I clearly imagined how we felt back then. I've blown it up in my mind, beyond reality.'

Behind him he heard Charles say brightly, 'Long time no see, mate. Glad I had the right number when I left that message for you.'

He turned and tried to act normal. 'Yeah, sorry I forgot my manners and didn't ring you back, to say I was coming.'

He'd been out collecting the kids when Charles left his message two weeks back, then busy with meal preparation and hounding reluctant children into bed, ready for their grandparents to pick them up next day and whisk them away for the school holidays. He'd almost forgotten the message and nearly didn't come today.

'No worries. Details of time and place and 'come if you can, no need to reply' seemed sufficient as notification for a reunion.'

Jack nodded but was in no mood to chat.

Charles took up the slack in the conversation. 'I hear your consulting business is going great guns. Still travelling a lot?'

'Not seeing as much of Asia as I was.' He should tell his old friend the reason why.

'I saw you talking to Sarah before she left in a hurry. Did you scare her away, mate?' Charles gave him a friendly slap on the back.

'Your guess is as good as mine.' Jack shrugged and took a swig on his beer.

'And I've had no chance to ask where Jenny is. Too busy with the kids?'

Jack took a second gulp of beer before replying. 'Jenny's dead.'

Charles reeled back and stared at him. 'What! Oh my God, I'm so sorry. When did this happen? How?'

'A car accident. About a year ago. While you were overseas, probably why you didn't hear. She was on her way to pick up Tom and Lottie from her mother's. Killed by a drunk driver.' It still seemed like yesterday, every time he thought about it.

'Is that what upset Sarah?' Charles scratched at his head in a distracted way.

'No, I didn't get the chance to tell her.' He tilted his beer can and gave it a slosh. Almost empty. Charles had better have plenty more where that came from. 'She seemed very agitated. Said she'd double-booked. But I got the feeling she was upset at seeing me. Did she know I was coming?'

'No, because I didn't know you'd be here for sure. I bumped into her in the street last Friday, by accident. Didn't tell her it was a reunion.'

'Was she with someone? When you bumped into her, I mean?' Why was he tormenting himself with a question like this?

'No, and I asked her if she'd like to bring someone, but she made a very odd remark about being footloose and fancy free. That didn't sound like her at all. She's never been that kind of girl. Do you think London might have changed her? That's where she's been for the past three years.'

'She didn't look like she's changed.' Seeing her standing there, looking so stunning and so alone, had taken him straight back to his Moresby days. Wistful despondency overwhelmed him and he slouched against the verandah rail for support.

'There's still something there? For you, I mean.'

'It'd be better to let sleeping dogs lie.' His honest answer would be yes, but then he might let down his guard, so he preferred prevarication. 'I tried to contact her years ago, to apologise for turning my back on her. She never answered my letter.'

His throat tightened. She'd probably found herself a new love.

Meanwhile, he was trying to cope with being a single parent to two kids devastated at the loss of their mother, staying strong for Tom and Lottie by keeping things on an even keel for them. Just being around was important. Shopping. Cooking. Supervising homework. Saturday morning sports. Organising their play dates with their friends. Keeping up his own work schedule. No time for any dating of his own.

'I reckon you're just saving face. What do you really feel?'

Pressed by his friend, honesty won out. 'What do you think? It was hell back then. Losing her. I know I had to do it, but it was hell. It feels like I've just lost her again.'

His glum voice betrayed his sadness. Seeing Sarah again was like a miracle. A very short-lived miracle. When she materialised out of thin air, like a genie out of a bottle, he'd almost dropped his drink. Clumsily he'd tried to break the ice, to talk, but she'd frozen him out. There'd been no time to tell her about Jenny before she quickly disappeared again.

Charles was silent for a moment, as if nervous about the best way to respond. Then he said, 'I never told you how upset she was that day I took her to the airport in Moresby.'

'No need to rub it in.'

'I wrote to her once, because I thought she had real guts to do what she did and I admired her for it.' Charles bit his lip, looking worried. 'I wish I'd known about Jenny when I invited her to come today. It might have made a big difference to her staying and talking to you.'

'Turning to matchmaking?'

'If I knew how to contact her these days, I'd give it a try. She lives overseas. That's all I know.'

'We all move in different circles these days.' And she was out of his reach.

'Given how you feel, I'll ask Carolyn to get her contact number if she rings tomorrow, and I'll pass it on to you.'

'I'd really appreciate it.' Despite his fear that she'd found someone new, he'd risk chasing after a phantom who lived on the other side of the world.

'Where are the kids today, then?'

'With my parents, on the family farm. School holiday time.'

'So you can stay for a while?'

'Right now, I feel like drowning my sorrows.'

'You've got a few to drown, mate. Come over with the others, they're keen to see what you've been up to of late. It might take your mind off things for a bit.'

He stayed on at the party longer than intended. Had more to drink than he'd planned. Sitting in the dark on this park bench on Kurraba Point, the headland near the Williams' home, was as good a place as any to quietly sober up before he got back into his car and drove any further. He stared at an amazing moonrise and took another gulp from the water bottle he kept in his car.

He stood up and paced around like a tiger. He groaned. *She did to me what I once did to her— turned her back and walked away, as if I was a pariah. She seems determined to cut her ties with her old life.*

He sighed heavily, gave a resigned shrug, and stamped back to his vehicle. As he drove home slowly along the peaceful back streets, he hoped he'd sleep tonight. He faced a long drive in the morning to pick up Tom and Lottie from the farm.

A super-sized orange moon hovered in the eastern sky. It was so spectacular and unusual that Sarah, her headache dispatched by medication and copious quantities of water, drove from her hotel to Middle Head at Mosman to watch its progress as almost imperceptibly it glided upwards from the ocean's dark horizon, floating, like a soccer ball in slow motion. Other cars had brought other spellbound eyes to watch the phenomenal display.

It was not the light of a silvery moon illuminating their vehicles. Tonight's moon was special, its aura lighting the harbour with a golden glow the colour of love. 'Australia is really putting on a show for me,' she thought, 'keeping me emotionally tied to its beauty. But how I long to step back three years and be bathed once again in the real glow of the love light in Jack's eyes. Relying on the glow of a heavenly body for my emotional sustenance is not enough.'

She reflected on the party. In inviting both her and Jack, Charles probably thought he was doing the right thing, giving two people who might have something meaningful to say to each other the opportunity to meet unexpectedly in neutral territory. Though he should have warned her, so she could arm herself in advance.

Did Jack really think he could saunter over to me as if nothing had happened and engage in polite chit chat?

As the moon rose higher overhead, Sarah drew in a deep breath, sighed it out sadly, keyed the ignition and headed off home to pack her suitcase with the items she'd brought with her on leave. Tonight was her last night in Australia for the foreseeable future. On the golden oldies station of her car radio, Frank Sinatra crooned his signature song 'I've got you under my skin'. She pressed a hand to her heart. *And Jack, no matter how hard I try, I can't scratch you away.*

CHAPTER TWENTY-NINE

Sarah's new posting was in Washington, at the World Bank. She'd applied for the position because of her interest in development economics, an interest sparked by Jack when he'd been her boss, and won the position because of her experience in PNG and her reputation as a country risk analyst.

She rang Carolyn from the airport before breakfast on Monday morning to apologise for her brief appearance at the party, feigning the excuse of a migraine which had been coming on her all day, combined with unfinished preparations for her imminent departure.

Carolyn said, 'That's not what Jack told Charles. Jack said you told him you double-booked. Charles wants a word.'

Her husband came on the line. 'Jack really wanted to talk to you.'

She assumed that Charles, by now, had long since told his wife about the reason for her sudden departure from Moresby. 'Why didn't you tell me it was a reunion? That he was coming. I thought it was just us three, and your kids.' Sarah's indignation echoed in her voice.

'I didn't know for sure if he'd come. And I thought you might not come if you thought he might be there. We all wanted to see you.' He paused. 'I don't get it. Why did you leave in such a hurry? Are you trying to avoid Jack?'

'I didn't realise he'd have that effect on me until I saw him again. It gave me a shock. I wanted to get away.'

He persisted. 'What's your contact number? We need to stay in touch.'

'Haven't got one at present. I'm off to the States in under an hour. I'm at the airport as we speak, calling from the public phone there,' she said. She wanted them to know she was indeed leaving Australia, and wasn't making up the story about her travel preparations. But she didn't say this was a new posting. The way she phrased it, she might have been going on holiday. Or back to London via the USA, as if on a round-the-world ticket.

'I'm truly sorry I couldn't stay. Now that I have your address, I'll catch up with you next time I'm in town.' Despite her jittery nerves, she did her best to sound bright and cheery. 'Have to rush now, or I'll miss my flight.'

'But Sarah, Jack wanted to tell you ....'

'Sorry Charles, crackly line. I can't hear very

well. Noisy flight announcements. Give my love to Carolyn and the boys. See you soon, I hope.'

She rang off without leaving her new work contact number, denying Charles the opportunity to pursue his obvious interest in her plans.

Whatever Jack had to say would only upset her again, so it was best left unsaid. No use him trying to contact her through their mutual friends. Mystery and geographic distance would surely kill off that idea. America was a big place, even if it became known, eventually, that she'd gone there to work. Flights from Sydney ended on the west coast and she could be anywhere in the USA after landing at Los Angeles.

She'd be desk-bound in Washington, but the prospect didn't worry her. With more on-the-ground practical experience than most analysts, she expected her work to be fascinating but relatively straightforward. Having leisure time in one of the world's most interesting cities, and mixing with some of the world's most interesting people, was a prospect to savour. She was familiar with the city, as she'd previously visited to attend a conference on country risk and made the contacts which led to her job offer in Washington.

Her favourite place was just outside the city, at Mount Vernon, George Washington's former home. Such a simple home, set in a perfect garden. One day, if she ever owned a country pad, she'd create a garden just like it, with its riot of autumn foliage. It contrasted dramatically with her newly purchased home in McMahons Point, which offered barely enough room for a single feature magnolia tree.

Her days in Washington flew by. By comparison with the tropics, or even London, the passing seasons dramatically defined the passage of time. Baking hot in summer, freezing cold and snow-bound in winter, visually spectacular in the autumn or fall, when brilliant foliage which coloured the landscape red, yellow, orange and gold fell to the ground as a richly patterned carpet.

She lived in a small apartment in fashionable Georgetown. Washington gave her easy opportunity for many interesting weekend trips. To Gettysburg. To Williamsburg. To the Amish country outside Philadelphia. To the ivy-league Princeton University. By train to New York for the weekend.

Her plans for anonymity worked well. She maintained contact only with her immediate family in Australia and her oldest friends like Beth, and heard no more of Jack for the whole three years she spent in the US.

He still intruded on her thoughts. There were many more seminars, many more business dinners, many more eligible men, except that every other man she met fell short. They just weren't Jack.

To minimise the pain of looking, wishing,

remembering, she'd destroyed all the photos of their family outings together and now she had no souvenirs of him, other than his impact on her. He held significance to her far beyond what he ever realised.

All these years later, she still wondered what her true significance had been to him.

CHAPTER THIRTY

Waiting for his first client to arrive, Jack browsed through today's copy of the *Fin Review*. For once, sport dominated the front page. Next week's Melbourne Cup. Even in Sydney that horse race had become a Mecca for the corporate world. A flutter of interest stirred his mind. He wasn't a betting man but the event was a rite of passage for an Australian and he must attend himself, one of these days.

Idly he turned the pages. In an article about women beginning to make their mark in banking, a name jumped out at him. Sarah Robinson.

His pulse raced. Sarah. *His* Sarah.

Wait. He counted up the years. Maybe someone else's Sarah by now.

According to the journalist's story, she'd recently returned from three years with the World Bank in Washington and was newly appointed as a director of a leading merchant bank in Sydney. The last he'd heard, she lived in London. She'd come a long way in the world. Going overseas had made her career. He was glad for her. Women were held back so blatantly in Australia's misogynistic society. Even he, a man, could see how unfairly women were treated.

If only he'd known she was with the World Bank, he could have tracked her down easily. He'd had a contract with that organisation once himself, in his PNG days. A pang of hurt rippled through him. *She didn't use my name as a referee.*

The article mentioned her role in a different section of the World Bank to the department which recruited him. *It's a massive organisation, tentacles everywhere. I guess it's no surprise that they never contacted me about her employment credentials.*

She'd never written. Never answered his letter. But he'd give anything to see her again.

He didn't think it appropriate to turn up uninvited and possibly unwanted at her Sydney office. That might be awkward for both of them.

He rang the Victorian Minister for Agriculture at the last moment and belatedly accepted his earlier invitation to join his party at this year's Melbourne Cup.

Plan A—he hoped to find Sarah there. He prayed her company would seize the opportunity of introducing her to the corporate high-fliers who flock to the Cup. Where else would their paths cross socially these days? He'd make damn sure to spend most of his time scanning the crowd, looking for her.

Meeting her at the Cup might seem coincidental to her, and thus non-threatening.

Plan B—his fall-back plan. Hang around outside her office next week and waylay her as she left, pretending to be just passing by. He wasn't too confident of that plan. Most senior executives prefer to park under their high-rise offices and drive out of subterranean caverns without a backward glance at random pedestrians. He did the same himself.

His client arrived. He put his paper aside, a slight fizz in his mind. Next week couldn't come quickly enough. There'd better be a spare seat on the plane to Melbourne on Tuesday.

CHAPTER THIRTY-ONE

At Flemington Racecourse, Sarah sat in the Members' Stand with several corporate guests invited to the Melbourne Cup.

Her new employer, eager to introduce her to their guest list of Australia's business elite at the earliest opportunity, had asked her to perform the duties of co-hostess at their marquee.

The Melbourne Cup, the highlight of Melbourne's Spring Racing carnival, brought an entire nation to a standstill. For three minutes on the first Tuesday afternoon each November, all eyes and ears tuned to its broadcast. In the metropolis of Melbourne, the entire day was a public holiday. Even interstate, work stopped at lunchtime for Melbourne Cup lunches at the office. Everyone either bet on the race directly, or took a ticket in a 'sweep', a form of lucky dip. It cost a dollar or two to enter the sweep, with the total sum collected divided amongst those who'd drawn the winning horse and the two runners up.

It was a day to see, and to be seen, even for the roses at Flemington. Carefully cultivated for the occasion, the roses featured in news broadcasts if unseasonal weather dimmed the prospects of them reaching full bloom on the day.

Women spent months planning their outfits, and milliners made their fortunes at this time of year. Competition amongst the fillies of the human variety was keen as they tried to attract selection by the judges for the 'Fashions on the Field' competition.

The race event, dating from 1861, had built to cultural icon status and its fame had spread far and wide. After the British model, Jean Shrimpton, scandalised the world by wearing her short white shift at Flemington in 1965, with no hat or stockings or gloves as convention dictated, visitors began to pour in from overseas. The race committee adjusted the race length from the Imperial distance of two miles to the metric distance of 3,200 metres, better understood in international racing circles.

Never having been to the Cup herself, Sarah felt a mounting sense of excitement. One couldn't help being affected by the air of vibrant anticipation surrounding her as the scheduled time for the big race drew closer. Part of the fun was spotting familiar faces amongst the attendees. She joined in, scanning the festive crowd standing on the lawn in front of the Members' Stand. Among so many interstate and overseas visitors, she must recognise someone.

Wait a minute. Her breath caught, and her heart pounded like a jackhammer. Was that Jack, standing twenty feet in front of her? The stranger had his back to her, but this man had the same confident stance, legs slightly apart, as Jack. He turned occasionally to speak to his companion, and she noted the same facial profile, the same unmistakable alert and penetrating look directed at the man beside him.

If it was Jack, he'd aged well. No bulges in the wrong place. No premature grey hairs cursing his mid-thirties. He was still tall, still solidly built but not overweight, still fair-haired and tanned, although his hair had darkened a little. In all the years she'd known him, this was the first time she'd ever seen Jack, if indeed it was him, in business attire. The rear view of his well-tailored suit, carefully fitted to broad shoulders and tapering down over his hipline, flattered his manly shape as much as the cotton shirts and shorts of the tropics had.

It was as if her London dream, years ago, releasing her from memories of Jack, had never existed. Seeing a man who even looked like him changed everything.

Her memories flooded back. She'd been right to trust Jack. He'd been a man of his word. He'd never left Jenny and come looking for her, but oh, how she'd missed him. Everything about Jack. The way he thought about the world. How he looked. The way he walked. The way he talked. His laugh. His musky aroma. The way he made her feel. His body close to hers. So many foolish little things reminded her of him. The sudden jolt of nostalgia took her breath away, like slamming headlong into a brick wall, or diving into a cold swimming pool on a hot day.

She didn't miss Andrew this way. From their mid-teens she and Andrew had been together for almost a decade, but he hadn't got under her skin in those ten years the way Jack had done.

Eight long years had passed since Andrew had left. He lived back in Sydney, in a nearby suburb, and she sometimes bumped into him at the local supermarket. She always said hello, but neither felt the need to stop and chat. Andrew had been right. They'd drifted apart many years ago.

She stared at the man in silence, as her companion Helen chatted amiably beside her. 'Oh, but my dear,' Helen exclaimed 'Just look at that hat. Front row of the stand. Have you ever seen anything like that bunch of fruit sitting on top of anyone's head? That's Tina Devine, Robert Devine's wife. And that's Robert beside her, talking to the Premier, currying favour for his latest inner-city development project, no doubt. These men, they never miss an opportunity to talk about business, do they? Tina must have spent a fortune on that hat, but my dear, would you wear it?'

Sarah giggled in a distracted way. She still had

her eye on that stranger, even if half an ear was listening to Helen, the wife of a major Melbourne-based client. After her marriage, Helen never worked again for a living, she told Sarah, and she enjoyed her days playing tennis and lunching with the girls. Helen was fortyish, and rather matronly but well-groomed and well-dressed in the rather predictable fashion choices of Toorak's society ladies.

Helen was a trained corporate wife and knew how to make small talk in the company of her husband's business contacts. Sarah had little in common with her lifestyle, but she admired Helen's cheerful and chatty social graces and reflected on the life she herself might have led if Andrew had been able to sire children.

Or if she'd been with Jack. This was painful territory. She blinked back a tear and tried to tune in again to Helen's sociable chit chat about clothes and people. Helen seemed to know the life history of just about everyone parading before them, including where they'd gone to school, where their children went to school, where they lived and who was 'on' with who.

Sarah's new role would require her to visit Melbourne regularly on business, so she found this aspect of Melbourne's life fascinating, after her own life as an international executive. Melbourne was such a large city to display such incongruous and charming similarities to the intimacies of village life in England. No wonder so many English and European companies based themselves here rather than in Sydney. Not only was the climate and the vegetation more akin to that of Europe, but the lifestyle was also similar.

Helen continued to point out the rich and famous of the Melbourne scene. Sarah kept half an ear tuned in to her commentary, enough to make suitable murmurs of acknowledgment, but found herself irresistibly drawn to staring at the disturbing back view of a somehow familiar stranger.

The man who looked like Jack apparently didn't notice Sarah sitting twenty feet behind him in the Members' Stand. His companion was telling a long and involved story, requiring the listener's attention. While the Jack look-alike frequently cast surreptitious glances at the crowd surrounding him, her stares at his back didn't prompt him to turn his head right around to look directly into the stand behind him. She couldn't tell for sure if he was Jack.

Even if it was him and his eyes came to rest on her in this crowded stand, he'd be unlikely to recognise her in Melbourne Cup mode, stylish hat and sunglasses obscuring her face, after the light frocks and sandals of the tropics. She recalled that they'd also worn casual attire to that abortive luncheon party. He had no visual cues for how Sarah might look today.

Formal business attire was the norm for her

now, but she remembered a comment he'd once made, that he liked women either simply and plainly dressed, or dressed up to the nines, fully elegant, with all the right jewellery and accessories. Either way, he liked to feel that a woman cared about her appearance and didn't adopt sloppiness as a way of life. Was this his response to the rather casual ways with which Jenny approached life? He'd never criticised Jenny, but he might have wished for something else. She felt that if Jack could see her now, he would approve.

It was almost time for the big race. The massive crowd pressed round the two men she studied, blocking them from her view as twenty-four horses thundered along the track and pounded to the finish line to the cheers of one hundred thousand spectators.

After the race, when the crowd thinned and gradually dispersed, she could no longer see the man who looked like Jack.

Was it a mirage? It was like stepping back in time. Sarah felt disoriented. With the greater wisdom and maturity of her extra years, she bore Jack no grudges and hoped that his life had been happy. Where was he living now, and what was he doing? Was he still married to Jenny, sticking his marriage vows? How had the delightful Tom and Lottie turned out?

She continued to wonder, too, whether he'd

suffered afterwards from their hurried but passionate parting, or whether he'd soon forgotten all about her. She remembered the way he'd ignored her in the street. He obviously wanted her to stay out of his life, to avoid complications.

But this assessment couldn't be completely correct. She remembered his attempts to be friendly at Charles' luncheon party. Could it possibly be that, with his wife not present at that party, he might have been trying to take advantage of an opportunity to test out the waters for an illicit affair with her? Had he turned into a rat? Men were like that, weren't they? He might have thought it possible now they were no longer living in the same small community.

She quickly brushed another tear from her eye as the pangs of her own suffering jabbed at her heart. She'd never found the husband and family relationship she'd craved, despite the many men who'd wooed her without penetrating her baffling reserve.

By necessity, she'd looked to other areas of her life for fulfillment, especially her work. Concentrating on work brought its own intellectual stimulus and rewards and helped fill up her days. She'd prided herself that she'd developed into a mature woman, able to cope with whatever came her way. Able to cope with men's unwanted attentions. Able to cope with being around other people's children. Able to see that love begins when you learn to accept and love yourself and no longer look needily outside of yourself for love.

She thought she'd successfully put Jack behind her—until today.

'Is anything the matter, Sarah? You look a little upset,' came Helen's solicitous enquiry from Sarah's side.

'A speck of dust seems to have blown into my eyes, that's all, or some pollen. Sorry Helen, my allergies can cause a little trouble sometimes.'

She sat up straight and clenched her jaw firmly. This train of thought had to be squashed. Plenty of people would envy her lifestyle, the travel, the restaurants, the famous people she knew, the money she earned, her personal independence and autonomy. Just because she was lonely for the right companion was no reason to feel sorry for herself. So she wouldn't. She would try to count her blessings.

'Come on,' she said, 'let's return to our marquee and drink some champagne as a toast to the winner. Did you happen to back the winner?'

'No, but I backed the horse which came second, for a place, so I've had a little luck,' responded Helen with a laugh.

They joined the exit queue and slowly filed out of the Members' Stand, along with the rest of their party. They ambled slowly across the lawns, back towards the area which housed the corporate hospitality tents.

Helen continued to walk with Sarah, as the men had joined up with other members of their group heading for the bookies, clutching their betting tickets, eager to claim their winnings. Unusually for the Cup, the favourite had won the race, so the odds were not high and the winnings were modest. But one of Sarah's other guests had picked the trifecta, and he was jubilant. Helen's husband was collecting her more modest winnings on her behalf.

'Sarah?'

Her heart missed a beat as Jack's firm voice sounded behind her. There was no mistaking that manly baritone.

She turned nervously. There he was, striding towards her from the Member's lawn, not a mirage at all, accompanied by his male colleague. Jack's usual broad smile was missing from a face filled with uncertainty and hope, as if cautious about mistaking her identity but not wanting to miss the opportunity of speaking to her.

As he reached her, she whispered, 'Hello Jack.'

'I was sure it was you, when I saw you walking across this way with your companions. Last week's story in the press came to my attention, so I've been looking out for you all day.'

His companion grumbled good-naturedly: 'I wondered why you've been so twitchy. If you'd accepted my invitation in time, you'd have enjoyed a better lookout point from the stand. And I'd have been able to see the race.'

Jack gave an apologetic grin. 'Better luck next year, mate. At least you had a win.'

He returned his searching gaze to Sarah. 'I saw your profile as you turned to say goodbye to the two men you were with, and I knew straight away.' He stretched out both arms towards her, grasped her firmly by the shoulders and kissed her gently on both cheeks, in the European greeting style. 'It's been a long time,' he sighed, 'too long.'

She was an expert at handling the polite, business-like kisses women received on social business occasions when a handshake seemed inappropriate. Jack was now clearly a business executive, and his two kisses should have been no different. The difference was the out-stretched arms, imploring her to enter his personal space. The proprietorial grip on her shoulders sent an urgent message to her brain that this man harboured serious designs on her.

Her body sent its own warning signals. A chaste kiss on each cheek in front of an audience didn't normally send a shiver down her spine. Or prompt a heated response in more private parts of her body. In fact, the last time an uncontrollable shiver had travelled up and down her spine was the last time she'd touched Jack. No-one had turned her on since that day in his office, nearly seven years ago, when she'd said goodbye. He still used the same brand of aftershave, which blended with his own muskiness to stamp him as unmistakably Jack. It was strange how one's sense of smell could so instantly revive significant memories.

Her colleagues may have noticed the shiver, but they couldn't possibly know of her sudden secret sensations of heat and moisture.

This was dangerous territory, calling for the ice-maiden treatment. Jack might have dropped unexpectedly back into her world, but she'd not allow him to disturb the hard-won equilibrium she'd fought so long to achieve.

Instantly on her guard, Sarah responded in a manner befitting her well-honed professionalism. 'It *has* been a long time, Jack.' Her smile did not meet her eyes as she performed the required introductions. 'Helen, this is Jack Martin, who was my boss many years ago. Jack—my guest, Helen Maxwell.'

'Pleased to meet you,' simpered the suddenly coquettish Helen.

'Forgive me,' said Jack. 'I've forgotten my manners. Meet Rob McIntyre, the Minister for Agriculture in Victoria. I do a bit of consulting work for him. Rob, this is my former colleague Sarah Robinson, the best analyst you could hope to find.'

Everyone gave polite half-smiles and shook hands.

Jack said, 'I hope I introduced her correctly. It was years ago that I knew her as Sarah Robinson.'

He turned towards Rob. 'Do you have that problem too? It's never clear whether women in the workforce are using their maiden name, or their husband's name, as their professional name.'

Sarah realised Jack had jokingly dealt with not knowing her current matrimonial condition. The problem was mutual. She said noncommittally, 'Sarah Robinson is still my name, Jack.'

This should remind him that many women, once established in a career under a maiden name or the name of a first husband, retained that name even if they married. Building up a quality reputation took time. Men took pride in developing a good name for themselves, and increasingly women in the workforce could see this was an issue and refused to change their name, no matter what a husband might wish.

Sarah moved on to less treacherous ground. 'How are you, Jack? What an unexpected pleasure meeting you here, of all places. And how are Jenny and the children?'

That should prove a suitably innocuous reminder, in front of his companion and Helen, of the cause of a great deal of past or potential heartache. As well as damping his ardour, if it existed, this reminder to herself was helping to control the almost-forgotten shivery sensations which had been building up in her own body.

Jack's gaze didn't flinch. 'I'm well, as you can

see, but I'm sorry to say I have some bad news for you.'

Her nerves jumped to attention. Had something happened to Tom? Or Lottie?

'Poor Jenny died in a car accident four years ago. She was driving, but it wasn't her fault. A drunken driver ran a red light. He died too.'

Sarah splayed her hand against her breastbone as she tried to calm her racing heart. He rushed on: 'Luckily, the kids weren't in the car. Jenny was on her way to pick them up from her mother's house.'

With these few words, he conveyed to her a succinct and potted version of a highly distressing time. Her sexual awareness of him and its related tension instantly dashed out of existence.

'Oh, Jack, that's dreadful news,' gasped Sarah. 'Truly dreadful. I didn't know. I'm so sorry.'

'Yes, terrible,' contributed the soft-hearted and horrified Helen, 'I'm sorry too.' In Helen's rather cocooned world, bad things didn't happen to nice people.

'Thanks,' said Jack. 'It does take a while to get over something like that. The kids had trouble recovering from the trauma of losing their mother, but they're both doing well now.'

Sarah was aware of their respective companions and the difficulties of meaningful conversation under the circumstances. Watching Jack gazing hungrily at her, she was sure that neither wanted their companions to share any more of their exchange of such personal memories.

After an awkward silence for a few moments, finally he said, 'I have a lot to tell you, Sarah. I'm in Melbourne for a few days. Would you be free for dinner during that time, by any chance, so we can talk?'

Sarah gazed longingly at him, her spirits mysteriously lifting. But she remained cautious. He'd just told her that Jenny was no longer his wife. But did he have another wife? Or a live-in lover? Was that what he wanted to tell her about? He must have, as he'd never sought her out in the years since Jenny's untimely death. Why didn't he tell her that piece of news at Charles' lunch?

The answer flashed through her mind—she never gave him the chance. And she'd made sure she was almost impossible to find.

Did she dare to find out if he was now on his own too? She had to seize the opportunity, or go to her grave wondering.

She didn't want to appear too eager to see him again, as she didn't want Helen to pass on too many titbits of gossip to the ladies who lunch. Trying to sound blasé, she replied, 'Only tonight, I'm afraid, if it's not too long a day for you. I'm returning to Sydney tomorrow.'

'Then tonight it is,' he confirmed. 'Where are you staying?'

'At a boutique hotel in South Yarra,' replied Sarah. 'Now that I've experienced it, I'll make it my home away from home when I come to Melbourne on business. I've had enough of the same-sameness of international hotels.'

'You jetsetter, you,' he teased.

She gave him an embarrassed look. 'Didn't mean it like that. I like to see beyond a city's CBD. My hidey-hole is only a short taxi ride to the city, but that drive along the Yarra provides fantastic views of the city skyline, the curve of the river, the arch of the bridges, and the efforts of the rowing crews.'

'Don't forget those magnificent trees and their seasonal splendours,' Helen chipped in.

'It must be why Melbourne has the reputation of being so civilised, with so congenial an atmosphere.' There, that should please Helen.

'Special place alright,' he agreed. 'Sometimes I go for a run along there, when I'm in Melbourne on business. It's close to town. Can I pick you up?'

'Thanks, but no thanks. I'll return to my suite and freshen up, then catch a cab back into town to meet you somewhere.' She didn't want to be beholden to Jack for the return journey to her own hotel. Better to be an independent agent, as tonight could be dangerously upsetting for her.

'OK,' said Jack. 'I'm staying at the Sofitel.' With a cheeky grin at her he highlighted that his personal choice of accommodation was opposite to hers. Melbourne was proud of its newest, high-rise international hotel. 'Let's meet there, at the restaurant on the thirty-fifth floor, at seven thirty.'

She knew the reputation of that new restaurant, already famous for its prize-winning chef and its panoramic view over Melbourne. 'Wonderful. I'll see you at seven thirty, and you can tell me all your news. It'll be good to catch up.'

As they continued their progress back to the corporate hospitality area, Helen said with scarcely concealed enthusiasm, 'Sarah, that man's a real hunk. It sounds as if he must be a free agent after that dreadful accident of his wife's. I can tell he really fancies you.'

'You reckon? I haven't seen him for years.' She tried to downplay her connection to Jack.

'How could you lose touch with him, of all people? All of us ladies who lunch are so jealous of women like you, with all your brains and beauty and style. We all pray our husbands will return to us in the evenings, when we know they come across women like you in the workforce. Now that I've met you, I can't understand why you weren't snapped up years ago.'

Sarah laughed at Helen's frankness. 'It's a long story.' One she was not about to tell. Feeding Helen some juicy gossip was not on her agenda.

'Look out Helen, we're right in the path of a spirited thoroughbred here.' It was a fortuitous distraction that they were crossing the track which led from the racecourse to the horse stalls. Helen's alarm at being up close and personal with a real live horse, and its steaming deposit near her daintily clad feet, took her mind off the scent of an interesting topic of fascinated speculation for her next ladies' lunch.

'Good Lord, that horse nearly ran me down. And I nearly stepped in that mess. Ugh. Thanks for warning me. I hope someone cleans it up quickly. Ugh, animals. But it was a magnificent creature, wasn't it? Did you see the way it snorted and tossed its head? And did you notice its ankles? So narrow to carry the weight of such a large animal. Was it a he or a she or an it, do you think?'

Sarah laughed good-naturedly at Helen's prattle and said, 'It was a stallion, Helen.'

'How did you know that?'

'I once worked in that world, the Department of Agriculture, Stock and Fisheries to be precise, and you get to notice the bits attached to animals.'

'Silly me. I didn't think to look.' Helen adjusted the angle of her hat as they reached the corporate tent. 'I haven't met someone like you before. Jack obviously respects you. My husband sings your praises. Wait till I tell the girls about you.'

She spotted a friend and waved. 'Excuse me. There's Annabel.' Helen drifted away for a gossip session.

Helen was easily distracted. But Sarah was not. As she paid attention to her other guests, the back of her brain focused on the answer to one question. Could it be true Jack still fancied her? She'd been too flummoxed at seeing him to notice his reaction to her, to pick up any spark of his old interest.

Excitement and nervous energy started building in the pit of her stomach. It was only a few more hours before she'd see Jack again. In private. The day at the Cup couldn't end fast enough as she dreamed about tonight.

Even after finalising her duties as hostess at her Melbourne Cup event, she'd have plenty of time to prepare herself for her date with Jack.

And to prepare herself for a Jack without a Jenny. What would the evening reveal?

A sixth sense told her that he hadn't changed from the person she'd known.

But she'd changed, hadn't she? She was closed off, wary, and jaded. She now functioned in the world on automatic pilot, keeping up the façade of a successful businesswoman. He probably wouldn't find her attractive, once he found out that the innocent young woman he'd once known had disappeared to be more like a hermit crab, a loner, maybe with a soft inside but with a hard shell on the outside.

Until today, nothing much for years had aroused her emotional interest, although plenty engaged her intellectually. Today Jack had stirred her memory of a time when the world was a beckoning place.

Tonight was a rare treat, something to look forward to. No, she corrected herself firmly, someone to look forward to seeing. Jack. *At last. I'm not half dead after all. I should duck my head out and take a chance on life.* Life as most people knew it, but not her.

Back at South Yarra, she surveyed the few items hanging in the cupboard. She was used to travelling light, but fortunately she'd packed one of those demure little black dresses and plain black high-heeled court shoes without which no woman's wardrobe is complete. Just in case. It always paid to be prepared for all social contingencies when one was a director of a merchant bank.

With Jack on her mind, she flashed back to the clothing she'd worn in Port Moresby and cringed at the memory. Trying to keep up with fashion trends sweeping the world from London during its swinging sixties, she'd worn mini-skirts. Culturally inappropriate in PNG, especially on her field trips. Women's thighs, not their breasts, were the turn-on for PNG's men. Why hadn't Jack said something to her?

She hoped he'd like this dress tonight. Much longer, but it showed off her slim but shapely figure to perfection. She ate well but didn't overeat, so her clothes hung well on her. The heel height of the shoes emphasised her trim calves and ankles without forcing her to topple forward onto the balls of her feet when she walked.

'I'm assessing myself almost like Helen did with that horse,' reflected Sarah, 'but at least my ankles look strong enough to carry my weight.' She grinned with amusement as she inspected her feet.

The just-in-case dress and shoes had solved her problem of what to wear to dinner. But what about her face?

She peered at herself in the harsh and unforgiving neon light of a bathroom mirror. Not too many wrinkles. Having a redhead's pigmentation had forced her to stay out of the sun as much as possible, even in those carefree days in PNG. What had been a beauty disadvantage in her youth was paying off in her thirties. Relative to other women of her own age who were becoming weather-beaten and prune-like, her fine translucent skin was possibly her best feature. She'd need little makeup.

It was mainly the freckles on her arms and hands which showed the impact of the harsh Australian sun. Since her dress had long sleeves, she was unconcerned about her arms, and she hoped Jack would concentrate on her face this evening, rather than her freckled hands. *Get a grip. He never cared a hoot about my freckles in the past.*

She'd applied fresh nail polish that morning, and her genteel activities today had averted chipping damage, so she didn't have to complete any running repairs with the bottle of varnish in her toiletry bag.

She smiled ruefully to herself as she noted that another of her old-fashioned ways was also paying off. She drank little alcohol, or coffee, but had always loved her cups of tea and they contained the anti-oxidants helping to reduce the impact of ageing. No-one believed she was over thirty. She'd scarcely aged since Jack last saw her, three years ago.

As for her hair, she'd already had a trip to the hotel's recommended hairdresser early that day, trying to look her best as a corporate hostess for the day. He'd washed and conditioned her super thick hair to tame its wildness and had gently blow-dried it to encourage the riot of curls to burst out from under the bit of nonsense which masqueraded as the obligatory hat, an essential item for every self-respecting woman at the Melbourne Cup. The hat was fortunately so minimalist that it hadn't squashed her hair flat.

Yes, once she'd showered, if she squeezed a little conditioner onto her hands and ran them through slightly dampened hair to fluff it out again in the right places, she'd still look presentable, despite wearing a hat all day.

Her mental inventory completed, she decided that her physical appearance would be under control and as attractive as she could manage at short notice. Why was she worrying anyway? Jack had never cared in the past what she looked like.

But he'd noticed that special dress on that fatal New Year's Eve. And Sarah wanted him to notice her again. She wanted to attract his attention tonight. She needed his attention tonight.

Feeling desperate, she sprayed a shot of Chanel No 19 behind her ears and on her wrists. Her favourite perfume always gave her a burst of extra confidence.

But what about her inner self? Could she keep her feelings under control? Did she want to? An insistent little voice inside her head said 'no, no, no.'

Another little voice said, 'What if he has remarried? How will I deal with my disappointment over that?'

The blood drained from her face. Thankfully, that insistent inner voice returned. 'I don't think he has. It didn't feel as if he has.'

Her tension eased slightly. 'I'll just have to wait and see.'

She placed her order for the taxi early, giving herself plenty of time to get into the city. The taxi companies would be busy ferrying all the Melbourne Cup revellers between celebratory venues.

It was altogether a most auspicious day to bump into Jack. She'd absorbed the city's good-humoured vibe, the infectious magic in the air, the air of great excitement. Everyone was ready to party tonight. Could she embrace the party mood, let down her guard and completely relax with Jack?

CHAPTER THIRTY-TWO

At seven thirty it was close to sunset, with the dusk settling over Port Phillip Bay. The gathering darkness would later show off the fairyland view across a stylish city. The lights of over three million inhabitants would out-twinkle the faint emissions of the billions of stars of the Milky Way sweeping across the heavens above them.

Her taxi driver had his radio tuned to 3MP, the easy listening station, and the soft sounds of Jim Croce's lyrical masterpiece 'Time in a Bottle' calmed her nerves as they drove towards the city. She closed her eyes and breathed in her indelible memories of Jack and tried to imagine how time with him might stretch into the future.

'We're here, lady.'

Her eyes shot open and she fumbled for her wallet to pay the driver.

The hotel doorman ushered her towards the lift, which whisked her physical body calmly upwards while her mind raced in circles like a crazy child.

Jack had chosen a seat facing the entrance to the restaurant and rose quickly from the table the minute he saw her arrive. A welcoming smile lit his face. He looked childishly happy to see her.

This was a good start, she thought, suddenly panic-stricken. Then her inexplicable joy at seeing him took hold and the same spontaneous smile erupted on her face.

His words of greeting were also reassuringly direct. 'It's made my day, seeing you. My year.'

Once again, he kissed her on both cheeks and seemed loath to break the contact but, ever the gentleman, he pulled out her chair and helped her take her seat. She sank into it, feeling rather shaky after the repeat performance of the kisses he'd bestowed earlier that day. He'd always raised her body temperature and sent her lower body into a frenzy, so that her legs felt slightly rickety and her insides wobbled like jelly.

'Will you have some champagne with me?' He gestured towards the bottle immersed in the ice bucket beside his chair.

Sarah noticed he had already taken a few sips from the glass on his side of the table. He'd arrived early. A sign of his eagerness to see her?

'I'd love some. It's my favourite celebratory drink.' The waiter appeared on cue and poured her a glass of Dom Perignon.

French champagne. What a perfect choice for

today. Over-indulgence in champagne was the signature statement for a day at the Cup.

She'd heard all the tales about Melbourne's four-seasons-in-one-day weather and what happened to the revellers on the first Tuesday in November after a long day in the hot sun, or the cold and rain, drinking too much champagne and eating too little food. In the late afternoon the trams and trains of Melbourne overflowed with crowds of race-goers: men with suit jackets slung over shoulders, opened collars and loosened ties, escorting ladies in skewwhiff hats, some ladies wearing bare feet and dangling their high heels in their hands. Clutching their racing programmes, they laughed loudly and clung to each other to stay upright, using public transport to ensure that a drink-driving charge, or worse, did not spoil their big day out.

But not Sarah and Jack. In the big league, corporate-wise, neither had over-indulged in champagne at the Cup and both were headache-free, so tonight they could allow the champagne bubbles to evoke a strongly celebratory mood. Sarah raised her glass in response to Jack's toast of 'here's to us.'

'To us,' she repeated, and smiled back at him for the second time in the space of a few minutes. God, it was good to see him again.

The waiter departed after serving her drink, and topping up Jack's glass. He spoke in his well-remembered forthright fashion: 'I couldn't believe my eyes when I spotted you on the Members' lawn today. You've been on my mind for years. Let's have a second toast. Let's drink to us finding each other again.'

They raised their champagne flutes again and gently chinked them together, eyes locked, not speaking, not touching hands, avoiding the dangerous sparks of contact. This toast meant something deeper than the actual words he'd chosen.

After taking a healthy gulp of his champagne, Jack continued: 'It's so wonderful to be here with you. We have the whole evening ahead of us, and I don't want to start by treading on treacherous ground, so please tell me about your day today. Then I'll tell you about mine. There'll be time later for all the important things that need to be said before the night is through.'

He'd said evening to begin with and then it became night. Was this a Freudian slip? Sarah shivered a little. What would the night bring?

There was plenty to chat about when you'd spent the day at the Melbourne Cup. The only genuine reason to feel unhappy on a day like today was if you'd lost a fortune making unwise bets on the races. Sarah hadn't, and she relaxed. 'The roses looked spectacular today,' she began.

'That they did.'

She looked at him, expecting him to make a better contribution than that to her pathetic attempt at small talk. The amused glint in his eyes proved he was teasing her.

'That deals with the roses then,' he laughed. 'What's your next topic?'

She entered the conversational game more confidently. 'How about the Cup itself? Have you ever sighted it, other than at the presentation ceremony?'

'Indeed I have. The owners of the champion horse visited the corporate tent adjoining ours, brandishing their prized three-handled trophy. They were generous enough to let us all hold it, for commemorative photos. That was pretty special.'

'So you'll have a permanent reminder of today.'

'Most definitely. Today was my lucky day. My horseshoe was hanging the right way up when I got out of bed this morning.' Jack was hinting at a different dimension to his luck that day. He abruptly changed tack. 'My host, Minister McIntyre, was impressed that I knew you.'

'That's nice of him. You impressed Helen too, only she chose the word hunk to describe you. You won yourself a fan there.' They both laughed. He'd always seemed oblivious to his good looks. She saw no need to pass on the rest of Helen's comments.

Instead she mimicked Helen's shocked response to the idea that she'd nearly stepped into the horse dung. She laughed. 'Could you see a genteel and oh-so-refined Toorak matron surviving in the tropics, in the conditions we once lived in?'

That brought her back to reality and her sense of the ridiculous. Here she was playing the good-mannered corporate entertainment game with him. Jack, of all people. He'd seen her sweaty face caked in dirt on hot and dusty roads—her wet hair plastered to her skull in mountain streams—her spectacular dive off those water skis. He'd held her in his arms on the dance floor. He'd seen her cuddling his children, and them cuddling into her. He'd seen her laughing and crying. He knew how she operated at work. He'd kissed her thoroughly and passionately. He'd seen into her very soul. Jack knew her. So why were they playing this game?

She looked at him and giggled slightly. The champagne was going to her head. She'd have to watch herself. His eyes crinkled as he smiled back at her. He knew what she was thinking, and she didn't have to say it.

But she did. 'Jack, we don't have to be polite and sophisticated strangers.'

'No,' he agreed, 'we could take up where we left off. Trust you to notice the roses at Flemington. You still love your gardening?'

At that moment the waiter came to take their order and broke the mood of increasing rapport. Sarah ordered a light entrée of smoked salmon, followed by her favourite meal of chicken breast with a coating of mushrooms and grilled cheese and lightly cooked vegetables. Jack ordered oysters and a grilled steak with vegetables.

They'd already shared nearly a full bottle of champagne. Neither was a big drinker, so they decided against ordering a bottle of wine to accompany their meal. One glass each would do. Sarah ordered pinot gris, and Jack ordered cabernet sauvignon, both from the best range on the wine list. Quality not quantity suited them both.

While they waited for their meal to arrive, Jack returned to where he'd left off. 'I remember you as a keen gardener. I also remember you were a novice in the workforce then, and look at you now. Hosting a group of top executives at the Melbourne Cup. Impressing Ministers of State. Well done, Miss Blue Eyes. You've made it. Let's drink to your success.'

Sarah relaxed a little more at Jack's old term of affection for her. With the third toast, the champagne bottle was almost empty. And Sarah's heart was melting all over again. This man was so positive. So ready to notice others and not brag about himself. He made her feel so good and so happy she could fling out her arms and jump for joy, like a child.

His champagne glass chinked against the cutlery as he set it back on the table and gave her the proud parent look: 'As Ms Sarah Robinson you've travelled down some different paths from me since we first met. I'm still passionate about my work, but it remains pretty well-grounded in the soil, while you now operate up there in the stratosphere, overseeing the movement of megabucks around the world every day.'

He was teasing her again. Perfectly confident within himself, his tone showed he was genuinely proud of her achievements. He'd never been a man to feel threatened by the success of others. And he'd never shown the slightest sign of chauvinism. Once she'd been Mrs Robinson to him, now he'd comfortably shifted to Ms.

Jokingly she replied in the same vein: 'All thanks to your professional training. You gave me a lot of confidence in my abilities at work, and then ...' Her voice trailed off as she remembered what had pushed her into another world.

'I know, Sarah, I know. Leave it for later. Here comes our meal. We should try to enjoy it.' And they did. They were hungry. A day at the Cup was a tiring day. All that fresh air and sunshine had built up an appetite.

She enjoyed watching him eat his meal with gusto. He had a man's appetite. For more than food, she wondered, not for the first time since she'd sat down in this restaurant. Did he still have the same appetite for her as before? She hungered for him as her imagination led her into wild and exciting territory. She reprimanded herself. *Stick to safe topics.*

'Tell me all about Tom and Lottie. Do you have any photos?'

'But of course. What kind of dad do you think I am?' Out of his wallet came the latest school photos. 'Fifteen and twelve. Both of them at high school this year.'

Sarah studied the pictures as she recalled past times. 'They were such lovely kids, Jack. I can still feel Lottie's trusting little arms around my neck. She was like a koala bear, always ready for a cuddle.'

Her examination of the photos continued. 'Tom looks so grown up. He's got your eyes. He's going to be a force to be reckoned with, I can see that.' She looked across the table at him. 'You're too young to have teenagers.'

'Don't forget the reason,' replied Jack rather contritely. He grinned ruefully at her.

Lottie was proudly wearing her badge as her class captain. 'I see she's taking after you. A born leader, like her father. So pretty too. She looks a bit like her mother. You must miss Jenny a lot.'

'Yes, she left a hole behind her. You develop a special bond when you bear and raise kids together. We were so young when we became parents. We struggled, *and* we had some good times together.'

Sarah felt a sudden surge of jealousy. She wanted what he had experienced with Jenny. Had he noticed her slight change of mood?

The waiter cleared away their plates and Jack reached for her hand across the table. He'd spotted her shoulders sag when he mentioned those good times with Jenny. 'You remember what you were saying when our meal arrived. How I gave you confidence in your abilities—until your voice trailed off. I have something to say that I've wanted to say to you for many years now. But only in person. That's why it's so good to see you tonight.'

He gave her hand a gentle squeeze of encouragement, pleased to see her expression lift.

'Everything I ever said to you was true.' He kept his gaze firmly focused on her expectant face. 'When I found you all those years ago, when the kids were virtually babies, I'd already made my commitments in life, to Jenny and the children who needed me and to myself out of pride. I had the ongoing responsibility of two youngsters.'

She nodded slowly. 'That's why I left, remember?'

'I do, but hear me out. We were happy enough until I met you and realised the meaning of the word soulmate. After that, I knew why my life felt so flat at its core. Jenny and I didn't actually fight or anything, but we both knew intense feelings were missing from our marriage. The feelings that you and I shared. The passion for life. I wanted you to know that.'

'Those feelings overwhelmed me, like a tidal

wave.' Her downcast eyes and faint sigh signalled to him her distress at recalling those emotional times in PNG.

He scrutinised her reaction for a few seconds before he pressed on: 'Three years ago, when we last met so briefly, I wasn't in a good place myself.'

Her eyes lifted, curious, like a child wanting to hear a new bedtime story.

'We all missed Jenny, especially the kids. They were staying on the farm with their grandparents and I had a free weekend, for once, so I was hugely glad to be invited to that party at Charles and Carolyn's place. I imagined some welcome camaraderie with some of my old workmates. A drink or two to drown my sorrows. All the while hoping you might be there too, by some miracle.'

'My presence that day *was* by pure chance.'

He watched her face cloud over again, like one of those days when the wind blew scudding clouds across the sky, intermittently exposing and hiding the sun.

He needed to clear those clouds away, bring back the sunshine.

But first he had to point out the bleeding obvious. 'And history repeated itself, like in Moresby, when you did to me what I'd once done to you—you turned your back and walked away, as if I was a pariah. You seemed determined to cut your ties with your old life because Charles and I both tried to find you afterwards, but you made sure you couldn't be found.'

Sarah nodded in silent affirmation.

'I wangled an invitation to the Cup today in the specific hopes of finding you. Thank God I did.' He smiled at her and gave her hand a gentle rub with his thumb. Did she thank God too?

'We almost missed each other.' She gave nothing away with that answer. Then her eyes bored into his. 'Did you just want to tell me about Jenny?'

'Of course I wanted you to know about Jenny, for obvious reasons.' He sighed heavily and squeezed her hand more firmly. 'Of much more importance, I wanted you to know that you meant everything to me back then, and I've really missed you.' His eyes implored her to believe him.

The seconds ticked past. She said quietly 'Thank you for telling me at last, that I meant something to you.'

'Oh yes, my dearest Sarah, you certainly did.'

He'd used the past tense. Was it over? Was he just trying to make his excuses to her?

Her stomach quivered in unease. Something was missing here. She remained silent and waited patiently for him to continue.

'The Sydney papers last week outlined your brilliant career, but didn't mention your personal life. You must have a husband and family by now, but I notice you haven't breathed a word about your private life all evening, so tell me about it. Who's the lucky man?'

So that's why he was treading carefully. He assumed she must have a new partner, even though she'd abandoned the wedding ring strategy years ago, for costume jewellery. These days a wedding ring was no longer an essential trophy for a woman. Thanks to the likes of Germaine Greer, many women felt free to live with a man without marrying him.

The tears pricked her eyes as she gazed steadily at him. 'There's no husband and family, Jack, just my work.' Her love for him had cost her everything she'd wanted.

She watched him absorb her simple statement. He was quiet for a moment before saying slowly, 'I see. Then I'm doubly sorry. Sorry for what happened then, and sorry for what it cost you.'

Another tear escaped her control. Jack watched it slide unchecked down her cheek and said slowly, 'For all your polished veneer of a high-powered executive, I know you're still the same Sarah as before. And I know where your priorities still lie.'

She looked at him. Yes, this was still the same insightful Jack alright. But she kept her counsel. It was bad enough that the occasional tear was giving her away. Her mouth mustn't quiver as well.

'Ever since that day I turned my back on you, I've wanted to express my sorrow for hurting you so much. The memory of your puzzled, hurt face has haunted me for years.'

'I was devastated.'

'I know Sarah, I know. I'm so sorry. I still don't know why I did that. Self-protection, I guess. I knew I couldn't resist you. You were, you still are, such an incredibly beautiful and desirable woman.'

'Even at the ripe old age of thirty-four?'

'I've known you since you were twenty-four. Nothing's changed, for me.'

'Thank you.'

'Jenny never realised my feelings towards you. At least I hope not.' He squeezed her hand.

He leaned across the table and with his free hand he wiped away the fresh drops of moisture gathering at the corners of her eyes. 'Don't cry. Don't cry. I'm hoping for a happy ending to this story.'

She continued gazing at him, evaluating his explanation of events of the past few years.

'From what you've told me tonight, you deliberately kept a low profile as a bureaucrat in Washington. I wasn't sure of your surname, but I made quite a few international calls trying to locate the right S. Robinson, before I decided that any telephone listing under the surname Robinson was obviously a silent number. I had no real clues about where to find you. Don't forget my world is agriculture, not high finance.'

Sarah's brain was in overdrive, trying to digest all that Jack had said. The outward show of her tears only hinted at the range of emotions which had flooded her body as his confession unfolded. Surprise. Sorrow. Regret. Relief. Hope. Eagerness.

Jack paused, as if wondering why Sarah remained so silent. He changed tack. 'Did you know that Tom and Lottie still remember those outings we had? They sometimes talk about the nice lady who used to play with them. Lottie was too young then to remember your name. Tom always reminds her. I think they'd like to see you again.'

Not like him to sound so reticent, so indirect. She watched him shift uncomfortably in his chair, eyes wary, as if he feared she might close the door opening to the future and turn back into the room full of pain from the past. Then he sat up straight and looked at her longingly. 'I can't wait for you to meet them now.'

'So you want to see me again?' Her blue eyes engaged steadily with his hazel ones.

'What do you think?' His eyes begged her to say yes.

His explanation rang true to her. She, too, had experienced the stubbornness wrought by hurt feelings and knew what it had cost her. She felt comfortable with him, as if they belonged together, despite the painful memories and the long years which had elapsed since their last contact. It was like meeting up again with the other half of yourself.

Two pairs of eyes gazed at each other across the dinner table, communicating messages they did not have to vocalise. Their hearts had been calling to each other all evening. The passion they'd felt for each other, always repressed and dormant for so long, had been smouldering from the instant they first clinked their champagne glasses.

His eyes were a window to his soul. Shining out of them was the glow of a dynamic human being, a responsible man, a caring father, a perceptive friend, an intelligent professional and a kind person. But most of all was an awareness of her and the person she was. Mutual appreciation as before. Irresistible sexual magnetism.

The discovery of a soulmate made for a heady mix of feelings, summed up in two words. Total happiness.

Jack stretched his other hand across the table, loosened the fingers gripping the stem of her wineglass, and thus grasped both her hands with both of his.

He whispered, 'Still waters run deep. Calm on the surface. Underneath—a strong current of passion. We have both been pining for our long-lost love. I still love you. You've been my secret love for all these years. You knocked me sideways from the first day we met. Did you know that? Right from my first sight of Miss Blue Eyes, always my private name for you. And when we shook hands, it was all over. I was a goner.'

"You mean that?'

'For ten years I've felt like that about you. For ten years I've wanted you. And that was even before I realised you were such a clever little rose amongst the thorns of that disparate group in that remote tropical town. Despite my best endeavours I soon grew to love you, as well as want you. I struggled hard and mightily to remember my marriage vows and existing commitments until that fateful New Year's Eve, when I couldn't help myself.'

Sarah's eyes filled with tears as he broke through her defences. He was the one person with the right combination of physical attributes and mental perspicacity to reach her and bring her alive, as he had before.

His eyes bored into hers, looked right into her. No need for overt display: it was all in the eyes and inside the head. Soulmates instinctively know how the other one feels.

There was suddenly no doubt at all what would happen next. It was no longer the occasion to order dessert and coffee and maintain conversation, whether it be polite or deep and meaningful.

Jack called the waiter and charged the meal to his room account. They rose without another word and silently left the restaurant.

The hotel lift carried other diners. Could they

sense the sexual tension in the air? Jack stood beside Sarah, as close as was possible, his left hand clenching her right hand tightly, as if he would never let go. Their arms rose from their joined hands like two straight sentries, rigid with tense anticipation.

In the hotel corridor a bell-boy was delivering the luggage for a late-arriving guest. 'Good evening, sir,' he said to Jack as they approached his room. Jack gave a brief smile of acknowledgment and glanced sideways at Sarah. She glanced back. A very good evening was about to become a superlative evening.

The door between the public world of propriety and their own private, joyous world within Jack's luxurious Melbourne hotel room stood before them. 'Alone at last' came his strangled voice as the door slammed shut behind them, and he rained kisses on her as ardently and urgently as he had once before, and as she'd given up dreaming that he ever would again.

They couldn't discard their clothes fast enough. Jack pressed Sarah against the door and they made love standing up, both too aroused to wait one second longer. It was over in a flash.

Their first hunger slated, they remained joined at the hip as they backed down the hallway into his bedroom and collapsed together on the bed for a second frenzied burst, their bodies almost exploding with the need to find release again. Their superheated skin, racing hearts, laboured breath, indescribable build-up of ecstasy, and explosion in an overwhelming climax was like nothing she'd ever experienced.

Languorous stupor followed. Recovery time was swift. The slightest move from either of them found Jack ready to deliver, and Sarah ready to receive his precious gift of nature. Over and over. She hoped it would never end.

'Sarah, darling Sarah, you have done wonders for my libido. I need you so much. I want more of you, so much more.'

'Jack, my own Jack, please, don't ever stop.' Jack's slow hand remorselessly worked its own brand of magic as it explored her body. His lips and tongue were other instruments of sweet rapture.

By morning, exhausted, they rested quietly in each other's arms after their long night of continuous love-making. 'I didn't know it could be like this,' he whispered.

She snuggled even closer. 'Neither did I.'

'We are both free to marry now, my darling.' His thumb caressed her cheek in gentle soothing strokes. 'In the grand scheme of things, who cares about careers. Yours or mine. We have both proved already that we can adjust to living and working in different places, with different people, in different circumstances. But we've kept on needing each other, through thick and thin.'

He turned her body to face him, kissed the tip of her nose and continued with his soft words of encouragement: 'We can work something out to make us both happy. Keep your professional name, I don't care. I just want to see love light shining out of your eyes.'

'It should be blinding you already.' She leaned across for another kiss, and one thing led to another.

When he came up for air he said, 'You're still young enough to have kids, several, if that's what you want. Plenty of women have kids in their mid-thirties. I'd love to have a second family if you were at its centre. I always wanted more kids, and Tom and Lottie would love it too.'

His entreaties enticed her, holding up the pot of gold at the end of Sarah's rainbow. She snuggled closer into his arms and, with a cheeky stroke, provoked another erection.

'Still in my prime. If you only knew how much I always wanted to give you the baby you craved.' He puffed out his chest.

She looked at him and couldn't resist an affectionate grin. He sounded suspiciously like an alpha male in the animal kingdom trying to promote the benefits of his mating capacities to a choosy female.

He responded with a grin of his own, reassuring her that his self-deprecating humour had survived the years intact.

Then he frowned slightly. 'Come to think of it, we might have already made ourselves a baby. I was too enamoured to care.' His face cleared. 'Thank heavens for the new morning-after pill. Should we ring your doctor after breakfast? Or do you still want that baby as badly as before?'

Years of pent-up emotions overwhelmed Sarah. All things bright and beautiful were finally happening to her. For a brief moment she was too choked up to speak.

He grumbled impatiently, 'For God's sake, woman, put me out of my misery. Will you marry me?'

Her face almost cracked with the force of her smile. 'I say yes I'll marry you, no to that pill and yes to that promise of a baby.'

ACKNOWLEDGMENTS

'Still Waters Run Deep' is a work of fiction which happens to be based on various real-life experiences, scrambled up and re-arranged to become a genuine product of the author's imagination. The story is not intended to reflect on any actual person, living or dead.

I am grateful to my Melbourne friends Karen Dew, Jacqui Hagan, Lyn Payne, Martin Reddington and his daughter Charlotte, for their helpful comments on various drafts of this book.

Special thanks are due to my writing buddy Eliza Renton. Without her constant encouragement, patient re-reads and insightful, detailed feedback, this book would never have reached the hands of the reading public.

Once 'Still Waters Run Deep' was ready for readers, the ever-helpful Annie Seaton and Ebony McKenna took over the process of designing a cover and formatting this book for print.

A team effort like this lies behind every book reaching the market place. Many thanks to everyone who has helped this book along its journey.

ABOUT THE AUTHOR

Louisa Valentine, an Australian author, has long-since waved goodbye to her multi-faceted career in finance & economics and returned to her teenage passion for history, mystery and romance.

Her first novel *'Retreat into Paradise'*, an Australian rural romance of the old-fashioned variety, is set close to Melbourne.

Her second novel, *'Trading Secrets'*, introduces a little mystery to a family story set in the Sydney financial world – and an infertility clinic.

Her third novel, '*Still Waters Run Deep*', is a story of longing, set in spectacular Papua New Guinea in the 1970s.

Yes, Louisa Valentine's romantic fiction covers a lot of ground.

She lives a double life as an author. As Louise Wilson she has also published nine non-fiction books (in print format only). These bring previously untold aspects of Australia's fascinating history to life in well-researched and award-winning historical biographies and family histories, starting with the First Fleet of 1788.

WANT TO READ MORE?

If you enjoyed reading 'Still Waters Run Deep',
why not try my earlier books?

'Trading Secrets'

Nicola Pearson is a new recruit to the Federal Bank in Sydney, hired to devise a new system to manage the trading risks of the bank. It is the mid-90s and she has to prove herself professionally and intellectually to win over the dealers, especially their boss Tom Forrester. He has recently returned from a three-year stint in London to run the Federal Bank's financial trading operations.

Nicola has been left in the lurch by her ex-husband and does not trust men, lacking confidence in her judgment of them although she is confident of her workforce skills. She lives quietly, keeping her private life to herself.

Tom is also divorced, following a marriage experience which left him very disillusioned. The world sees him as living in the fast lane and Nicola is not his usual 'type' but something about her calls to him. He gradually recognises she is bottling up a secret. Does he hold the key to changing her life?

Get your copy here:
https://books2read.com/Trading-Secrets

'Retreat into Paradise'

City girl Hannah Stockton writes histories as her day-job and family histories in her spare time. Needing a temporary escape from a violent boyfriend, she takes up an advertised position as a live-in caretaker 'with light duties' at a country retreat outside Melbourne. The owner, Philip Boulton, is a hunky high-flying banker who visits on weekends to attend to his small herd of cattle.

Hannah is dismayed to discover that Philip has been taught all he knows about farming by his next-door neighbour, who lusts after Philip and resents Hannah's presence. Hannah can't tell whether Philip is 'more than friends' with his guru.

Philip has recently discovered a family secret. Given his profession, he's sensitive about this fact becoming public. Fearing Hannah's skills as a family history researcher, he keeps her at a distance while he processes his secret.

Meanwhile, as her 'boss', he helps Hannah to overcome her fear of cattle and she learns to love country life … and Philip.

Get your copy here:
https://books2read.com/Retreat-into-Paradise

BEFORE YOU GO

If you'd like to hear about future stories
by Louisa Valentine, please 'Follow' me on
www.facebook.com/LouisaValentineAuthor.

Or visit www.louisewilson.com.au

Remember, authors spend countless hours
conceiving, drafting and perfecting stories,
aiming to provide readers
with a few hours of reading pleasure.
Authors appreciate all the assistance they can get
with spreading the word about their book.

Please help in one or more of the following ways …

- What is your rating for this book?
- Share or Tweet that you finished it.
- Tell friends & family if you enjoyed it.
- Leave a review on your online sales outlet.
- Leave a review on Goodreads.

THANK YOU

www.ingramcontent.com/pod-product-compliance
Lightning Source LLC
Chambersburg PA
CBHW020300120726
47904CB00001B/280